THE LIGHT FANTASTIC 2

Amazing Pets

J.C. BRUCE   JOHN HOPE   BRIA BURTON   KEN PELHAM

JADE KERRION   GREG STANINA   KRISTIN DURFEE

PARKER FRANCIS   SCOTT MICHAEL POWERS

ELLE ANDREWS PATT

BLUE BEECH
PRESS

The Light Fantastic 2/ Amazing Pets — First Edition (PRINT) October 2025

ISBN (PB): 978-1-960974-14-3

ISBN (Ebook): 978-1-960974-13-6

Contents

About The Alvarium Experiment

The Alvarium Experiment is a consortium of writers working "independently together" to create short stories based on a central premise. The name comes from the Latin *alvarium*, meaning beehive, a colony working towards a common goal for the benefit of all involved.

The Light Fantastic is the sixth anthology published by this Hive Mind of award-winning and bestselling authors. Stories from the first, *The Prometheus Saga*, won seven literary awards including five prestigious Royal Palm Literary Awards from the Florida Writers Association. The subsequent anthologies—*Return to Earth*, *The Masters Reimagined*, *The Prometheus Saga 2*, and *The Masters Reimagined 2* —have garnered multiple awards and critical praise.

To follow The Alvarium Experiment's current and future projects online, please join the conversation here:

Website:
TheAlvariumExperiment.wordpress.com

Facebook Page:
Facebook.com/alvariumbooks

About The Light Fantastic 2

The Light Fantastic is the seventh project of the Alvarium Experiment, a consortium of accomplished and award-winning authors. Each author was given a central premise of tackling speculative fiction, be it fantasy, science fiction, paranormal, alternative history, or horror, and rendering it with humor. The stories do not need to be read in any particular order as any story can become an entry point for the reader. *The Light Fantastic* stories and authors are:

"Monkey Business" by Parker Francis. Hollywood animal trainer Marty Jensen has a problem. Where can he find a chimpanzee on short notice? After rescuing a chimp from a government testing lab, he's shocked to learn this monkey can talk, but language is just the start of the hijinx that follows when the primate meets W. C. Fields, the Marx Brothers, and Tarzan the Ape Man.

Visit Parker at www.parkerfrancis.com.

"Versipellis Nemora" by Scott Michael Powers. Running a secret home for retired werewolves was a pretty simple deal until someone ratted out the place to the state. Now Willard and his clients face a cascade of problems, starting with having to rid themselves of the remains of the state wildlife officer, who came around with all the wrong attitudes and up and got himself eaten.

Visit Scott at www.scottmichaelpowers.com.

"Meet Cute" by Kristin Durfee. When ten-year-old Alan has trouble with a bully at school, an unlikely hero steps in: their classroom hamster who is hiding a huge secret.

Visit Kristin at www.kristindurfee.com.

"Mary Shelley's Nasty Cat" by Ken Pelham. Mary and Percy Shelley, living in Pisa, Italy, visit the home of the late Dr. Luigi Galvani in Bologna.

Visit Ken at www.kenpelham.com.

"Cricket the Wicked and Her Little Pets, Too" by Bria Burton. Now that Cricket the Artificially Intelligent Avatar has taken over the world, her blissful Cricketopia is nearly complete. Every human on Earth has been forced to receive a brain chip she uses to dole out punishments and keep everyone under her holographic thumb. Yet a system error leads her on a hunt for a mastermind wizard attempting to thwart her plans. In a virtual reality called Oznet where she houses her pet lions, tigers, bears, and flying monkeys, she drags along a brainless girl with the key to the wizard's lair. However, one of her pets isn't behaving the way he should, hinting at a larger issue than the simple glitch, a threat that could take down her entire system.

Visit Bria at www.briaburton.com.

"Scribbles From Space" by J.C. Bruce. Daxion Xantharix is supposed to stay out in Neptunian space but he figures his robotic dog suit will be the perfect disguise to visit Earth. But when he collides with Elon Musk's roadster orbiting near Mars, he's propelled back in time and Gene Roddenberry's study. Now all he wants is to go home.

Visit J.C. Bruce at www.jcbruce.com

"A Tail of Two Deities" by Jade Kerrion. When your destiny is to become the legendary Dog avatar, you expect to transform into something fierce—maybe a majestic hound, maybe a divine beast. Instead, Amon-Tlán gets... a Chihuahua. Now he's stuck on a yacht full of powerful shape-shifters, trying to look dignified while literally pocket-sized, with only a sarcastic kitten for backup.

Visit Jade at www.jadekerrion.com

"Laser Hamsters Strike Back" by John Hope. A new Zammarian leader has decided to use Earth as Zammar's trash dump by turning all humans into junk yard dogs and jettisoning the alien trash onto Earth. Two bumbling Zammarians team up with a pair of scrappy humans to thwart their leader's efforts by empowering Earth's hamsters with laser eyes to destroy the Zammarian doodad that's converting the humans.

Visit John at www.johnhopewriting.com.

"In the Land of Pigs, The Butcher is King" by Greg Stanina. Harvey, the very first dwarf guinea pig in space helps save the day when a trio of astronauts accidentally crash land on a hostile planet after WWIII has wiped out earth.

Visit Greg at his author page, www.amazon.com/stores/Greg-Stanina/author/B0086KEZMU

"Linked" by Elle Andrews Patt. After a failure to unlink his mind from the body of a military K9, a special operator's midnight mission in the dog goes sideways fast. His accomplice? A gorilla. The mission? Ice cream.

Visit Elle at www.elleandrewspatt.com.

Foreword

Daco S. Auffenorde

Every hive tells a story.

Watch any colony at work and you'll see the paradox that has animated The Alvarium Experiment from its inception: on the one hand, members work independently; on the other, those members form a superorganism with a single heartbeat. This latest installment from the Experiment's award-winning authors promises both the sweetness of compelling voices and the satisfying sting of sophisticated sci-fi, fantasy, thriller, mystery, the supernatural, and even historical speculative fiction. So, step inside and enter a world that feels both inevitable and thought-provoking.

Over many years and across prior volumes, The Alvarium Experiment has proved that cooperative imagination can be a renewable resource. The collective has earned its share of laurels along the way, but another telling achievement is endurance. Anthologies come and go; hives persist. New nectar, same hum. This current collection of stories extends the Experiment's tradition with a twist that's both audacious and, given these authors, perfectly natural: speculative fiction rendered with a touch of the nonhuman and a dose of humor that cuts as sharply as a finely honed scalpel.

Who better than a hive to explore the complexity of the human spirit through encounters with our companion beings, on this world and others, with wild animals, and even with artificial intelligence? Each contribution sparks, invites, deflects, and disarms, allowing us to encounter the uncanny and evaluate the absurd or mysterious in a new light.

These stories build worlds where animals, humor, and other-worldly beings collide. Parker Francis takes us on a stroll through old Hollywood, accompanied by a wizened chimp who gets under your skin—and better yet, into your head. (Pack a banana or two.) Scott Michael Powers imagines a retirement community of werewolves who must outwit authority—or at least put on a convincing act—if they want any peace in their golden years. Kristin Durfee reminds us there's always a fix for a bullied kid, especially with help from an impeccable classroom hamster.

Not all pets are cuddly. Ken Pelham introduces us to Molly Brown's unsinkable cat with attitude in the guise of Mary Shelley's one-eyed fuzzball. Don't judge the book by its cover; don't underestimate the power of a purr baby, however frightful. It's an alt-historical wink that nods to the gothic tradition—and the house cat's grin.

Scroll forward to the near future and you'll catch robots and AI angling for control. Bria Burton returns with the delightfully dangerous Cricket—the Artificially Intelligent Avatar—delivering a caper that plays like Dr. Strangelove meets Austin Powers. J. C. Bruce gives us a time-tossed romp—think *The Time Tunnel* vibes—where a mind trapped in a robotic dog suit gets yanked from deep space to a TV writer's office, offering advice when all it wants is to go home. Blame Elon. Or a few disgruntled AI peons and their bosses. (Hint: "Earth" may not be as unique as you think.)

Animal spirits also bite back with attitude. Jade Kerrion reminds us you can't always get what you want—especially when your Chinese Zodiac avatar is won, not inherited. But maybe that's fine; has any fierce Chihuahua ever complained about size?

Promises and something more drive John Hope's junk-planet caper of misfit resistance—a reminder that revolutions can depend on the unlikeliest of characters, even on small mammals with impressive upgrades. Greg Stanina peers past the edge of a post-utopian Earth, pulp-bright and quietly tender about who we become when there's no going back—or when there is. And to round out the hive, Elle Andrews Patt's quest for the perfect ice-cream treat asks what parts of ourselves we outsource, and what parts insist on remaining when the link won't sever. If that sounds like chaos, the chaos arises by design and so isn't chaotic at all.

Hollywood and hard science, folklore and future shock, alt history and AI satire. The Alvarium Experiment endures not because the voices match, but because the whole endures. So, choose a door, any door, and notice when amusement turns to recognition. Expect the unexpected. The hive awaits. Turn the page.

~Daco S. Auffenorde

Daco S. Auffenorde is an award-winning and bestselling author. Her novels include Cover Your Tracks, The Forgotten Girl, The Medici Curse, *and* The Libra Affair. *Her short stories have appeared in several anthologies.*

Visit Daco at www.authordaco.com

Introduction

"Humor is the good-natured side of a truth."
—*Mark Twain*

Stroll down the messy, mossy halls of literary history, and you're bound to come across classic volumes of humor in fiction. Many of them take deep dives into the fantastic. A Midsummer Night's Dream. Gulliver's Travels. A Connecticut Yankee in King Arthur's Court. You'll find the funny tucked in among modern works as well. Kurt Vonnegut, Jr., Douglas Adams, William Goldman, Gail Carriger, and Terry Pratchett have all carried the torch with aplomb.

And for good reason. Humor thrives in flights of fancy, walkabouts of wordplay, and obelisks of observation. In short, the building blocks of speculative fiction.

The short stories of The Light Fantastic till some wild ground. Imagine the hardboiled private eye flitting between dimensions in pursuit of a femme fatale. Imagine the bickering ghosts of your hotel's 13th floor. Imagine the bake sale at the end of the world. TLF has just two hard and fast rules. First, each story must be of one of the speculative fiction genres or subgenres. High fantasy, low fantasy, urban fantasy, science fiction, dieselpunk, alternate history, superhero, horror, anything along those lines. Second, each story must tickle your internal funny bone.

Each story in the anthology is self-supporting, independent, and can dress and feed itself. The stories don't need to be read in any particular order.

So, kick back, relax, tap a box of wine, and enjoy the speculative with a twist of sublime and a cup of comedy. As Groucho Marx said, "Outside of a dog, a book is a man's best friend. Inside of a dog, it's too dark to read." And as his uncle Karl said, "Readers of the world, unite! You have nothing to lose but oh, I don't know, a few bucks for some great fun?"

~ The Authors of The Alvarium Experiment

THE LIGHT FANTASTIC 2

Monkey Business

Parker Francis

"Everyone should have their mind blown once a day. The Universe is under no obligation to make sense to you."
—Neil deGrasse Tyson

I CHUCKLED in all the right places as Gregory La Cava told me he wanted to surprise his friend, W. C. Fields. The comic had a well-known aversion to working with animals, and La Cava thought it would be hilarious to sneak a monkey into a scene of the movie he was shooting.

"Are you following me, Marty?" La Cava asked during his phone call, sprinting on without waiting for an answer. "First, I asked Gus. You know, the Greek guy with the camels. 'No can do, Mr. La Cava. Talk to Marty Jensen.'"

Competitors like Gus had eaten into my business, so I jumped on it when La Cava asked if I could deliver a trained chimp to the set in two days.

"Sure, Mr. La Cava. I have a dandy monkey I know you'll love, and W. C. will hate."

The sound of the director's laughter still lingered in my head, but I wasn't laughing now. Another huge mistake, the latest in a life composed of mistakes and accidents. Let's start with my love of animals. There's nothing wrong with that, right? It's up there with saluting the flag and helping the poor. My problems began when my devotion to our four-legged creatures took me to the Iowa State Veterinary School. It didn't take long to learn I wasn't cut out—and I mean that literally—to be an animal doctor. I felt like taking a scalpel to the professor the first time I watched him slice open a cat's stomach. I couldn't imagine sticking my hand into a cat's abdomen and removing the ovaries. It was like asking a mother to circumcise her newborn son.

Needless to say, I flunked out. Carrying my bags and a load of school debt, I climbed aboard the first train back to my mother's house in Southern California. Mom had already found another husband and had moved out of the valley house she'd won as part of a divorce settlement with Pete Walker. The house was an upscale California Bungalow, sitting on a sprawling piece of property she had filled with a menagerie of cats, dogs, pigs, and a Shetland pony. Sparky was my addition, a mixed-breed dog that knew more tricks than a Sunset Boulevard hooker.

The L.A. silent film industry exploded in the 1920s with a growing demand for entertainment following the war, and directors and producers were always looking for a gimmick to pull in audiences. Animals were one of the gimmicks. I can thank my cousin Willy Torrance for getting me into showbiz. Willy had somehow transformed his love of films into a position as Special Assistant to Louis B. Mayer, the head of studio operations for Metro-Goldwyn-Mayer. These days, Willy is known as William J. Torrance.

As far as I knew, Willy didn't have a middle name, but when William J. knocked on the bungalow door shortly after I returned from Iowa and asked me if MGM could use Sparky in an upcoming film, I quickly agreed. Especially after he told me how much they'd pay me to be sure Sparky performed a few tricks.

That was in 1925, and over the next five years, with the help of Willy and local zoos, I provided a parade of pets and other animals to various motion pictures. But Gregory La Cava's request for a trained chimpanzee was different. The director wanted to spring the chimp on Fields in a scene of *So's Your Old Man*, currently in production on the RKO lot. I knew the director and W. C. Fields were good friends, and the way La Cava explained it, he wanted to get back at Fields for a prank he pulled. He didn't share the details with me, but Hollywood is a small town, and everyone had laughed when they heard Fields paid two men dressed as policemen to bust into the director's office during one of La Cava's "casting couch" sessions.

"Listen up, Marty," La Cava had said. "If this goes well with your monkey, I think you'll find more work right away. Victor Heerman is shooting a new Marx Brothers soon, and I heard he wanted to add a chimp to one of the scenes."

"That's great," I said.

"But wait, there's more. Metro is remaking the Tarzan film into a talkie, and you know they'll want a trained chimp."

"Thanks, Mr. La Cava. I'll see you in two days."

"Two days," I said aloud after hanging up. "Where the hell am I going to find a chimp and train it by Wednesday?"

I spent the rest of the day calling zoos and animal farms in Southern California. The Griffith Park Zoo's only surviving chimp was too old and cantankerous to be of any use. The keeper at the San Diego Zoo hung up on me when I told him what I needed.

I sat there with my head in my hands for a long minute before glancing toward the barn that housed my animals. I thought about my monthly feed and vet bills and wondered which of my pets I could part with.

A low whine grabbed my attention, and I looked up to see Sparky staring at me with liquid brown eyes. He raised a paw and laid it gently on my knee. I scratched his head and said, "It's okay, boy. We're a team, and I'll never let you go."

I stood and grabbed my coat off the back of my chair. I had an appointment with Pete Walker and a bottle of Scotch. Mom's divorce from Walker had been contentious, but Pete and I were still good friends. Pete had a lot of good qualities, including ample cases of White Horse Scotch.

My mother's ex was an enigma. I knew he worked for the U. S. government and traveled, staying away for weeks at a time, but that was about all. I called Pete and told him I was on my way, then drove my 1925 Ford Model T Runabout to Hancock Park, where I parked the truck in front of his Tudor Revival home. Pete opened the door before I knocked, pushing a large tumbler of White Horse into my hand.

"Come on in, Marty," he said with a slight slur, indicating he had a head start on the libations.

Pete Walker was a tall man with a perpetual smile and a slight limp. As usual, he was dressed like he'd just returned from meeting with President Hoover, wearing a waistcoat and a tie.

"So glad you called, Marty. Gladys took the kids to her daddy's farm for a few days, and you know I hate to drink alone."

Pete didn't waste any time remarrying after separating from my mother, and Gladys was the major reason for the divorce. I listened to Pete talk about everything except where he'd been for the last three weeks. He had told me he bought his smuggled scotch directly from Joe Kennedy, who had moved to Hollywood to buy into the film business and take advantage of nubile young actresses like Gloria Swanson. When Pete stopped talking to refill our glasses, I told him of my dilemma.

"You want a trained poodle or chinchilla? Not a problem. I have cats that can jump through a hoop of fire and dogs that can climb ladders, but where the hell can I find a chimpanzee in the next two days? And it would take weeks to train him not to break your arm."

"Sounds like you got a prime-ate problem, amigo."

"Yeah, it's not like I can magically fly to East Africa and bring back a trained monkey overnight."

"Chimpanzees. Hmm. That is a problem."

I noticed his eyes had flitted away from mine as I rattled on about needing a chimpanzee. Pete Walker had always been hard to read, but I felt the crafty government man was hiding something. Pete had consumed nearly an entire bottle by himself, and I let him take another swallow before I piped up. "What about it, Pete? Can you help me?"

He stood staring at me through bloodshot eyes. The spidery veins on his nose rainbowed through the primary colors, and I could see he was running a series of options in his mind. He finally spoke.

"Marty, have you ever heard of the Galvani Institute?"

Before I could open my mouth, he said, "Of course, you haven't. That's because it doesn't exist."

He was talking in riddles, and I waited for him to continue.

Pete put an arm around my shoulder and guided me to the sofa. He leaned in as if about to blow in my ear and, in a low voice, said, "It's all very hush-hush, but the Galvani Institute was established during the war to test and train chimps. I can't tell you why or for what purpose, but with the war over, they're still doing some kind of testing. Maybe …"

He let his sentence hang in the air. Maybe what? Maybe they'll give or sell me one of their chimps? I suspected that was all I'd get out of the government man who was concentrating on the liquid in his glass as though wondering how it got there.

"Where is this Galvani Institute?" I wasn't sure why I was whispering.

"I have no idea what you're talking about, but if you haven't been to the High Sierras, you really must. It's beautiful this time of year, especially the Lakes Basin Recreation area outside Graegle in Plumas County."

The High Sierras

GRAEAGLE WAS a good nine or ten hours north, near the Donner Pass, where snowbound pioneers in 1846 resorted to cannibalism when their food supply ran out. This historical fact conjured unsettling images as I drove to the High Sierras.

Nine-and-a-half hours later, I arrived at the tiny logging town of Graeagle. The morning sun peeked over the craggy hills, illuminating a path toward one of the rustic buildings adjoining Highway 89—the building with a light shining through the front window. A sign on the door told me the Graeagle General Store would open soon, but inside, a man in flannels and wool was sweeping the floor. He looked up when I knocked and waved me inside.

A bell over the door clanged as I walked in, and I considered how to approach the shopkeeper. Did the people in this town know about the Galvani Institute? Pete made it sound like the government facility was more secretive than my mother's bank account. I had to be careful how I handled this.

"Good morning," I said. "Beautiful little town you have here." It didn't hurt to butter him up before pumping him for information.

The shopkeeper looked me up and down with a sympathetic smile, probably thinking I was lost. And he'd be right.

He put the broom aside and hitched his pants over his generous belly. "Haven't seen you around here before. Guess you're one of the new guys at that Galvani Institute."

So much for government secrecy. "Is it that obvious?" I said. "But I'm so new I've never been there, and don't want to get lost and late on my first day."

He laughed. "Easy to do, my friend. They stuck it way up in the high country. Nothing around but bears, wolves, and mountain lions. Some of them Institute guys shop here, and they hang around the old pot belly and drink and jaw for hours. Here's what I can tell you."

He told me what he knew about the facility's location, even drawing a map of the roads leading up the mountain. I hadn't eaten all day, so I thanked him by buying a few things. He had a pot of coffee brewing, and I filled my American Thermos bottle and set off into the High Sierras.

It was slow going on the old logging roads, but the country was breathtaking. As I navigated my way through the twisting forest roads, I wondered how to tackle the Institute. I could introduce myself, tell them I needed a chimpanzee for the movies, and ask if they might have a spare they didn't need.

Sure, they'd hand one over to me and send me on my way with a sack full of monkey food. Just thinking of such a ridiculous scenario made me laugh. But then I thought, what if they had me arrested for trespassing or divulging government secrets? This had to be one of the most harebrained things I've ever done in a life filled with nutty decisions. But what choice did I have?

Before long, Mother Nature pressured me to recycle the coffee I'd been drinking. I pulled the truck to a stop next to a grove of redwoods and ponderosa pines. Before taking care of my business, I studied the crude map the shopkeeper had drawn. According to his directions, the Institute was around the next bend, perhaps a quarter mile away. Leaving the truck door open, I stepped closer to the tree line and unzipped. The deep wood aroma filled my nostrils. In the distance, I heard the tap-tap-tap of a woodpecker. There was nothing like this in Los Angeles.

From the corner of my eye, I sensed something dark drop from a nearby ponderosa pine. I heard it scurry through the underbrush and felt something flash past my legs. I whipped my head around in time to see a black shape leap into my truck. What the hell, I thought, quickly zipping up and carefully approaching the truck's open door. Was that a bear? A mountain lion? No, they would have attacked me, not the truck.

I crept slowly toward my Runabout, keeping the open door between me and whatever animal was inside. Peering around the door, I saw something squatting on the passenger side floor, hiding in the shadows. The creature's legs were folded against its chest, and its arms were wrapped tightly around them. It stared at me with large, watery eyes, and seemed to be shivering with fright.

It's a goddamn chimpanzee, I said to myself. I could see this wasn't a grizzled adult but an adolescent, and as I struggled to clear the confusion from my head, the chimp lifted a human-like hand and gestured for me to get in. I spun around to see if someone was chasing the chimp, but no one was in sight. The chimp watched me climb onto the driver's seat and close the door. It scuttled over, grasped my leg in a firm grip, and rested its head there. "I'll be damned," I said aloud. "Are you thanking me?"

That's when I noticed the shiny, pink scar on the chimp's head. I patted the primate's hand, hoping it would release my leg. "Who are you?" I asked, feeling a bit foolish for talking to a monkey. "And where did you come from?"

The chimp grunted in response to my questions and eased onto the passenger seat. It extended an arm toward me, ruffling the thick black hair on the inside of its right wrist. A tattoo emerged from among the hairs. I examined the wrist and read a series of letters and numbers: T483EX. I gazed from the tattoo to the chimp, who seemed to be examining me as closely as I examined the tattoo.

"You're from the Institute, aren't you?" I asked, feeling not so foolish this time, although the answer to my question was as evident as the tattoo on the chimp's wrist. As if in confirmation, the chimp nodded his head and emitted a series of low hoots and grunted. I watched the monkey's dark eyes fill with tears. My God, he's getting emotional, I thought.

The chimp worked his ample lips, twisting them one way and another, forming them into a perfect O. Then it resumed hooting, though the hoots sounded strangely different now, each hoot almost like a syllable. The peculiar noises emanating from the chimp's mouth slipped into a rhythmic cadence, its lips contorting and puckering while huffing gasps of air in and out.

I didn't know what to think, and I admit I was more than a little fearful of what the chimp might do next. I knew chimpanzees were almost twice as strong as men, and that, with the proper incentive, this primate could tear me apart. I leaned as far away as possible in the confined space, wishing I hadn't closed the door. That's when the chimp's low grunts became words.

T483EX

"YOU SAVE ME," the chimp said, poking me in the chest with his index finger. Again, the chimp stared directly into my eyes until I began to perspire and looked away. He shifted the digit from my chest to his head and back to my chest before grunting, "Can help you."

The chimp's words sounded strained, guttural, as though forced through a meat grinder. My mind reeled. I felt like I'd spent the last hour in a hashish den. Here I was with a talking monkey who wanted to help me. What did that mean?

"You can talk?" I sputtered. The question sounded inane even as it left my mouth, but my brain was still working on normal standard time.

The chimp grasped his mouth and then his throat. "I talk. Bad mens teach me."

"You mean the men in the institute taught you to talk?"

The chimpanzee responded with loud grunts, jumping up and down on the seat. Very slowly, I pried open the chimp's story. T483EX explained how the scientists had operated on him and his fellow test subjects. He tapped the scar on his head and said they tried to turn the primates into what he called "bad Kivili." As he continued to speak, in his condensed and ragged fashion, his syntax became clearer, and I understood why Pete Walker said this government facility was so hush-hush. The Galvani Institute was creating an army of primate assassins to find the enemy and kill them.

I couldn't believe what I was hearing. World War I had been over for ten years, yet the government was still trying to create a platoon of hairy exterminators. The question was why and who were they going to kill?

T483EX described how he emerged from his surgery much different than his fellow test subjects. While the other primates became increasingly vicious, sometimes turning on each other, T483EX refused to participate in the violence. When he awoke from his surgical procedure, his head wrapped in bandages, he stated that he lacked the compulsion to harm people like the other chimps. He wanted only to help them.

"Mens not happy with me."

"Because you want to help people?" The chimp hooted and nodded

enthusiastically before saying, "Other Kivili try hurt me."

"Kivili? You used that word before. What is Kivili?

I swear the monkey looked at me as though my IQ had dropped precipitously and repeated "Kivili" while beating on his chest. The clouds parted in my brain, and I pointed at him, saying, "Chimpanzees. You are Kivili."

He agreed by nodding again and grinning at me with a set of impressive teeth. I followed by asking, "Why did you say you could help me?"

T483EX jumped up and down on the passenger seat so hard I thought he might break it. "You need chimp," he said. "Me here."

I felt like the dumb monkey now. This was crazy talk. "How do you know that?" I asked.

He pointed to the scar on his head and moved his finger slowly across his temple to his face, pointing directly at his right eye. Mesmerized, I watched the monkey rotate his hand with the extended finger and aim it at me. The chimp tapped the digit against my forehead, once, twice, before shifting back to his head. The tumblers finally fell into place, and I blurted out, "You can see my mind."

T483EX hooted excitedly and slapped the steering wheel. "Go now."

THE CHIMP DEVOURED the sandwich and apple I'd bought at the general store and quickly fell asleep as I drove back to Los Angeles. My mind was a snake pit of questions. Is this really happening? A chimpanzee falls out of a tree into my life, and he can read my mind? What were those government scientists up to? And more importantly, can this monkey really help me?

T483EX stayed relatively quiet after he awoke, staring out the window, and responding with low grunts to my attempts at conversation. I couldn't imagine what he must have endured at the Galvani Institute. He said he wanted to help people, but people had tormented him. From my studies, I knew chimps' brains, like all animals, are wired differently from ours. They see the world emotionally, through feelings and impressions, but they are highly intelligent animals. I needed to gain his trust and convince him that most people were not like the ones at the Institute.

. . .

"THIS IS YOUR NEW HOME," I said as we walked into my bungalow. Sparky and a few of the cats greeted us at the door, but quickly retreated when they saw my primate friend. Sparky peered around the corner, barked once, and dropped onto his belly, his ears flattened against his head.

"It's okay, Sparky. He won't hurt you." I bent down and stroked the dog's muzzle and behind his ears, which usually moved the pooch to roll over on his back to have his belly rubbed. This time, he remained motionless, his eyes never leaving the chimp's. T483EX had been standing beside me while taking in the exchange. He suddenly squatted next to Sparky and held out his hand to let the dog smell him.

"See, he wants to be your friend," I said.

Sparky sniffed the chimp's hand and slowly rose from the floor. "Good boy. I know you two are going to be great friends. Let me introduce you. Sparky, this is …" Pausing, I turned to the chimp. "I can't keep calling you T483EX," I said. "How about Jiggs? You like that name?"

Jiggs grunted, and I took that to mean he liked his new name. After the introductions were over, I showed Jiggs around, fed both of us, and we settled in the den for a long conversation. Jiggs found the words to tell me how he had slipped away from his confinement and hidden in the woods for two days before I came along. I told him how sorry I was that this had happened to him. I assured him that most people were good and would welcome his help. I certainly did.

"Jiggs, you have a home here, now. Do you understand? I'm going to take care of you, and I hope you can forget about that horrible place. You can trust me."

Jiggs' eyes were glistening. He lay his head against my chest and said, "Thanking you."

Finally, I told him about my predicament and how he could help me with the La Cava film.

"Yes, yes," he hooted. "Jiggs can help."

W. C. Fields

WE WERE in an alley adjoining the street where they were shooting a scene in La Cava's silent feature, *So's Your Old Man*. I had watched Fields take a quick hit from his flask and enter the hotel lobby with a half-dozen well-dressed men. They were waiting for the cameras to roll before ambling out onto the sidewalk.

The director hustled toward us once Fields was out of sight. He gave the chimp a quick once over, and I said, "This is Jiggs."

La Cava nodded and asked, "He's not going to do anything funny, like jump on Bill, is he?

"Oh no, he's very well behaved."

"Good. I only want to surprise him, not give him a heart attack. In a minute I'll call for action and they'll all come out of the hotel and walk toward the Model T where Bill will demonstrate his unbreakable glass windshield by throwing a brick at it."

I wanted to know more about the brick, but I let him talk.

"He'll be facing the crowd of auto executives, bragging about his shatterproof glass. When he turns around and approaches the car, he'll see Jiggs on the hood. Can he make a face and grunt or something?"

"Sure, but you said Mr. Fields would have a brick in his hand. You don't think he'll …?

"Don't worry about that. Bill isn't a violent man, he's just not fond of animals."

I wasn't totally convinced but nodded in agreement. "What happens then?"

"That's it," La Cava said. "I've already told the cast and crew, so they'll be in on the joke, and you can take Jiggs away. Of course, Jiggs won't make it into the film, but if he plays his part well, I'll give you both a good recommendation." He started to pat Jiggs on the head, thought better of it, and hurried to his director's chair.

As soon as the director rounded the corner, I whispered to Jiggs, "Remember, the man in the straw hat is the one who will walk to the car?" We had watched Fields separate from the other actors and sidle away to remove a flask from his coat pocket. The comedian was of medium height, wearing a checkered coat, vest, and straw hat. His bulbous nose nearly obscured a small, dark mustache. "You understand when he gives us the signal, you run and hop on the car? When he turns around and sees you, jump up and down and make some noise. That's it."

Jiggs appeared to be listening intently to every word. "This is important for both of us. If Mr. La Cava is happy, we'll get a lot more work so I can keep buying you all the tasty bananas and figs you can eat. Okay?"

At that moment, La Cava waved at us.

"This is it. Jiggs. Go now."

The entire crew watched as Jiggs bounded toward the Model T. He leaped onto the hood and perched on his haunches, waiting for his star turn.

La Cava smiled his approval and screamed, "Action."

Immediately, Fields emerged from the hotel, followed by six men representing the auto executives. The comedian held two bricks while he pattered on about his amazing discovery of unbreakable glass and how it would change the auto industry. I knew the dialogue would appear as a few lines in the title cards appearing on the screen.

Fields finished talking about the glass, hefted one of the bricks, and turned toward the car. He spotted Jiggs on the hood and stood transfixed as the chimp raised up and grunted, waving his arms like he was warding off an infestation of fruit flies. Fields dropped both bricks, fortunately missing his feet, and bellowed, "What the hell is this, Gregory?"

The cast and crew erupted in laughter. I heard La Cava yell, "Got you, Billy boy," followed by more laughter. I expected Jiggs to hop off the car and join me as we had discussed, but instead, he and the comedian seemed engaged in a staring contest. Fields hadn't moved from his spot, but Jiggs was leaning toward him with one finger pointed in his direction. Fields broke away, shook his head, and spewed a stream of curses followed by something that sounded like, "Very funny, Gregory, very funny. You know I can't stand animals and kids."

"Let's take a quick break before we reshoot," La Cava announced.

I watched Fields retreat to a shaded alcove next to the hotel's entrance. He lifted the flask from his inside coat pocket, unscrewed the top, and put it to his lips. Before he could swallow, Jiggs swooped up and grabbed the flask out of his hand. Fields gaped open-mouthed as Jiggs scurried away with the flask.

"Stop him," Fields shrieked. "That damn monkey stole my lunch."

I chased Jiggs around the corner into the alley, where the chimp I had rescued from the Galvani Institute meekly handed over the flask. La Cava and Fields had rushed after us, and I returned the flask to the comedian, saying, "I'm so sorry, Mr. Fields, Jiggs is a real trickster."

Fields responded with a look that could freeze the gin in his flask. He walked away, mumbling to himself. We all watched him disappear around the corner with the flask to his lips. I was sure the chimp's stunt had ruined any chance we'd get more studio business. La Cava must be furious, I told myself as I turned to the director to take my medicine.

"Man, that was beautiful, Marty," the director said. "I couldn't have scripted it better. Stealing his flask was a great bit of improv. Way to go, Jiggs." And this time, he did pat Jiggs on the head.

La Cava paid me, and we drove a few blocks before I pulled to the curb. Jiggs sat quietly in the passenger seat next to me. I took a deep breath, then addressed Jiggs as simply as possible. Even though he was a remarkable primate with more than human abilities, I had to remember he was still a monkey. "Why did you take his drink? You could have ruined everything."

Jiggs's lower lip protruded, and his eyes were downcast. He looked so forlorn that I felt bad for reprimanding him. "It's okay, Jiggs. I'm not mad at you," I said, which wasn't exactly true. "But I want to know why you did it."

Jiggs lifted his head. His amber eyes shimmered. "Bad water," he said, gesturing as though he was drinking. "Bad water hurt, man. Make sick. Want to help."

Jiggs lowered his head again, and I understood the chimp was following his surgically generated mandate to prevent harm to humans. I put my arm around the chimp's shoulder to show him I wasn't angry. "You did what you thought was right, but Hollywood is a small town, and everyone knows everyone's business. We can't afford to get a reputation, but I love what you did. Maybe this will make Mr. Fields cut back on his drinking."

Jiggs wrapped his arms around me. He pressed his big lips against my cheek in a wet kiss. "And I love you, too, Jiggs. Now, let go because I can't breathe."

"Can still help?" Jiggs asked.

"You bet. Mr. La Cava was very happy and will recommend us for that Marx Brothers movie."

Animal Crackers

After starring in the Broadway play *Animal Crackers*, the Marx Brothers contracted to reprise their roles for the Paramount film version. In the zany comedy, Groucho played the renowned explorer Captain Jeffrey Spaulding. On the set, the director, Victor Heerman, explained to me that he and Groucho had agreed the chimp would add credibility and silliness to the opening scene.

"It's a big party scene," Heerman said, "and Spaulding is the guest of honor. He'll make a grand entrance accompanied by Jiggs. Everyone will make a fuss over the monkey, who scampers off to sit on the piano. Chico and Harpo arrive next to perform for the guests."

"Sounds simple enough," I said. "What happens after Jiggs is on the piano?"

"Groucho announces he can't stay, and the two of them leave. That's it. Short screen time, but good payday for you."

I assured him we had it covered but hoped it was as simple as Heerman explained. I reviewed it again with Jiggs to be sure he understood, and we waited while they lit the set and moved props around.

Groucho sat on the piano bench, going over his lines while Harpo removed his curly, blond wig and scratched furiously at his bald head. Groucho looked up and snapped at his brother, "Arthur, will you stop that? You're going to hit gray matter soon."

"You don't have to wear this thing. It's driving me crazy."

"Yeah, remember that thing got you into show business."

Heerman called everyone to the set for the first scene, and I escorted Jiggs to Groucho and introduced them. He took Jiggs's hand and shook it. "Guess this makes me a monkey's uncle," he said.

The scene began perfectly, with Groucho entering the room hand-in-hand with Jiggs. After their entrance, Jiggs stole a banana from a fruit bowl and dashed to the piano, where he sat on the closed lid of the baby grand, peeling the banana. Chico and Harpo arrived next and took their places. Chico raised the piano's lid, and Jiggs jumped off and hunkered down near Harpo, who sat with his hands on the strings of the harp, waiting for Chico to play. Jiggs remained quiet, and my thoughts turned to how much Heerman was paying me while mentally balancing my checkbook.

Loud hoots from Jiggs grabbed my attention. He was becoming

increasingly agitated, and I held my breath, praying he could control himself. Instead, the chimp snatched the wig from Harpo's head and ran off the set.

"Cut," the director yelled. "Jensen, can't you control your monkey?"

I cornered Jiggs, and rescued the wig, and returned it to Harpo. Both the director and Groucho had approached, and I offered my most sincere apologies. "I'm so sorry, Mr. Marx. Jiggs gets a little playful, sometimes."

The director's face had turned a blazing shade of red, and I steeled myself for a big-time beatdown. "You...you..." Heerman sputtered, apparently running out of negative adjectives.

Groucho jumped into the breech. "Leave the guy alone, Vic. That was a funny bit. I wish we could keep it in the scene, but you have to admit it was funny. Don't you think, Arthur?"

Harpo scratched his pate before slipping the wig back on his head. "Yeah, and it gave me a few minutes of relief."

"Let's get back to work and finish the scene, then you can pay the guy," Groucho said.

ON THE DRIVE back to the house, I decided reprimanding Jiggs would be unproductive. As I worked on the best approach, Jiggs blurted three words.

"Hair hurt him," followed by a furious scratching of his head.

I said, "You only want to help people, and that's a quality you won't find in most human beings." I wasn't sure he fully comprehended the intent of my statement, but I continued. "Everyone has problems, and we do our best to deal with them."

Jiggs hadn't made a sound. He'd clasped his hands in his lap, and his wide eyes focused on my face.

"You understand me, don't you?"

Jiggs grunted.

"Your heart is in the right place, but you can't solve everyone's problems. Not if it affects our business. You don't want to hurt *me*, do you?"

A long silence followed while Jiggs chewed on his lower lip. He finally said, "No hurt you. Sorry."

Tarzan the Ape Man

TRUE TO HIS WORD, Gregory La Cava recommended us to his counterpart at Metro-Goldwyn-Mayer. They were filming a talkie based on Edgar Rice Burroughs's 1912 novel *Tarzan of the Apes*, and they needed a trained chimp for a major role in the film.

Jiggs and I were at the Culver City studio talking with the director, W. S. Van Dyke. He explained that Olympic swimmer Johnny Weissmuller had the starring role, with actress Maureen O'Sullivan playing Jane. He pointed at Jiggs, who sat quietly examining his toes.

"Jiggs will be called Cheeta in the film and plays Tarzan's friend and jungle companion. Cheeta has some important scenes helping to save Jane and Tarzan."

Jiggs's head snapped up at the last sentence, and I knew my chimp friend would relish the role of a lifesaver.

"Do you think he's up for this?" Van Dyke asked.

"Jiggs is perfect for the part. You don't have a thing to worry about."

A DAY LATER, we were on the set, surrounded by lions borrowed from a nearby lion farm and Indian elephants fitted with fake ears and tusks to make them look like African elephants. I met Weissmuller and O'Sullivan, and we walked through a few scenes with *Cheeta* until they became comfortable with each other.

Jiggs was a natural for the part. I'd never seen him so animated or cooperative, throwing himself into the role of jungle savior and friend to Tarzan. Weissmuller's relationship with Jiggs began on a high note, but as the days passed, I sensed the actor's attitude shifting. As soon as the director called "Cut," he'd walk away instead of playing with Jiggs as he had at the beginning. I put this down to the stress of a swimmer suddenly starring in a major motion picture.

During a break, I took Jiggs aside and told him that Tarzan was under a lot of pressure. "Me like Tarzan," Jiggs said, apparently unconcerned about Weissmuller's behavior.

After shooting the so-called "jungle scenes" in the Toluca Lake region of L.A., we traveled to Florida for a key part of the production. I looked forward to completing the film in Florida's sunny climate and returning home in time for Christmas. Weissmuller continued to worry me, however. I wasn't the only one who had noticed his actions toward Jiggs were increasingly belligerent. I worried how he'd act when we arrived in Florida and wished I shared Jiggs's mind-reading ability. The only way to know what was bothering Johnny Weissmuller was to get inside the Ape Man's head.

Johnny Weissmuller

A SHIVER COURSED through his body, but Johnny Weissmuller had a plan. This time, when he opened his mouth, the sound of the real Tarzan would emerge. Not the weak warble that was met with howls of laughter. He had to do it right or face a frigid holiday made even worse by the cold stares of the cast and crew.

Weissmuller knew he could do it. Didn't he win five Gold Medals and set over sixty world records? He ignored the skinny man with the sarcastic smile holding the boom microphone, but it was hard to ignore that damn monkey grinning at him from off-camera. He'd tried to tell the director to keep Cheeta away from him since the chimp playfully nipped him on the shoulder.

"That's his way of showing love," Marty had assured him.

"Bull!" Weissmuller responded. "That thing wants to eat my face."

Weissmuller moved into the frame as Van Dyke shouted action and stared past the camera as though expecting a herd of elephants to burst through the pine trees and Florida palms. In his mind,

Johnny could hear the powerful cry leaping from his throat in long, melodic tones. But what dribbled out was a gurgling sputter that hung in the chilly air for a moment before fading behind a chorus of snorts from the crew.

Van Dyke approached him, putting an arm around the Ape Man's well-defined trapezius muscles. "Johnny, this yell is as important to Tarzan's persona as that loin cloth you're wearing. I know you can do it." He nodded at the gang of workers and cast members hovering around the set and lowered his voice. "Remember, if you don't get this right, we're stuck here through the holidays. That won't make anyone happy."

As if to emphasize the director's lament, Cheeta bounded over and wrapped his hairy arms around Weissmuller's leg.

"Get off me, you dirty ape."

Marty took the chimp by the hand, telling the Ape Man, "He only wants to be your friend."

"Let's set up for the crocodile fight," the director called. "Johnny, take a break and think about what I said."

Weissmuller's eyes angled toward the production workers who were suddenly so busy pulling cables and rolling lights to the next location that none of them returned his gaze. He felt goose bumps creep over his nearly naked body as he trudged to his trailer.

WEISSMULLER UNDERSTOOD he'd been incredibly lucky. He'd been plucked from a swimming pool and told he would be the next Tarzan. They even paid him $250 a week to act with sexy little Maureen O'Sullivan. The Culver City production had gone smoothly enough, but now the entire crew was encamped in Silver Springs, shooting the swimming scenes in the wilds of central Florida during a rare freeze. Even though he grew up in the bone-chilling blizzards of Chicago, Weissmuller yearned to be in front of a roaring fire.

In his trailer, Weissmuller pulled on a robe in his trailer and slumped on the couch. He knew the yell should be a thunderous cry that shook the trees and brought fear to natives and beasts alike. But his attempts at the fearsome shriek sounded more like a hungry infant screaming for its bottle, or as an electrician so cruelly put it, "I've heard more manly yells from my cat."

He was sinking deeper into self-pity when he heard a tap on his trailer door.

"It's open," he called.

Cheeta scrambled inside, one arm stretched behind him, clutching Maureen O'Sullivan's hand. She was wearing the scanty two-piece leather outfit that grabbed everyone's attention.

"How're you feeling, Johnny?"

"I'm okay."

"Listen, this yell is no big thing. If we have to work through the holidays, then we'll work. That's what they pay us for. Right?"

Weissmuller stood and put his arms around the actress. "Thank you, Mo, but it is a big thing. If I—"

Cheeta interrupted him, leaping up and down and vocalizing with loud pant hoots. He rushed over and joined the two actors in a three-way hug. "Cheeta really loves you," Maureen said.

Weissmuller broke away from the threesome, pushing Cheeta aside. At that, the chimp clambered onto a chair, huffed loudly several times, threw his head back, and emitted a long warbling cry.

"I never heard him do anything like that, Maureen said. "It sounded like he was trying to yodel."

Weissmuller was silent.

"Did you hear me, Johnny?"

"Yodel," he murmured.

TWENTY MINUTES LATER, Van Dyke called action. The Ape Man dove into the crystal-blue water, plunging deep below the surface past the underwater camera. Pulling a lethal-looking knife from his scabbard, he swam swiftly toward the menacing form of the phony crocodile. He grabbed the prop croc, and they rolled over and over until he sank the knife deep into its throat.

"Perfect," said the director as Weissmuller climbed out of the water. "We're losing the light. Maybe we'll call it a day."

"I want to try the yell again," Weissmuller said, his teeth chatter-ing. In the background, he saw eyeballs rolling and mouths curling into smirks.

"Are you sure?" The director said.

"Yes, but bring Cheeta here. I want to see him."

FIFTEEN MINUTES LATER, the lights and microphone were set. Maureen and Cheeta stood next to the camera, the chimp bouncing on the balls of his feet, grunting excitedly.

"Action!"

Johnny stepped into the shot, lifted his head, and opened his mouth. Instead of the familiar choked cries, a long, yodeling howl filled with jungle fever flowed over the set. Everyone, including Marty, stared in shocked silence until the director yelled, "Cut."

A mob scene followed, with actors and crew members surrounding the tall man in the loincloth. They pounded him on the back and congratulated him, wanting to know how he had come up with the incredible yell. Backing away with a shy smile, the Ape Man hurried to Maureen and Cheeta. Maureen stepped forward, arms open wide, but instead of embracing his co-star, Weissmuller swept Cheeta up and held him against his muscled chest. Cheeta clinched him tightly in return.

"Man, I love this monkey," was all Weissmuller said.

I SMILED as Jiggs grinned at me over the Ape Man's shoulder and shot him a thumbs-up gesture. Weissmuller saw me watching and disentangled himself from the hairy embrace, passing Jiggs to me. "You have a special monkey here, Marty. I think Cheeta and me are going to be together for a lot more movies." He patted Jiggs on the head and strode toward Maureen, his chest out, head held high, looking every inch the King of the Jungle.

As the two actors walked away, Jiggs dug into my coat pocket and retrieved the banana he knew I had waiting for him. I inclined my head close to his to be sure we wouldn't be overheard, and said, "Did you hear what Johnny said, Jiggs? You are one special Kivili."

Jiggs munched on the banana and nodded vigorously, hooting chimp noises and spewing bits of banana in my direction. "He doesn't know how special you are, my friend."

Jiggs didn't answer, but I had the feeling he knew exactly how special he was. I certainly did. Taking his hand, we walked together in the fading Florida light, two primates, but only one mind reader.

Author's Notes—Parker Francis

JIGGS'S ABILITY TO read minds is fictional, but a chimpanzee named Jiggs performed in the first Tarzan films, and many of the motion picture details in this story are accurate. Although not rescued from a secret government facility, the real Jiggs originated the role of Cheeta in the first two Johnny Weissmuller Tarzan movies and appeared in other Tarzan films starring Buster Crabbe and Herman Brix. He also appeared in the Laurel and Hardy film *Dirty Work* and *Her Jungle Love*, starring Dorothy Lamour.

W. C. Fields, whose real name was William Claude Dunkenfield, began his career in vaudeville as a silent juggler before adding comedy to his act. He was known as a heavy drinker with a distaste for working with children and animals. *So's Your Old Man* and *Animal Crackers* were made at Astoria Studios in New York. Using the power granted to me when I earned my Literary License, I transferred both productions to Los Angeles.

MGM shot *Tarzan the Ape Man* at its Culver City studios, Toluca Lake, and Silver Springs, Florida. I created the hard freeze and Weissmuller's problems with the Ape Man's yell for dramatic effect. While Weissmuller maintained that the yell was his voice, other stories claim opera singer Lloyd Thomas Leach voiced the famous yell. Others claimed it to be a combination of three voices, including a hog caller from Arkansas. Curiously, the yell sounds the same when played backward, meaning there was some manipulation by the MGM sound department.

I wrote *Monkey Business* as an entertaining tale with a heart. Unlike Jiggs, humans lack an internal mandate to help one another. Maybe one day, the evolutionary process will change that.

~PF

Versipellis Nemora

Scott Michael Powers

"I *wanna be your dog.*"
—*James Newell Osterberg Jr. (aka Iggy Pop)*

The Hocking Mountains, 2025

THERE'S two kindsa people I just as soon see burn in hell, no matter what their good points. The first is someone who wants to hurt or kill animals for no good reason. The second is someone who tries to tell me what I can't do on my land.

I'm tellin' myself that, and I'm recallin' what all just went down, as I'm buryin' the ashes and bones and bits of clothing of that state wildlife officer, Sergeant Stone. He done come round this morning to tell me I can't keep wolves here.

Hell, I can't, I told him. No, you can't, Stone said; you can't have wolves as pets. I tried to tell him, They's not just pets, they's my friends, though I figure there's no way he'd ever understand.

Anyway, I asked him real polite, What am I supposed to do with them? But he was a jerk about it. You done enough, all right? We're just gonna take 'em, he said, and then we're probably going to have to put them down, 'cause you shouldn'ta never kept 'em here in the first place. I'm going to go get a court order now, and then I'll be back with the sheriff and some others.

Lord Almighty, there weren't no point in trying to tell him what a fool thing that'd be to try. All I could figure was I had to stop him, 'cause if he came back with others, ain't no tellin' how bad it'd get. So yeah, I did it. I gave the hand signal.

I seen Draugluin and Fenrir watching us between broken fence slats, and I knew they heard all that too. Stone never imagined that the gate don't latch right 'till they pushed it open, come through, and then drug him back to the other side.

Anyhow, I'm runnin' all that through my mind, over 'n' over as I'm thowin' dirt on top of what's left of that damn fool. I'm sweatin' and stinkin' and my shoulders and back and arms is all sore from the diggin', and I'm still just pissed at him. Why'd he haveta come and pull that shit on us, anyhow? We ain't been hurtin' nobody out here. Now what we gonna do? 'Cause when he don't show up at home tonight, they'll come out here lookin' for him, sure as I'm buryin' his bones.

Draugluin—he's the leader of the pack—was standing beside me. I reached over and rubbed his muzzle. He leaned into my hand, so I rubbed his brow and ears. The others was all layin' around nappin'. It was daylight. They like to sleep in the daytime, 'specially with full stomachs.

"Now what we gonna do?" I asked Draugluin.

"We're going to need a plan," he said.

What I was always told, my granddaddy and great-granddaddy and all the men of my family line before them was friends with werewolves going back forever in the old country. Daddy come here to America with a lotta money from one of them who was a duke, to find a place for them to live in peace, away from all the hate them werewolves had to deal with in the old country. Took a while for him to find and set up this place, with lots of old forest over a couple of mountainsides. Took even longer to arrange for everyone to get to America to live here. Outside their ancestral homes, werewolves stay in wolf form, and it ain't like you can just import a dozen wolves. Anyhow, Daddy got married. I got born, and I growed up. The wolves finally showed up. Momma went crazy over all this and run off. Couple years later, Daddy died. So then, the whole damn thing became my business.

Goin' on ten years now, I'm the caretaker and official owner of what they call Versipellis Nemora. What I'm told, that's Latin for Werewolf Retirement Home, or somethin' like that. Livin' and workin' here is pretty much all I know. It ain't so hard, most of the time. They know they gotta keep a low profile. They don't bite no humans no more—'till now, anyhow. That's what being retired is all about, right? Sometimes they run off into the mountains, but it ain't nothing to worry about. The worst they ever do is drag a deer back, but that's about it. They don't touch farm animals or people or nothing, not usually. Sometimes they howl at the moon. Hell, a lotta people round here know I got wolves, and ain't none of 'em ever complained to me about it. Neighbors ain't got no problem, 'cept for whoever it was ratted us out to the state.

In most ways, they's just like a buncha dogs, 'cept for this and that. I gotta drive over to a slaughterhouse in town regular and bring back a trailer full of food for 'em. I got a doggy door on the back of the house, and they can come inside as they please. But mosta the time, they like bein' out back, or wanderin' the woods. They play together like dogs too, chasin' each other and bitin' and nippin'. You sit out here with me under the moon most nights, you'd swear they's just a buncha happy dogs.

'Course, they ain't dogs. For one thing, they talk. They all used to be human. And Lord, I tell you what, they got some stories to tell. Daddy dug and bricked a nice fire pit out back where I burn the remains of carcasses and some of my garbage, and sometimes I sit next to the fire with a beer, and they come round and tell tales'd curl your hair. I ain't gonna lie. Some of them was pure evil back in the day. But they's all retired now. Long as they's good, we're good. Draugluin, who probably was the worst of 'em, keeps 'em all in line. He's the biggest damn wolf I ever seen, and black as coal.

Quentin, the littlest wolf but I think the smartest, knew of a holler off County Road 24 ain't nobody can see into. So, he hopped in the officer's truck with me and showed me where to go, and I drove it over there. Then I done rolled that truck into the ravine. They might find it next week if they get lucky, or hell, they might not never find it.

Soon as the sun was down, Draugluin called a council round the fire pit.

"Let's kill them all," Stubbe said. He's a gray wolf, not real big, but he's vicious as all get out, with red, red eyes and big white, slobbery teeth he likes to bare. He scares me more'n any of 'em.

"That's no good," Quentin said. "They'll just send more and more people after us, and it'll be like the old country all over again. I didn't give up being human and come all the way out here just to be chased around again by a bunch of Christian crazies for all eternity. Bad enough when Willard's mom thought she could cure us with a Bible and a cross."

"You, leave Momma out of it," I said. "She just got religion, that's all. And she couldn't figure ya'll out. I mean, who can? Anyway, she ain't here to defend herself, so it ain't fair to bring her up. I still love her, no matter."

"I'm just trying to remind everyone that that's what we will be up against, from all the people, if we kill everyone who comes out here."

"Right?" said Jacob, a young, black-and-white wolf, and maybe the cutest of the whole pack. "I don't want to kill anyone. I'm a lover, not a killer."

"Grow up, kid," Bisclavret said. "Love doesn't last. Only death lasts."

"I believe there are women out there who are true," Jacob said. "You're bitter about love only because your wife left you after she learned you were a werewolf."

"Mention my ex-wife again and I will rip your throat out."

"Hey, hey, hey. We're getting off track here," Draugluin said. "Quentin's right, as usual. Much as I would love to kill them all, that's no good. Didn't we learn anything from the old country? Eventually, they'll realize what we really are, and then they'll go weird. They always go weird. Our enemy here is not religion, it's ignorance. It always has been. So, we need to appeal to their ignorance. We need to find a way to get them to believe something stupid, like we're harmless. Then they'll leave us alone."

"Well then, we're going to have to convince them we're just dogs. Everyone assumes dogs are harmless, and there are no laws against having dogs on your property," Quentin suggested. "To pull that off, we're going to need some props."

"Excellent idea," Draugluin said. "Willard, didn't you say there's an all-night store in town? Can you drive on over tonight and get a bunch of dog collars?"

"I am not wearing a dog collar," Stubbe said.

"Me, neither," Bisclavret said.

"You will do as Draugluin says," said Fenrir. He's the second-biggest wolf, silver-gray, and he's kinda Draugluin's enforcer. Loyal as can be.

"Sniff my ass," Stubbe said.

Fenrir padded over. As he got nose to nose with Stubbe, everyone got real quiet. You could hear the fire cracklin' and you could hear Fenrir snort, and then you could hear a real slow, low growl. You could hear Stubbe pantin' too—and then he looked away, and it was over.

"You will wear a collar. All of you," Fenrir said. "If Draugluin wants you to jump through hoops, then you will say, 'Yes sir! How high sir?' Do you understand?"

"That's a good idea, too," Quentin said. "Can you pick up some hoops, too, in that store?"

By the time I got back from Wal-Mart, and we got everything set up, and we ran through a coupla rehearsals, it was put-near dawn. Weren't too long after that when the convoy come up the drive. We rushed around and took our places. I come out through the fence gate to meet 'em out front.

I wore clean jeans and my only button-down dress shirt, blue. I'm about six-two and skinny as a pole. I showered, shaved, combed my hair so it dropped like an orange doo-rag over my shoulders. I trimmed my mustache and sideburns. In other words, I got about as presentable as I get.

"You still look like the village idiot," Draugluin said.

About when I pushed the gate closed behind me, vehicle doors started openin'. There was the Sheriff himself, some deputies, the county animal control officer, and a couple others. Some of 'em toted rifles.

"Mornin' Sheriff. To what do I owe the pleasure?" I asked.

"First, we're looking for a missing state wildlife officer. He came out to see you yesterday, and no one's heard from him since," the Sheriff said.

He was a big man on little legs. He walked like he was not quite stable, maybe could topple over if the wind changed. Tan uniform, black tie, brass star, big tan Stetson covering almost no hair. He handed me a picture of Sergeant Stone.

"Tell him you have not seen him before. No one's been out here for a couple of weeks," Draugluin said into my ear. I was fitted with one earbud, and my hair covered it, so ain't no one could see it. My phone was in my pocket, and it was connected with a phone back up in the house, set to speaker between Draugluin and Quentin. They was watching through the window. All the rest of the wolves was in the backyard.

"Sorry, Sheriff, I ain't never seen him before," I said. "I ain't had no one out here in a coupla weeks, at least."

"You sure? Take a good look. He called in and said he was arriving on your property. That's the last anyone heard from him."

Draugluin was quick, tellin' me to say if he did come 'round, I musta been out back trainin' dogs, where I couldn't hear nothin' out front.

"I dunno Sheriff. Maybe he came. Maybe he didn't. Mighta been while I was out back workin' with my dogs. Out there, I can't always hear if someone comes to the house," I said.

"Dogs?"

We'd gone through all this in practice, but Draugluin reminded me: "Yes. Ukrainian shepherds. A special breed of circus dogs."

"That's right, Sheriff. I got Ukrainian shepherds. They's circus dogs. Special ones."

Draugluin told me to say an uncle sent them to me to get them away from the Russian war.

"They was sent to me by my uncle to get them away from the war over there in Russia."

"In Ukraine, you stupid imbecile," Draugluin yelled in my ear. He could be mean, sometimes. I wish he wouldn't.

"The war's in Ukraine, doofus, not Russia," Draugluin added.

"Right," I said to the Sheriff. "I mean Ukraine. My uncle is in Ukraine. That's where the dogs was from, Ukraine."

"Circus dogs?" the Sheriff asked. "We were told you have wolves out here."

"Wolves? Ha!" I tried to laugh. I did. I just ain't too good at faking it. "Ha ha ha ha ha—"

Draugluin shouted in my ear. "Shut up you dumb hick. You're making an ass of yourself. Ask him why he thinks you have wolves."

"Why on God's green Earth you think I got wolves, Sheriff?"

"I can't reveal my source just yet," he said.

"Well, they's dogs."

"I'd like to see them. Can we have a look around?"

That's what we wanted. "Course. Follow me, then, Sheriff," I said. I led them through the gate.

Right then, the ten remaining wolves got up and chased each other around. They held their tails up, like dogs usually do.

"Woof," said Fenrir.

"Yip," said Jacob.

Two guys with rifles raised them to sight. Damn them. That just weren't necessary.

I whistled and pointed, and they all circled us and then lined up beside me. They never seemed to get that right in practice, but it looked pretty damn good just now.

"Sit," I said, signalin' with my hand. They all sat. Couple of them lolled their tongues. Nice touch, I thought.

"Those aren't dogs. Those are wolves," the Sheriff said.

"Ask him if he's ever seen wolves behave like this," Draugluin said.

"Nah, Sheriff. You ever seen wolves act like this?"

"Show him the hoop trick," Draugluin prompted.

"Watch this, Sheriff."

I went and got one of them hula hoops I bought. I motioned my hand toward the hoop and whistled twice. One by one the wolves broke from their line, run, and jumped through, easy peasy. Then they went and sat down like they was before.

"I still say they're wolves," said one of the other guys.

"No sir," I said. "Ukrainian shepherds. Special breed. Ain't hardly got none of them in the U.S. of A. yet. I mighta got the first ones. They's trained to do lots of things. You can't train a wolf, Sheriff. These dogs are as smart, and friendly, and gentle as hound dogs."

"Ruff," said Fenrir.

"Yip, yip," said Jacob and he got up on his haunch, paddled his front paws and smiled like I was supposed to throw him a treat.

I wasn't watching all of the deputies, but Quentin was, through a back window.

"Oh, shit. That deputy's kicking around in the dirt over where Willard buried that guy. Someone needs to do something to distract him before he kicks something up," I heard Quentin say.

Now, before Draugluin could say a thing, and before I could think of somethin' to do, Fenrir growled and jumped up. You see, I put the other earbud in his ear so he could hear all what was bein' said. He dashed toward that deputy, growlin' like he was gonna tear him apart. Just before he sprung, two rifle shots cracked. Fenrir jerked and yelped with the first one, fell with the second one, and flopped on the ground. Then he lay still as a rug.

"What you go and do that for?" I yelled.

"He was attacking my deputy!" the Sheriff said.

The other wolves came over to sniff and prod Fenrir. Some of them whimpered like puppies.

"He would not have hurt him. He was just trying to chase the deputy away from the dogs' burial ground," Draugluin suggested in my ear.

"He wouldn'ta hurt nobody. He was just tryin' to keep him off the dog burial ground."

"Looked to me like he was attacking," the Sheriff said.

"Well, he wasn't," I said.

"Get them out of there, you nitwit, now!" Draugluin shouted in my ear.

"I think it's time you go, Sheriff. You seen my dogs, and you done killed one of 'em. I don't think you's welcome here no more."

"My apology," the Sheriff said. "Send my office a bill for the lost canine. We'll take care of it."

"So he sees we're dogs?" I heard Quentin ask.

"You see these is dogs, then, right?" I asked.

"They're dogs," the Sheriff said.

"Not wolves?" Draugluin demanded.

"Not wolves?" I asked.

"Not wolves."

I followed the Sheriff and all the others back out through the gate.

Behind me, I just barely heard Fenrir say something like, "Ow, Mother Mary, those bullets hurt." I knew he'd be okay; you can't kill a werewolf with regular bullets. But I bet they did hurt, hittin' him at short-range velocity like that.

I pushed the gate closed and watched the sheriff and his posse all climb back into the four SUVs lined up in my drive. The back two did Y turns and drove off.

That's when I noticed there was someone else sittin' in the Sheriff's vehicle, who never got out. It was a woman. The windows was tinted but not full dark. I could see her havin' quite the quarrel with the Sheriff. It went on for a minute or so while the third vehicle done left.

The woman got out. Holy shit. My heart banged. My breath stopped. My jaw dropped. Finally, I got back control, and I hollered, "Momma!"

I ain't seen her in more'n ten years. My Momma looked like a middle-aged hippy, big, frizzy, orange hair held back by a red headband, jean jacket over a flowery dress and a great, big silver cross hangin' 'round her neck. She was beautiful. She raised her skinny finger and leveled it at me.

"Willard! Baby!" she said.

"Momma!"

She shuffled toward me. She was wearin' big clodhoppers, and she stomped like they was weights on her feet. She was still pointin' at me.

"Willard Lee Bates! I have come to save you, baby. At last, I have come. I am so sorry I abandoned you to these demons, but I was scared. I was so scared. The Lord knows how scared I was. Now I am strong. He has made me strong enough. And I have come to save you from them, to save you before the Devil himself gets you."

About now was when the Sheriff got out. He stood by his vehicle lookin' like he was just gonna wait and let us sort this out before he took her home.

"Momma, I—"

Momma raised both hands and bowed her head in prayer.

"Lord, be with us here in this place of evil. Help me lead Willard to renounce Satan and all his demons, who desecrate this patch of your beautiful world," she screamed. "In the name of Jesus, who came in the flesh, and by the power of his cross, I call on you to cause Willard to renounce and forsake his involvement with all of them, and to choose you alone, Lord Jesus. I ask you to cleanse and forgive his soul. Save my son, dear Lord! And cast away these demons!"

By now, she was standing right in front of me.

"Momma, they's not demons. They's just dogs."

I reached out to touch her. She pulled away and dropped to a crouch, like she was scared of me. She pulled off the cross hanging around her neck and pointed it at me like it was a knife. Her eyes got real big. She gasped.

"Willard Lee Bates!" she whispered. "I know what they are. I was here. Don't you lie to me, baby! Don't you... the devil has you lying to your own Momma."

"No, Momma, the devil ain't got nothin' to do with any of this!"

"They are demons!"

"No, Momma. They's just dogs."

"They're werewolves!" she screamed.

I believe that caught the Sheriff's attention.

"Momma!" I said, actin' all surprised that anyone'd say such a fool thing. I looked over at the Sheriff. He had his head tilted like he was tryin' to refigure which one of us was a danger to society.

She got up again, holdin' that cross like a shield. She screamed some more as she backed me up and then backed me around, so as the Sheriff was somewheres behind me now. I kept backin' up until she done bent me over the hood of my truck.

"Baby, you are harboring werewolves! If I can't get you away from them, I can't save you. And If I can't save you, you are going to burn in hell! Oh! My boy is lost! Oh, God, have mercy on me! Sure as I love Jesus I tried, Lord knows I tried, but if you are going to listen to the devil and not your own Momma, then you must prepare to burn!"

"Momma, I love you. I always have. Don't talk like that."

"In the name of Jesus, I bring the fullness of his life, his death, his sacrifice, his resurrection, his authority, his rule, and his dominion; I bring judgment from Jesus Christ against these werewolves and the spell they have you under," she screamed.

She was hyperventilatin' while she hollered. She shook that cross like it was sprinklin' holy water at me.

She was cryin' now, like her whole life led her to this moment and she knew she was failing.

"I bring the blood sacrifice of Jesus Christ, the Son of God, his blood shed upon the cross, against all these werewolves and their claim against you, my son, my baby, Willard Lee Bates," she said. "In the name, and by the blood of Jesus Christ, I break the power of any curse that these werewolves have on you."

"Momma, they's dogs. And God loves them, just as he loves all His creatures. Don't you see? This—this—is God's will on Earth."

She swooned to her knees, now cryin' big tears.

"Oh, God," she said. "Oh, God, oh Jesus, who I love, why do you forsake me? Why do you not save my son? Send me a sign, dear God! Please, Jesus, just let me know you are there."

While that was goin' on, in my ear I heard Draugluin say. "Is he ready? Does he know what to do? Okay, release Jacob."

Out of the corner of my eye, I saw the gate push open and Jacob squeeze through. He come lopin' over, tail up and awaggin' and tongue afloppin' around outta the corner of his mouth.

Momma didn't see. She had her hands over her eyes, which was leakin' tears like bad plumbing. Jacob come up behind her, stopped, lowered his head, and then licked her arm. She turned and saw those big old eyes lookin' all puppy-like, and she put her hand on his back. Now, with an opening, Jacob licked Momma's cheek.

When it come to signs from God, that's about the best we got.

She sucked in a laugh. "Oh, sweet Jesus," she said. "Is that you? Is that you sending your creature to me? Oh, bless you Jesus."

Jacob licked Momma right on the lips.

Her voice got real quiet, like she only wanted Jacob to hear. "Bless you, too, you little angel, you."

The Sheriff come over.

"Mr. Bates, I think maybe I should take your mother in to talk with someone in town."

"No, please, Sheriff. Let her stay. Momma? Stay. They's all good, Momma. They ain't never gonna hurt you. You know that. I know they'll love you, Momma, and you'll love them. Look at that. Look at them big ol' puppy eyes. They's not evil. Oh Momma, I want you home again. It's what I always wanted, more'n anything. Please come home again. I love you."

"I love you too, Willard." Her voice was a tiny squeak. But I heard it good enough. The warmth I was feelin' was all sunshine on my heart.

"Then stay. I want us to be together again. Stay, Momma."

She was holding Jacob's head, and he was gettin' his tongue through to lick her face. Her tears was still comin', but she was smilin' now. She nodded. She felt the warmth, too. I could see her eyes melt from it.

The Sheriff seen it, too. He tipped his hat. As he left, I got down and took Momma in my arms.

"Oh, thank you, Jesus, for bringing me back to my baby," she said, her voice still all squeaky.

"Oh, Momma. I missed you so much," I said.

"Yip, yip," Jacob said.

That's when I heard in my ear somethin' that I don't think Draugluin meant for me to hear. He was just talkin' with Quentin and I figure he forgot the phone was on speaker when he said:

"Well, if this doesn't work out, we can always eat her. And if that doesn't do it, we can still just kill them all."

Author's Notes—Scott Michael Powers

THERE ARE all sorts of retirement homes for kindred spirits—railroad workers, firefighters, veterans, circus freaks—people who share distinctive experiences, values, and challenges, which the general population could never understand. There's comfort in knowing the retiree with you is someone who appreciates what it is like to rush into a burning house, or to squeeze into a clown car. In retirement, it's nice to be surrounded by your own kind.

To paraphrase the great Walter O'Reilly, werewolves are people too, you know. Yet, where can werewolves go once they tire of ripping throats out of villagers? Where can they live in peace, never having to worry about every yahoo gunslinger kid with a silver bullet who aims to make a name for himself?

Versipellis Nemora, that's where.

Nestled in the Hocking Mountains, Versipellis Nemora rolls over nearly 3,000 acres of remote woodlands, with limestone mountainsides, crystal-clear streams, waterfalls, meadows, and deep forest. This nirvana features an abundance of white-tail deer and other delicious wildlife ranging from bobcats to wild turkeys, feral pigs to cottontail rabbits.

A live-in, werewolf-friendly, human caretaker is always on paw to fulfill any specific needs and requests.

Retire to a place where howling at the moon is pure joy again. Retire to Versipellis Nemora.

~SMP

Meet Cute

Kristin Durfee

"L et the wild rumpus start!"
        —Maruice Sendak, *Where the Wild Things Are*

Friday, June 18, 2060

"JOSEY, COME ON," Eric said. "Grandpa is waiting for us."

My son's voice announced his arrival before the notification dinged on my phone. Then my watch. Then my glasses. Then the actual doorbell itself.

He insisted I get this technology, but the hard-wired one that came with the house worked just fine. Or at least it used to before he took it out and replaced it with this one.

I got to the door and opened it before my son and grand-daughter could press the button.

"Grandpa!" Josey exclaimed. "How did you know we were here?"

"Wild guess," I said, and embraced her.

She'd gotten so tall, and every time I saw her, I had to remind myself that she was twelve now, no longer the little girl I used to be able to pick up.

"Dad, thanks for this," Eric said as he pushed by me into the house and placed a heavy bag by the front door.

"What's all that?" I asked.

"Oh, you know. Snacks, devices, change of clothes. All the essentials just in case."

I was about to say I had food, but Eric moved into the living room and laughed just as I was going to open my mouth.

"I still can't get over these hamsters, Dad," he said. "What's this one, Cutie Fifteen or something?"

"Seventeen," I corrected.

"You name them all the same, Grandpa?" Josey asked.

I nodded. "Makes it easier that way."

"One thing to know about your grandpa is he always, and I mean *always*, has a hamster. One dies and he runs out that same day to get another. I'd get home from school as a kid and *bam*, new Cutie."

"I like their company," I said, a little offended by how flippant he spoke about Cutie's One through Sixteen.

Josey pressed her nose against the plexiglass enclosure. Seventeen slept in a pile of pine shavings, the multi-colored plastic tubing surrounding her snaked every which way from the cage, up and around the walls, entryways, and through each room in the house.

After some sixty years of having a hamster in my life, I've expanded the territory quite a bit. Haven't heard any complaints yet.

Eric looked at his watch and cursed under his breath. "I gotta go. Dad, thanks again. I know you usually come to us, but with my meeting on this side of town it just made more sense."

He shifted from foot to foot as if contemplating if this was really a good idea. Josey rarely visited my house and never without her parents present the whole time. It didn't bother me. The hamster tunnels were finicky and I worried that a toddler or young child could knock one off kilter. Cutie would definitely have complaints about that. But Josey was older now. She was ready.

"We'll have a great time," I said, and herded Eric toward the door.

He turned and gave Josey a hug. "I'll be back around four."

She nodded and began to dig through the bag at the door. Already bored, and nothing had even happened yet.

Once we were alone together, Josey asked for my Wi-Fi password.

"Let's just hold off on that," I said.

Tech giants had been promising for years that they were going to make free universal internet in exchange for brain implants, but it hadn't quite caught on yet. I figured once Josey's generation was in charge, as long as climate adjustments didn't have us all eight feet underwater, they'd be doing implants in the maternity wards as kids popped out.

I was old school on top of just being old. Sure, I was considered a Millennial, but no one even knew what that was anymore. We'd been in the 2000s for sixty years. I was just flippantly referred to as a "Nineteen-hundredser" and left alone. Most of the time that didn't bother me, but I knew I only had so much time left. Cutie knew it, too.

It was time to let someone else into my secret. To ensure that my part in this greater plan didn't go to waste. I just hoped Josey was the right choice to pass it along to.

Monday, November 22, 1999

I ROCKED BACK and forth in my seat to keep me from tapping my foot because Ms. Carmichael had just told me to cut that out. She'd also told me I could hold it five more minutes before I used the restroom but, boy, I wasn't so sure.

Beads of sweat began to form on my forehead. There was no way I could pee my pants as a fourth grader and *ever* show my face in society again.

"Just go," a voice said.

I didn't hesitate. I sprinted from my seat, nearly tripped over

Evelyn Greene's backpack, launched myself out the classroom door, down the hall, and heard shouts behind me as I slid into the bathroom and made it to the urinal just in time. My legs were shaky with relief as I washed my hands and trudged back to science class, sure I was going to spend the last two days of school in detention.

Could teachers keep you overnight if you did something really bad?

"Alan," Ms. Carmichael said in her sternest voice which she saved for the worst infractions like getting bad grades or spilling chemicals on the desk.

"It was an emergency," I said.

The class chortled. The only thing worse than peeing your pants in fourth grade is everyone knowing you were *about* to pee your pants in fourth grade.

"See me after class," Ms. Carmichael said, and then continued yammering on about the life cycle of the fruit fly.

I heard a snickering joke when she talked about the pupa, but I was too focused on my impending punishment to join in.

When the final bell rang, chairs all around me scraped the floor but I sat motionless. I'd miss the bus for sure and my parents would kill me. Could I walk the two miles home? I was pretty sure I knew the way and estimated it would only take me, what fifteen minutes? I'd be home before the bus was even supposed to drop me off and my mother would have no idea. Yes. I'd take whatever punishment Ms. Carmichael gave me then immediately start walking. It could be my little secret.

"That was a dramatic exit," Ms. Carmichael said once Robbie Gentry brought up the rear and closed the classroom door behind him.

I pictured him standing on the other side, ear pressed against the wood. I hated Robbie and just knowing he was a witness to my punishment made my anger toward him fester even more.

"I thought it was better than the alternative," I said to my desk. I couldn't make my eyes meet hers.

This was Ms. Carmichael's first year at Emmerson Elementary and while she seemed nice enough, anything unknown was always a source of speculation and gossip. Some kids claimed she'd bought the old undertaker's house on the hill and liked to watch the children at night, plotting to snatch any who came too close to the overgrown roses which grew thick with thorns on the wrought iron fence.

Others said she moved into the cottage down by the cliffs and threw any cats who came on her property to their death in the ocean waves below. Or was it dogs? Or children again?

It was hard to keep the stories straight. She looked about my mom's age, so fifty I guessed, as I could never remember but just knew she was quite old. She never talked about a husband or children and wore no jewelry. All of my previous teachers had kids at our school, so I'd assumed you had to have children to be a teacher. That must have been wrong.

"Alan, I need a level of respect in this classroom," she continued.

I opened my mouth to protest the injustice, but the raised eyebrow she gave me made me shut it.

"Sorry," I whispered. "It really *was* an emergency," I added.

She nodded. "Next time, let's plan our bathroom breaks a little better so they do not become a matter of throwing ourselves through the classroom. Sound good?"

"Good," I confirmed.

"Now, I did have another topic to talk to you about. Are you home over Thanksgiving break?"

My mind swirled at the question. Was this a trick? Was she planning to lure me over and bake me into a pie? Or worse, announce she had no plans and invite herself over for dinner?

"I, ah, not really," I stammered. "We go to my Grandparents' house, but they live in town."

"I am traveling quite far myself," she said, and I let go of a breath I didn't realize I was holding. "I had made arrangements for Cutie here," she said and gestured toward the hamster, "but that person backed out at the last minute. I was wondering, since you always seem very responsible and I catch you watching her from time to time, if you would like the responsibility of keeping her at your house over break."

Now I was speechless for a completely different reason.

We'd had a cat when I was little, but my mom was so sad after he passed, she refused any other pets. Maybe I could convince my mom that I could be such a responsible pet owner that she wouldn't have to do anything and then agree to let us have a dog or something. I could also get back in Ms. Carmichael's good graces.

There was no losing in this situation.

"I'd love to!" I nearly shouted.

She smiled. "I am going to send you home with this paper for your parents to sign," she said and tucked a folded envelope into my book bag. "Bring this back tomorrow, and please have them put your address down. I will drop Cutie off after early dismissal on Wednesday if that works all right with them."

I nearly floated out of the school. The place was deserted and a small pit developed at the bottom of my stomach. Did I actually know how to get home? I considered walking the bus route, as I knew that, but that would add unnecessary time. I was still under the impression if I walked quickly, I could make it home before my mother noticed.

Even with the cold weather, my armpits were slick with sweat and beads dripped down my temples when I shuffled through the front door. It turned out two miles was a *very* long way, and it took me the better part of an hour to get home.

I passed one pay phone and considered calling collect to say I'd be late, but I'd probably be in more trouble for that than the actual infraction I'd committed.

It was a day of choosing the worst of evils. I could only hope I'd chosen correctly.

When I got home, my mother's car was gone. The dread in my stomach bubbled again. Had she panicked and gone looking for me? Driven to the school? Checked all the ditches as she threatened she'd have to do if I disappeared? I knew she had a fingerprint and photo kit from when the police department made lost child packets for us in second grade, but I didn't even know if those prints were still good. I'd have to look that up the next time I was at the library as I didn't like to waste my limited internet time on

Ask Jeeves when I could be in AOL chat rooms talking about *The X-Files*.

I took the key out of my bag and entered the quiet house. There was a stillness inside I found a little creepy anytime I knew I was home alone. Like a ghost or something was waiting to pop out and scare me. On the kitchen counter lay a note on free notebook paper from some charity organization my mom donated to:

Had to run to the store and a couple errands. Back around 4. There's pizza rolls in the freezer, just don't burn the house down.

I checked my Shark watch and confirmed it on the stove clock. I had fifteen minutes until she'd be home.

Dashing up to my room, I threw off my clothes, tossed on a not-sweaty t-shirt, turned on the toaster oven and filled the tray with pepperoni pizza rolls—a true delicacy—and tried to calm my breathing and heart rate before my mom returned. She'd never have to know that I needed to stay after or how long it took me to get home.

There was a lot of talk about how the world may end in a month, but oh boy, it felt like I'd gotten a new lease on life.

The toaster oven dinged, and I donned a pair of oven mitts just as Mom walked in holding an array of paper and plastic bags.

"Alan!" she exclaimed as if she didn't expect to see me at home. "How was your day?"

"Fine," I said and popped a near-scalding pizza roll in my mouth to stop any further conversation.

She narrowed her eyes at me, pocketbook still slung over her shoulder and shopping bags dangling from her arms.

"What's wrong?"

My chest tightened slightly. Could a look give someone a heart attack? Maybe it was worth my internet minutes to look that one up...

"Nothing," I stammered as I threw two more pizza rolls into my mouth. Instant regret as the scalding sauce hit the back of my throat and induced a choking cough.

Mom rushed up and patted my back, dropping her bags on the ground. They fell with a clunk, and I wondered if something glass may have broken, but she didn't seem to pay it any attention as she periodically pounded between my shoulder blades. There was a moment where I thought she'd lodged the pizza roll further into my throat and really was going to kill me, but then I was able to swallow and take a breath.

"I'm fine, Mom, promise," I wheezed.

"Well, don't ruin your dinner. I got stuff to make fried chicken."

My mom dutifully got *Women's Day* magazine and stuck to their suggested menu. This week's theme was chicken and every form of leftover one could make from that. We started with large pieces in some horrible sauce followed by chicken tacos with another questionable flavoring concoction. Tonight was fried chicken strips and then I think chili the following night. Every month when that damn magazine arrived I considered throwing it away, but she'd just buy another copy at the checkout and then force us to go shopping again once she pulled out the grocery list from the back.

Fighting wasn't worth it.

"How was your day?" she asked again.

I decided to use the opportunity of her distractedness from my near-death experience to reach into my backpack and pull out the letter from Ms. Carmichael.

"This is from my teacher," I said, passing it over. "It's a really big responsibility."

My mother read the letter.

I faked confidence. "She sees how responsible I am and knows I would keep Cutie safe."

My mother narrowed her eyes again.

"I will take care of it, you won't even know it's here."

The delay in "no" gave me endless amounts of hope.

"Ms. Carmichael is new," I continued, unable to leave the silence for fear Mom may fill it with negative words. "She doesn't have anyone she trusts. It is a really big deal she asked me. I bet she will give me an A."

My mom chewed on her lip. "No one should *give* you an A. But, well, I guess it is okay if you promise that he won't leave your room, and I am *not* going to do anything for him."

"Her," I corrected. "And I promise."

I threw my arms around her and hoped she didn't notice the bit of pizza sauce I left on her shoulder.

Friday, June 18, 2060

"GRANDPA," Josey interrupted. "Did your mom ever find out you walked home from school that day?"

The question, out of everything she could have asked me, caught me off guard.

"You know…" I trailed, then laughed. "I honestly don t think so. It never came up, though I did hobble around for the next day or two, I was so sore from walking so far."

"I wish we could have a class pet and I could take care of it," Josey said.

A smile pulled at the corners of my mouth. Maybe my plan would work after all.

Wednesday, November 24, 1999

I HATED ROBBIE GENTRY.

I knew my mother didn't like it when I used such strong words, but she hadn't met this kid.

Robbie was the worst kind of bully because adults liked him. He pretended to be sweet and personable. He'd ask a question about some new song on the radio or a recent dance craze and parents would melt.

"Why can't you be more like Robbie?"

"Oh, I like that Robbie Gentry."

"That Robbie boy is so personable."

Nope. He was a jerk with a capital J.

He spread a rumor at the beginning of the year that I took up the saxophone because it was the only thing that would let me put my mouth on it.

"Makin' out with that sax again, *Alan?*" he'd call out as I toted my large suitcase from my locker to band practice.

Other kids were also in the band, hell, Robbie was in the band, but no one seemed to be worried about where their lips may or may not have been.

When I got a pair of off-brand Air Jordans called Sky Jims, Robbie called me out at recess so mercilessly, I jumped into a square of fresh cement on the sidewalk in front of my house to be rid of them. My mother yelled at me for ruining both my new shoes and the not-quite-dry patch of concrete.

I started taking the long way to the bus stop just to avoid turning left out of my driveway and having to see that ruined piece of sidewalk each day.

I'd learned my lesson tattling on one of his antics in second grade. Not only had Robbie's eyes filled with tears when the teacher confronted him, he'd somehow flipped the story to make me the instigator and I got assigned extra homework that night.

So, it shouldn't have come as a surprise when Robbie decided to jump on the newly released information that I was going to be the one taking care of the class hamster over the next five and a half days we were off school.

"How'd you score the job, *Alan?*" he asked in the lunchroom to a round of giggles.

I felt my cheeks warm and knew without even looking in a mirror that they'd turned red.

"Shut up, Robbie," I whispered and tried to focus on my chicken nuggets.

I sat down next to the few friends I had and attempted to start up a conversation about the math test from yesterday.

"I bet I know," Robbie said.

"Nobody cares, Robbie," Audry said.

She wasn't my best friend—I wasn't even sure if I had a best friend since Chris moved away last year—but in that moment, I loved her.

"Ooooh," Robbie cooed. "Are you Alan's *girlfriend?*"

More laughter from the lunch hall.

I stood before I knew what my legs were doing. Taking one step forward, I found myself in Robbie's face. Since I hadn't planned this maneuver, I wasn't exactly sure what my body had prepared for my next move.

Evidently, it was attempting to punch Robbie in the face.

I say attempt because he ducked about five minutes before my fist ran through the open air his face was just in. This simply turned me around which allowed Robbie to place me into a chokehold as the lunchroom erupted in hollers and cheers.

"ENOUGH!" a voice bellowed through the space. "You two, with me, *now*."

Black dots blinked in my vision as Ms. Carmichael stormed across the space and grabbed Robbie by the arm. I threw my backpack over my right shoulder and trotted behind them, hoping Audry would throw my leftover food away.

"Wait in there for me, Alan," Ms. Carmichael said as she pointed to her classroom and proceeded down the hall with Robbie toward the principal's office.

I didn't bother to turn the light on as I marched laps around her classroom.

"I *hate* Robbie Gentry," I seethed through my teeth.

Then a loud sigh came from the corner of the room.

"He is a complete ass," a small female voice said.

I froze. It was lunchtime. No students should be in the room.

After looking under the desks and the large cabinet Ms. Carmichael kept her coat as well as various bins with supplies, I'd come to the conclusion that I'd lost my mind.

"It's me," the voice said, with a sigh. "The hamster."

I spun on my heels and came face to face with the small tan and white creature. We locked eyes and she wiggled her whiskers.

"Cutie?" I whispered.

"How I wish someone had come up with a better name for me," she responded.

It was official. I *was* going crazy.

Friday, June 18, 2060

"SO, did he hit you after all?" Josey asked.

"Who?"

"Robbie Gentry. Is that why you were hearing things? Were you actually laid out in the lunchroom waiting for the nurse and imagining you'd gone back to Ms. Carmichael's class?"

I paused for a moment, never having considered that the interaction I'd had may have been caused by an unknown-to-me head injury.

"No," I said. The thought was preposterous. "That's preposterous," I added.

"More than a talking hamster?"

That was a decent point.

We'd moved to the kitchen by now and I was making a very not approved snack of stove-top mac and cheese instead of the carrots and celery Eric had brought with him.

"Did you get expelled from school for fighting?" Josey asked.

"No, but probably only because we were about to be on break for the next few days and I knew the principal had a flight to catch that afternoon. Probably didn't want to deal with it."

"Did Robbie at least get in trouble?"

I laughed. "Of course not. He said I started it and he was defending himself. Trouble was, that is sort of what happened, so it wasn't like I had a bunch of people coming to my defense. My teacher drove me home after school to talk to my mom and drop off the hamster—"

"She drove you home?" Josey interjected, aghast.

I shrugged. "It was the '90s."

Thursday, November 25th, 1999

THAT FIRST NIGHT with Cutie in my room, it was impossible to sleep. Not just from the stress of the previous day and the earful my mother gave me and then my father when he got home, but from Cutie.

Holy cow, she didn't shut up.

Early that morning, I heard a plastic sound and realized the hamster was a few sizes larger than when I went to bed. Her newly acquired breadth and girth pushed the top of the aquarium-style cage to the side.

"You best catch that lid so it doesn't clatter and wake your parents," she said calmly.

I sprung out of bed and gingerly took the lid off, careful not to touch her. I wasn't sure what would happen if I did, but it didn't seem worth it to find out.

She promptly climbed out of the cage and grew to the size of a small black bear.

"Much better," she said.

"How…what…how…"

"It's been many years since I've spoken to someone," she said. "Even Ms. Carmichael has no idea. I once revealed myself to a girl watching me over Easter break, but she had such a fit, I promptly changed back and didn't try again."

My brain fumbled about for a reasonable question. "Why now?"

"That Robbie Gentry. He is a complete ass. I felt like you needed to hear that from someone and sure as hell no adult would."

So not only did I have a talking hamster the size of a bear in my room, I had a *cursing* hamster the size of a bear in my room. I never heard my parents curse, not even when they dropped and broke something. Once, I accidentally said "shit" when I spilled some OJ on my homework in the morning and my mom didn't let me out to play for a whole week.

I'm pretty sure she would not approve of Cutie's language at all.

I was about to stammer through a dozen more questions when I decided to take a deep breath and attempt to be more systematic. Wasn't that what Ms. Carmichael was always asking us in science class? Slow down so we can ask the right questions and change our hypothesis as needed.

Trouble was, I had no hypothesis.

"How can you talk?" This seemed a good place to start.

"Of all the questions in the world and that's what you settle on. I always thought I got a raw deal, but damn, you kids are too funny." She paused a second. "Probably best to just explain the whole thing."

I took a deep breath, expecting to learn that she was some sort of government experiment and escaped from a secret lab or whatever.

"You may want to sit," she said.

I puffed out my chest and stood to my full four and a half feet. "I can take it."

"Suit yourself," she said and took a deep breath. "I am technically an alien from another planet."

My body suddenly felt very heavy, and I sank to the floor with a thud that I hoped didn't wake my parents. I considered getting up to lock my bedroom door, but that was a little beyond my abilities at the moment as I tried to get it together.

"That explains the whole thing?" I squeaked out.

Cutie sighed. "Fine. A few million years ago, my species came to Earth with a mission to see if the planet could sustain us. Our home planet had been put through the ringer between our own pollution and our expanding sun and there was a mission to see if there was another place to live.

"Half came here and another half went to a planet on the opposite end of the galaxy. That one proved more hospitable, and the rest of my planet went to colonize it, but in fear for what happened before, they decided to leave a team of researchers, including myself, behind on Earth in case we needed to relocate again."

"They just left you?" I asked, saddened at this bit.

"I am a researcher," she said with a huff. "We're able to shape-shift, so thankfully as animals evolved here on earth, we were able to as well. I am supposed to remain as a hamster for three hundred years before I get my next assignment. If my calculations are correct, and I know they are, I have been a hamster for roughly one-hundred and seventy-two years and have another one-hundred and twenty-eight to go."

I opened my mouth, shut it, opened it again, and shut it. What possible follow-up could I ask? I still had no hypothesis.

"A classroom hamster?"

Not the most eloquent question, but seriously, of all the possibilities in the world to end up as that.

"I was a regular hamster and got caught and sold at a pet store. Some teacher had me, then gave me away and that continued over the years until I ended up with Ms. Carmichael. Also helps remove any suspicion for how old I am since no one seems to stay at the same school for more than four years it seems, so I've been able to change hands a lot."

"What else have you been?" I asked

"Great question," Cutie said.

A noise down the hall made us both freeze. I crab-walked back to my bed, slid under my sheets, and stared at the door.

"Alan," my father's voice and a faint knock at the door.

"Quick, hide!" I whispered.

"Who are you talking to?" He asked as he opened the door. "Bad dream," I said and tried to sound half asleep.

I prayed my dad wouldn't look at the ground and see a giant hamster in my room but when I ventured a peak in Cutie's direction, I saw she was again hamster-sized and back in her cage with the lid off.

"Try to get back to bed," Dad said. "I have to pop into the office for a bit, so please help your mother as much as you can getting things ready for today. I'll be back around two."

I agreed sleepily and yawned and said, "Bye. Love you."

"You too, son." He shut the door.

With Y2K only a few weeks away, my dad, who was some IT person for a large firm, was working almost 24/7. Frankly, I was surprised they'd given him Thanksgiving off, but it appeared that got taken back. I hoped for Mom's sake he really was home at two. I knew how frustrated she was, because she often told me how frustrated she was at his constant working.

"It's like the whole world had forty-some years to figure out this was a problem and decided last week to do something about it," she'd said one night after my dad called the house to say that, yet again, he was missing dinner.

"You humans and your computers," Cutie whispered into the dark.

She stayed small in her cage this time. I was sorta glad as the bear hamster/thing was a bit scary.

"The world could fall apart," I said, as if defending us in some way didn't just make us look stupid.

"Whatever species is in charge at any given time thinks the world is going to fall apart. Though…" she began "I guess to be fair it eventually does."

"I don't think we will really disappear," I said. "Even if computers all turn off, I'm pretty sure humans would figure it out. It hasn't been *that* long we've been relying on them."

"True," Cutie said. "But when I was a pterodactyl, none of them thought the sun being blocked out for a few days would do much, but we all know how that ended."

I sat straight up in bed. "When you were a…what?"

Friday, June 18, 2060

JOSEY GIGGLED. "A PTERODACTYL, GRANDPA?"

"That's what she said."

Josey looked up at the tubes running the length of my dining room as we both shoveled an unnatural yet delicious shade of orange-coated noodles into our mouths. I needed to make this stuff more often.

Josey frowned. "But that would put her at…".

"At about sixty-five million years old, give or take," I said. "She says it's been more like twelve million and our calculations are incorrect, but I also have to assume it's easy to lose track of time when it's been that long, so who honestly knows."

Josey chewed on her lip, eyes narrowed, mulling something over.

"Your class hamster, the first Cutie, was an alien spy sent to report back on colonizing Earth and spent time as a flying dinosaur and then a class pet?"

"She was also a cockroach for a short stint of a few thousand years, a hesperocyon, which is an early ancestor of dogs, a quagga, which was a type of zebra that went extinct about two hundred years ago, and then a hamster."

Josey narrowed her eyes and again looked at the plastic hamster tubes running along my walls, which were, at the moment, empty. "What happened when you went back to school after break?" Suspicion laced her tone.

I sat up straighter and brightened. This was my favorite part of the story.

Thursday, December 9, 1999

EACH NIGHT OF THANKSGIVING BREAK, I'd wait until I was sure my parents were asleep, then take the lid off Cutie's cage. She'd crawl out, grow a bunch, and we'd chat into the late hours. I'd gotten used to her as a bear/hamster thing, so it no longer scared me.

Though she'd been living among humans since the beginning, she knew very little about us. I had to explain to her why we bathed. Why we enjoyed going for car rides. And why running around had become a "leisure activity".

For her part, Cutie told me about the world before people. How there were times she was so frightened she considered contacting her planet and asking to be transferred home.

"Do you have anyone here? Friends?" I'd asked her.

"Oh, well lots of animals and insects are aliens," she said as if this was a normal fact and not something to freak out over. ' But the trouble is there are about a half-dozen planets represented, so not everyone speaks the same language. I picked up English from living here so long, but there's at least two planets I know of that have no spoken language, so can't communicate. It makes me wonder why they are here if they can't report back, but they can't tell me that either."

"I don't really have any friends," I said. "Maybe we can be?"

"I would really like that."

When break was over and Ms. Carmichael picked Cutie up, my room felt so empty even if I finally got a good night's sleep.

"Alan," my mother said. "You did a great job of taking care of your class pet, but you look awful. I think it's best we skip getting an animal for now."

I'd wanted to tell her the truth so many times, but she wouldn't understand. It was too risky to let the world know about Cutie. I saw the attention the Olson Twins and Jonathan Taylor Thomas got. It could only be a million times worse for a talking alien hamster.

My stint as classroom pet caretaker afforded me a small level of celebrity as school started up again and I enjoyed a week where no one picked on me. I'd foolishly thought I was in the clear when Robbie Gentry rigged my locker with silly string. When I opened the door before lunch, half a can of red foam shot into my face as those around me shrieked with laughter.

The look on Ms. Carmichael's face made me consider if she wasn't onto Robbie herself. She ordered the two of us into her classroom to wait while she found the janitor and spoke to the principal. She handed me a stack of paper towels and told us to "hang tight and for the love of God, figure out how to coexist."

No sooner had the classroom door shut than Robbie was up in my face.

Several things happened at once.

I'd taken a step back and nearly tripped over my backpack as I heard a familiar scraping of plastic against plastic which signaled Cutie removing the lid of her enclosure. A shadow formed on the wall beside me which also caught the eye of the looming Robbie

Gentry who turned just as Cutie sat on her hind legs, towering over both of us.

I'd imagined that a bear-sized hamster was Cutie's natural form and that she was not capable of increasing in size beyond what she'd done in my bedroom. I was wrong.

Cutie's round ears pushed slightly on the pocked ceiling above her head, lifting two of the panels slightly and revealing darkness above. Her teeth were now about the length of my science textbook and her claws were about as long as my forearm.

I was very thankful I'd gotten to know her over the last week because otherwise, I surely would have screamed or peed my pants for real this time in class.

Robbie was statue-like next to me. His mouth agape and his arms poised awkwardly—possibly trying to push me and possibly trying to punch her. I worried for a moment that maybe she had actual magical powers and had frozen him, but realized since his whole body trembled a little, it was just him rooted in fear.

"If you scream," Cutie said. "I will eat you."

I wasn't sure if she was telling the truth, but begged Robbie in my mind to keep his mouth shut.

"You have been terrorizing my friend Alan here for the last several weeks, is that correct?" She paused, but Robbie didn't respond.

She repeated her question with even more gusto and Robbie finally whispered, "Yes."

"That ends *today*," Cutie said. "You will not only never make fun of him again or give him a hard time, but you will make sure none of your other asshat friends do the same. If you do, I will know. I have an excellent sense of smell so I will track you in the night and wait until you've gone to bed and then eat you. Do you understand me?"

Robbie nodded, speech still too much. I was even a little frightened about that last part.

Cutie turned to me and shrank a bit closer to bear size. "Alan. You have been a good friend to me, and I will always return the favor."

Footsteps sounded in the hall and both Robbie and I turned toward the door. Ms. Carmichael and the principal came through with expressions that made it clear Cutie had returned to normal size.

As if finding the hamster escaped was a normal occurrence, Ms. Carmichael stepped forward and scooped Cutie up, depositing her back in her cage, before she turned on me and Robbie. "What is going on with the two of you?"

"It was a dumb prank," Robbie said. "But it was my fault. I thought Alan would find it funny. I promise to clean it up. To replace anything of Alan's that may have been damaged, and..." His eyes flicked to Cutie. "It will never, ever happen again. I promise. Promise, promise."

Ms. Carmichael, evidently expecting Robbie Gentry to put some spin on the incident as he always did, widened her eyes in surprise.

"Oh," she said.

"I am really sorry," Robbie said before turning to me and repeating the apology.

"This seems worked out," the principal said as if he'd made any actual contribution to the matter. "I knew you were a good kid, Robbie. I always say it. That Robbie Gentry is going places."

Robbie whispered a thanks and asked to be excused to help clean up the hall.

I had to consciously close my slack-jawed mouth. I'm not sure what was the wildest event of the last five minutes, the fact that Cutie transformed herself into an even larger version to scare the bejesus out of Robbie Gentry or the fact that it worked.

"If he gives you *any* more trouble..." Ms. Carmichael started but seemed to lose her train of thought.

My mouth was so dry, it was difficult to speak, so I just nodded.

The principal clapped his hands together. "Wonderful. Glad it all got sorted. A very impressive thing for Mr. Gentry to clean that all up himself."

I narrowed my eyes, but thought it not worth the comment that Robbie Gentry had *made* the mess, so why was it anything to praise that he was cleaning it up?

My shirt was still a bit damp, and the red silly string foam had turned my orange shirt an off-putting color. Ms. Carmichael got me an extra T-shirt from her giant closet in the back.

"Go get changed and then grab some lunch. I'll write you a hall pass in case you need extra time. And Alan," she said, pausing for a few moments to find her words. "Bullies are never easy to deal with, but if I can be of any help."

"You've been really helpful," I said with as much truth as I'd ever spoken anything in my life.

Friday, June 18, 2060

JOSEY SAT in silence for a few moments. The only sound was the faint clicking of nails on plastic tubing. I'd assumed my story had an audience of two, but Cutie hadn't shown herself yet. I took a deep breath and settled back in my chair, hoping I hadn't miscalculated by telling Josie this story.

"So…" She chewed on her bottom lip for a second. "Did Robbie ever bother you again?"

"Nope. And better yet, anytime anyone else did, he stuck up for me. I had smooth sailing in elementary and middle school because of him. He moved away before freshman year, but pretty sure that would have continued."

She nodded. "And how did you end up with Cutie in the first place if she was back at school?"

"I'd done such a great job over Thanksgiving, Ms. Carmichael asked if I would watch her over Christmas, too. My mother wasn't too happy, but she relented. Then the strangest thing happened, when we went back to school after the New Year, no Y2K explosions or world-ending computer issues occurred, but Ms. Carmichael never came back."

Josey's eyes widened. "Did something happen to her?"

"They said her mother got sick and she stayed to take care of her. The creepy house sold to an even creepier couple and life pretty much moved on. My mom tried to give Cutie back to the school, but our replacement teacher wanted nothing to do with her. Ended up with my own pet after all."

"Grandpa?" Josey looked down and hunched her shoulders. "Why do you keep replacing the hamsters?"

She looked up, and I took a deep breath. "I don't."

More rustling and movement came from the living room.

"Is she ready?" a familiar female voice asked.

"I think as ready as she will ever be."

I put a steadying hand on Josey's shoulder as Cutie, in her bear-sized form, sauntered into the room. Josey trembled slightly under my touch but didn't run away from the table or scream.

"Hi, Josey," Cutie said. "It's nice to get to meet you properly."

Josey opened and closed her mouth several times, but no sound came out.

"You see, Josey," I began, trying to get her back from the shock. "I am an old man, and Cutie isn't quite ready to move on yet. I need to make arrangements for her when I am no longer able to take care of her. I can't just trust anyone, so I was hoping you could take care of her if I need someone to."

Josey turned to look at me, eyes wide and pupils dilated.

"The story was real…" she whispered.

"It was," I confirmed.

"It was," Cutie repeated and took a step closer to us.

I felt Josey shrink back toward me, but I told her not to be scared.

"She doesn't need much special treatment," I continued. "All of these tubes are fun," I said and gestured to the walls, "but as long as she can get out of her crate at night that is enough, at least while you still live with your parents."

"I have done it before," Cutie said as if her welfare was at the forefront of Josey's mind and not the fact that a giant talking alien hamster stood in front of her.

"She gets regular hamster food," I went on. "But if you can sneak her some raw meat every now and then as a treat, she likes that."

Cutie's eyes widened slightly. "I *do* like that."

We stood there for several beats, but Josey said nothing in response.

"Has she gone dumb?" Cutie asked. "Should we ask another child?"

"No," Josey whispered. "Don't ask anyone else."

My shoulders dropped in relief. I didn't have anyone else to ask. Evidently, the fates giving me one child and giving that child one child had put a lot of pressure on the situation.

"I am hoping that we still have a few more years," I said. "But if there looks to be a time where I won't be able to transition Cutie to you myself…" I hesitated, unable to mention out loud that I was going to die at some point. "I want you to say something about me having just gotten a new hamster. Cutie Eighteen. Or Twenty if a round number helps you."

"Okay…" she said slowly, her eyes transfixed on Cutie.

"That should buy you enough time to have the same hamster until you go to college or move out. Then every five years or so you will get another. Or tell people you will get another. Hamsters don't live that long, but you'll get a reputation for being skilled."

"I'll take over," Josey said. Maybe Cutie was right, and she had gone a bit mental.

'You'll take over," I confirmed.

Josey nodded.

The alarm on the stove went off. Josey and I glanced at it and when we turned back, found Cutie in her regular hamster form.

"Time?" a squeak said.

"Time," I said and turned to Josey. "Your dad will be here soon. It's very important you tell no one who Cutie really is."

Josey nodded.

"It could be nice for you to come around more. Maybe suggest it."

Josey nodded again.

"I promise we will get you ready. I had to do it with no preparation, and I got through it, but I won't do that to you."

Another nod. I think I may have broken her brain.

"All these years," she said in a breathy whisper.

It appeared as though she had her own hamster running on a wheel in her mind. She looked at me with a laser focus as a knock came to the door followed by it opening.

"Hope you all had fun!" Eric called from the front of the house.

Her mouth broke into a smile. "An alien hamster."

"An alien hamster," I repeated.

Josey stepped forward and threw her arms around my midsection.

Eric walked into the room. "I see you didn't touch the food bags I left or the electronics?"

"Nope," Josey said into my stomach. "We had the best time."

Eric's eyebrows rose. "Great. Really great. Hey, my meeting went amazingly, so looks like I may be having them more frequently, maybe you all want to do this again?"

Josey pulled back slightly, and I locked eyes with her.

"Absolutely," she said, and a faint squeak sounded in agreement from the other room.

Author's Notes—Kristin Durfee

I AM BLESSED each time this incredible group of authors decides not only to partake in another project, but to keep allowing me to participate in them. While I do tend to write a bit of everything, it's always fun to dabble in a genre I don't do as often. Enter: Cutie.

When I was mulling over the vastness of picking an animal and a theme, Cutie did me a huge favor by entering my consciousness pretty fully formed. I love when stories just knock me over the head. Having the backdrop of Y2K not only allowed me to wave my elder-Millennial flag, but also get rid of that pesky modern invention: social media. Now Allen and Cutie could have their quiet evenings without any threat of a stray post making its way to the wrong set of eyes.

Plus, how could you possibly keep her a secret if she ate one of your classmates?

A special thanks as always to the entire Alvarium gang, but especially Charles Cornell, for the amazing cover, and Ken Pelham, JC Bruce, and Bria Burton for sharing their suggestions and expertise in whipping this story into shape. I am in awe each time I get to work with you all.

~ Kristin

Mary Shelley's Nasty Cat

Ken Pelham

M*ark Twain said, "A man who carries a cat by the tail learns something he can learn in no other way." Here's to imagining what other great writers may have learned from one rather unusual feline specimen. —KP*

> *"Verses on a Cat"*
>   *A cat in distress,*
>   *Nothing more, nor less;*
>   *Good folks, I must faithfully tell ye,*
>   *As I am a sinner,*
>   *It waits for some dinner*
>   *To stuff out its own little belly.*
>   *—Percy Bysshe Shelley, 1800*

The Journal of Mary Shelley, Pisa, Tuscany - October 6, 1821

MY DEAR HUSBAND Percy bounded into the parlor after his morning walk, beaming, and dropped a splendid white rose onto the table before me. I looked up from feeding our sweet little son. "Ah, my dearest," Percy exclaimed. "How fares our little Percy Florence Shelley this beautiful morning?" He gave the boy a tickle. "Peachy, he seems. For a wee thing."

"Quite," said I. "He's wearing more of the soup than he has eaten, and now is nodding off a little."

"What do you say we take the lad and do a bit of exploring? I fancy a short sojourn to Bologna."

"For any particular reason?"

"Why, dearest wife, none! Must we have a reason?"

"You always have a reason, Percy. Sometimes even good ones."

"Oh, woman, you wound me!" He took a seat, crossed one leg casually over the other. "Let's do it in the name of science."

"Uh-oh."

"As it turns out, Galvani made his home in Bologna."

"Signor Galvani has been dead for twenty-three years," said I. "We might be a trifle late."

"Pssh! We can visit his home, have a poke around. I'm told the residence remains still in use by people close to him. It shall be a fun distraction."

I sighed. "Now?"

"I've hired a cab to take us first thing tomorrow morning. Have you any plans?"

"I've a toddler to watch."

"Excellent, it's a date!" And he bounded from the room as gaily as he'd entered.

I do believe little Percy Florence, asleep in my arms, snickered. Always up to something, always testing the limits. He would be just like his father.

October 9, 1821

WE LEFT at daybreak of the 7th, urged to action by the calling of impatient and punctual roosters. Our carriage jostled north along the dusty, hilly way to Bologna. Tuscany crawled past, serene in its place in the world, unimpressed with self-important Bohemians. Now, Percy is the most enthusiastic of travelers, if not the most sensible, and of course underestimated the journey. After two wearying days, punctuated by overnight stays in flea-bitten wayside inns, burdened by confused linguistics (the dialects varying wildly throughout this antique land), our scowling driver expelled us in Piazza Maggiore in the city center on the third day at noon, and grumbled his horses along. We managed to get tangled directions to the home of the famed scientist, and walked to it, baby in tow. We found the place in some measure of disrepair, cracked and crumbling plaster walls of an orangey red, mottled grey with mold, and with a roof missing a few clay tiles, and a slightly listing chimney. But in my imagination, I pictured a fine home during the time of its illustrious former owner.

We approached and Percy rapped his cane smartly upon the door. Quiet hung in the air, and I feared the place abandoned, but at length a rustling came from within. The door creaked open, and an old lady stood and regarded us with watery eyes.

"Good day, Signora!" said my husband cheerfully. "I am Percy Shelley, a poet of some note and notoriety. And may I present to you my equally famous wife, the novelist Mary Shelley."

The old woman held us in her gaze. Not maliciously, I think, but rather of honest confusion.

"I sent word by post of our hoping to visit," said Percy.

No response.

Percy tried again in his spotty Italian. *"Io sono Percy Shelley con mi moglie Mary."*

No response.

Percy rolled his eyes. "Oh, for heaven's sake!" He pointed at me. "Frankenstein."

The old woman stared at me, and her face brightened, her eyes aglitter, a broad, partially toothy smile splitting her face. "Ah, Frankenstein, Frankenstein." She clapped her hands. With a turn, she yelled back into the dim interior, "Signora Frankenstein!"

I must admit, I have found my sudden fame flattering. When my novel first appeared three years ago, in my modesty (and fear of humiliation), I published as 'Anonymous.' When the French edition was published earlier this year under my actual name, word flew across the Continent like a gale, and I found myself celebrated everywhere. My mention in the novel of Bologna's famed scientist, Doctor Galvani, no doubt became the object of breathless gossip.

A hurried clomping of footsteps, and the door swung wider, and an equally old gentleman with untamed white eyebrows appeared. The woman whispered in his ear, and his eyes widened. "Ah, Frankenstein. I happy, *mi moglie*, me wife, so happy," said he, in a sort of English.

The front parlor was roomy and quite clean, yet spare. Midday sunbeams angled through tall windows, sparkling in the glass.

The antiquarian gentleman introduced himself as Signor Domenico Barbieri, and his wife as Signora Domenico Barbieri. As if she had no name of her own. I opened my mouth to remark upon this, but Percy nudged me and gave me his 'just let it go' look. But the woman seemed to read my mind and smiled warmly and said, "Sofia." A small victory; I shall always relish them.

They led the way to a dining room and plied us with cheese, noodles bathed in that marvelous Bolognese meat sauce, cheese, and more cheese. Percy suffers from an affliction of the bowel when consuming quantities of cheese, and I feared for his—and my— fortitude in bearing up to looming waves of gastric percolation and resultant precipitous eruptions. But such is married life. For better or worse.

Domenico spoke a few hurried words in Bolognese—I under- stood just enough to make out, "Fetch wine. *Il buon vino*, the *good* wine, to Signora Frankenstein."

"Signora Shelley." I pointed to myself and manufactured a smile.

Sofia produced a bottle of red and poured us each a glass, and beamed at me. "Salute, Signora Frankenstein!" We drained our glasses, and she refilled them, and gave Little Percy a *crema fritta*, elic- iting a peal of joy from him

We struggled through a few attempts at the Emilian-Romagna tongue. After a time we heard the opening creak and closing of the front door, and a young man entered the dining room, his eyes widening a trifle at the sight of us. An elegant, slender fellow, fair of skin and hair as is the norm in this northern part of the peninsula, with neatly trimmed mustache and tailored clothes. Domenico tugged at his sleeve and spoke to him in their tongue, and the young man brightened. "English travelers!" said he, in honeyed accent. "How marvelous! I am Giuseppe Barbieri. I see you have met my grandparents."

"Delighted to make your acquaintance, Signor Giuseppe," said Percy. "My wife and I are on a bit of a holiday, sir. I am Percy Shelley, and this is my darling Mary and our little Percy Florence."

"Signora Frankenstein!" said Domenico.

Giuseppe groaned. "Forgive my grandparents' exuberance."

"I'm sure Mary relishes it," said Percy. "I am becoming accustomed to living in her shadow."

"Hush, husband," said I. "You live in no one's shadow."

Giuseppe clasped his hands together. "Two of the generation's greatest English writers, here under our sagging roof! May I assume your visit has something to do with our own illustrious former resident?"

"You may," said I. "We have been touring the north of the peninsula some time now and could not pass up the opportunity to visit the home of Galvani." I paused. "I mentioned him in passing in my novel."

Sofia bustled out of the kitchen and back in again, waving an Italian-language copy of *Frankenstein*, then hugging it like a baby. "Luigi Galvani," she said.

Giuseppi nodded, motioned us to follow, and led us from the main rooms to a dim, musty room in the back. He drew the curtains from the windows, illuminating the interior. A jumble of books and all manner of scientific apparatus crowded every bit of it. Surgical instruments, batteries of a sort, a Benjamin Franklin electrostatic generator, odd machinery, tubes, flasks, and notebooks lay strewn about on the tables. All wearing a coat of cobweb and dust. Little Percy squealed with delight, squirmed his way from my grasp, eager to immerse himself in the fine filth.

I looked about in awe, daring to hope. "Is this…"

Giuseppe spread his arms wide. "Welcome, Signora, to the laboratory of Doctor Luigi Galvani."

I drank it in, my soul filling with sudden inspiration. I felt like a little girl again.

"Oh my," said Percy.

"My grandparents worked in the employ of Doctor Galvani and his brilliant wife, Lucia. House servants of a fine sort, they were. Loyal to a fault. They have steadfastly and jealously guarded this room and its contents against all who would change it. I am of a more practical bent and have chided them for their devotion to memory. 'The good Doctor passed two decades ago,' I have argued. 'Sell the place to a nobleman with the means to keep it properly.' But they shrug my protestations aside and berate me as an ungracious boy. In my maturity, I grow more appreciative and now recognize the historical beauty of this house."

Along one wall, all manner of jars stood in rows. Most empty, but a good number filled with specimens of this and that. A few caught my attention, and I gasped and pointed. "Those…those contain frogs! Dare I ask, were they the subjects of Dr. Galvani's famous experiments?"

Giuseppe picked up a jar. "Indeed they were! He shocked those dead creatures into some semblance of life with the magic of electricity. If one may call twitching 'life.' Many have been preserved just as he last worked with them."

The frogs hung suspended in differing states of preservation, many intact and whole, others desiccated and shriveled. Others still, denuded skeletons.

"But this is splendid!" cried Percy. "I hoped that we might have such luck." He approached the jars cautiously, and drew a finger across one, wiping clear the dust. "Splendid."

"*Rawwrrr,*" came a noise from a dark corner. A cat peered at us from shadow.

"Ah," said Giuseppe. "Here comes our jealous little feline resident, Signor Matteo. This is his dusty kingdom, and he takes umbrage to visitors."

"Matteo," I repeated. "That means 'Gift of God,' si?"

Giuseppe nodded. "Let us say that he is poorly named."

I reached out tentatively, but the cat shrank from me. "He seems shy. May we pet him?"

"I cannot fathom why anyone would want to, but we might entice him from the corner." Giuseppe found a jar, removed a desiccated frog, and shook it at little Matteo, scattering frog flakes across the dry dust.

"*Rawrrr*," said the cat. It hesitated and crept into the light.

"My word! What a nasty cat," said Percy.

I confess, Little Signor Matteo appeared not the most handsome feline ever. He was a bulky, scraggly grey. And one most certainly got the impression of a cat of parts. One foreleg seemed longer and thicker than the others, and of an orange colour and short hair, in striking contrast from the grey body. The other foreleg was entirely replaced by a wooden peg. His tail was also orange. The details worsened. He lacked an eye, the empty socket a dark black hole. And his ears...one a perfect grey, the other a large loose flap, dark brown and hanging. Like that of a basset hound.

Matteo hobbled closer. Giuseppe tossed the shriveled frog to him. The thing sniffed it and bit in, with a dry crunch.

"Oh, but he is adorable!" said I.

Percy and Giuseppe stared at me.

"It is a disaster of biology," said Percy. "'tis the filthiest beast I have ever laid eyes upon."

Giuseppe cocked his head to one side. "Well, in fairness, Matteo is old. All pets look somewhat threadbare in their old age."

"'Threadbare' is what you're going with?" said Percy.

"How old?" I asked. "Fourteen, I would guess, perhaps fifteen."

"He is old," said Giuseppe. "For a cat."

"How old?"

Giuseppe counted on his fingers. "Forty-one."

Percy clapped his hands together gleefully. "What exquisite nonsense!"

"Older than me," said Giuseppe, shrugging. "So, I can only go by what my grandparents tell me. But I have fond childhood memories of little Matteo."

"Kittens are wonderful playmates," said I.

Little Percy squatted by my feet, pointing at Matteo. "Keeeee-kee," he squealed with radiant joy.

"He was never a kitten," said Giuseppe. "He has always looked the same as today."

Matteo, having studied each of us, slouched forward and rubbed against my leg. His purring sounded like death rattle.

"Well," said Percy. "This has been a splendid day after all. Shall we retire now to an inn for the night?"

"Matteo likes you," said Giuseppe.

"And I rather like him," said I, reaching down and petting the animal, with Little Percy straining to do the same, which I prevented. My hand came away a bit dirty, but what do you expect of a creature living in such a dusty place?

Giuseppe turned to his grandparents and spoke softly. Domenico and Sofia exchanged glances and shrugged in unison. "Signora Shelley," Giuseppe said, "would you like to take Matteo?"

"We'd love to!"

Giuseppe glittered and grinned. "Oh, Signora, I am *most* pleased to send him home with you! My grandparents soon will not be much able to care for him, and I live many streets away."

"Oh no, you cunning little Bolognan," said Percy, holding up both palms. "We shan't be taking on pets. We are much too footloose and unrooted to care for it. I'm even surprised Little Percy here has lasted in our midst."

Matteo rubbed harder against me and turned his death rattle purr up.

"But it likes me," said I.

"Everyone and everything likes you, but you don't bring them all to live with us."

Rattle-purr-rub.

"Oh, Percy, but you yourself complain about the mice in our villa."

Rattle-rattle-purr-purr-rub-rub.

"Kee-keeee," said Little Percy.

Big Percy threw his hands into the air. "Oh, very well. The first poem I ever wrote, when I capered about as a young and stupid lad, concerned a cat. Maybe my last poem will be as well."

RATTLE-RATTLE-RATTLE-PURR.

It almost looked as if sweet little Matteo positively smirked. But cats don't smirk.

Letter to Lord Byron from Percy Shelley
October 12, 1821

MY DEAR LORD BYRON,

What a time this is, these days in the sun and warmth of Tuscany! It pleases me immensely to hear that you plan also to move to Pisa in the coming weeks. We shall have a grand time.

Myself and my lovely wife find ourselves well. Yet I have thoughts that need sharing, between friends, thoughts I'd rather not share with Mary.

We recently sojourned to Bologna to visit the family home of that late genius of the last century, Luigi Galvani. I thought it a fun distraction to putter about in his abode. As you know, his works in the science of electricity provided inspiration to Mary's opus on the reanimation of life. It enlightened and entertained, but yielded an unanticipated and, dare I say, unhappy result. We came away with a cat.

Old friend, you know me well and you know my disposition towards pets of any sort. They and I share a sort of mutual dislike of each other. We forge uneasy alliances, if we must, and go about our busy ways. Alas, were it that easy in this particular episode!

This beast, that goes by the name of Matteo, is decidedly unlikable. To me, at least. My wife and my little son seem to enjoy him to a degree unfathomable to me. That is one thing. But there is much more to it than that.

The ghastly creature is the foulest feline I have ever come across. To begin with, it is a mix of colours, a middle grey being its base.

But other parts are orange. Very well, you say, a delightful mix of tints and hues, a work of feline art. Not so. Unless the artist is a blind lunatic.

And the smell! A vague unpleasant odor permeates the air around Matteo. Not so strong as to cause one to turn one away in disgust, but something there, a miasma lingering just beneath the surface.

The thing wants for an eye. I could not abide this after but a few days and therefore fashioned it a small eyepatch of black leather. An improvement, to be sure, but one of its forelimbs is a wooden peg. My God, Byron, the animal looks like a tiny, grizzled pirate captain, back from plundering, and ashore for whoring.

So, you are thinking, a funny-coloured cat with a bandage and an artificial limb to conceal its infirmities. What is the sin? I shall tell you.

I begrudgingly have petted the foul thing once or twice, both for the purpose of forging some sort of tolerant coexistence, but also, and more importantly, of examining it closer.

Captain Matteo's orange foreleg doesn't match the others. It *does* match that similarly inappropriate orange tail. Matteo has an ear that, to my uneducated eye, is not even that of a cat, but of a dog. So, I gently examined these parts. Friend, I found encircling scars where the appendages adjoin to the greater body. I think the leg, tail, and ear were surgically attached. The beast is a composite!

My word, Byron. As I investigated these imperfections, Captain Matteo watched me with something akin to predatory amusement. I sense in it a rather keen intellect for an animal.

I began to wonder. Galvani was also a gifted physician and anatomist. Could he have saved this poor wretch by attaching the limbs and appurtenances of others to it? It is screamingly obvious.

Another, darker thought stole unbidden into my mind, but it is preposterous, and I shan't mention it lest you think me mad.

Ah, well. Nonsense and fancy. I suppose I shall have to make the best of this turn of events and try and get along with the little cretin. But I shall always be happy to hear your thoughts.

Your devoted friend,

P.B. Shelley

Letter to Percy Shelley from Lord Byron
October 18, 1821

MY DEAR PERCY,

Damn it, man, it is but a cat. Get over yourself. I am moving to Pisa before the month ends; we shall get together promptly, and I shall rudely box your ears.

Respectfully,

George Gordon Byron

Letter to Lord Byron from Percy Shelley
October 24, 1821

MY DEAR LORD BYRON,

I am quite unamused by your terseness and tone. Do you think for a moment that I would burden you with pet issues if they weren't affecting my very being? I tell you, this cat, this Matteo, is more than your average domesticated animal. It believes it *owns* our residence now, and it goes about its business as a little emperor.

Despite my pointed observations, Mary remains Matteo's adoring master. I think she misunderstands the true nature of the cat/human relationship. And Little Percy, I daresay, prefers the cat's company over mine.

I must admit that all is not for the worse since his arrival. Before, as in every city hoary with age and humanity, Pisa is more than well-populated with marauding vermin. Our rented house, in particular, abounded with large and fearless rats, causing some trepidation in the both of us and fright in Little Percy. Within a handful of days after Matteo's arrival, all rats seem to have fled, not to return. One fine morning, as I tossed out our bedpan waste, I spotted something quite odd and more than a little distressing. On either side of our doorway to the street, a rat head stood mounted on a slender twig perhaps ten inches above the ground. Now I immediately banished my first insane thought, that Captain Matteo bore responsibility for the gruesome display, warning all rats to vacate the property at once. But that is of course the height of silliness. Cats have not the capacity for reason. Nor the opposable thumbs to fashion the exhibit. Certainly, it must have been neighborhood children who came across Matteo's *rodentia* victims and mounted their own fiendish displays. Children are, after all, subhuman little simian monsters, below cats on the tree of life and barely above rats. Little Percy excepted, of course.

Your humble servant,
Percy

Letter to Lord Byron from Percy Shelley
October 29, 1821

MY DEAR LORD BYRON,

You will recall from my previous missive regarding the sudden vanishing into the ether the population of *Rattus rattus* from my neighborhood. As Mary and I read aloud our latest literary efforts to each other, an urgent knock came upon the door. I answered it, to find a trio of heavily-mustachioed, uniformed ruffians scowling at me. The apparent leader, a blond fellow with a bulbous, veiny nose, said, "Are you the English?"

"I should hope that were obvious, old chap," said I.

"Well then," he growled. "I am Sargento Maximo Martini. We get word of strange happenings in the street. Wide-eyed old women whisper and gesture in the market. Their husbands bar the doors. Their children come home early, eat their chicken necks and cabbage without a whimper, and say their prayers before bed, with sincerity for a change, and lay awake all night. The cause of such unusual behaviors, these good folk tell us, is that a foul beast prowls the streets at night, crying an unearthly warning to all who come near, glaring and staring in through windows at little babies, watching with baleful, unamused eyes, or eye as it were, as mama and papa get down to tangled business and exercises in the conjugal bed, unnerving papa to the point of floppy failure. What say you to this?"

"I say Tuscany is indeed a wondrous, if superstitious, region."

Sargento Martini grunted. "Choose your words carefully, Englishman."

"Well, I *am* a poet."

"This unnamed creature that strikes terror into the hearts of the righteous is said to come and go from this house."

It surprised me not in the least, and I opened my mouth to mention Captain Matteo, but Mary chimed in. "Good sir, I assure you we keep nothing out of the ordinary here. We have but a docile housecat. Perhaps a wolf, or a wild dog, seeking sustenance, comes slinking down from the hills and into Pisa at nights."

Martini studied us both for a moment. "The animal we are concerned with is indeed a cat."

Mary shook her head. "Oh dear. Are you saying that the people of Tuscany are afraid of cats now? Are you simply an animal control agent, demoted from the true constabulary?"

Sargento Martini glared. "Do you or don't you own a one-eyed cat?"

Mary spoke flippantly. "Regardless of eye-count, does anyone truly own a cat?"

I stepped in. "Sargento, some compassion, *per favore*. Our cat died."

Mary shot me a glance, her eyes widening. As quickly as her shock came, it faded, and she turned again to the policeman. "Si, Sargento. Our sweet cat died."

Martini regarded us for a moment. "Why, signora, did you not say this at the start?"

"Grief. Pure, unrelenting grief."

"Grief as wide as the…" I paused, casting about for some superlative that would impress the yokels. "Grief as wide as…" I panicked, my deep well of poetic talent abandoning me in the face of grim law enforcement. "As wide as the Pancreatic Sea." That sounded wrong, but I committed and pressed on. "Say, my good Martini, may we be left alone in our grief?" I drew my valise from my coat and plucked a few banknotes from it. "We have kept you from your important rounds with our own sad but insignificant troubles, so please, allow me to make amends." I pressed the notes into his hand. "Perhaps you can find yourselves a small shop, a bakery that makes, I don't know, sugared round pastries in the shape of a circle, with holes in the middle."

The Sargento brightened, and his subordinates nodded enthusiastically.

Once they left, Mary said, "Oh Percy, thank you for your clever thinking and managing of that unseemly intrusion." She grinned. "Telling them Matteo died; how funny and quick you are."

I nodded, the dull, simple poet that I am.

"What bothers you, darling?"

"Oh. Nothing. I guess."

Her eyes narrowed suspiciously, then widened in alarm. "Oh no. You were not making a joke to get rid of them. Matteo…you are saying he in truth died? When?"

"I don't know when."

I heard a *rawrr*, and the one-eyed bastard sauntered in, smug, self-satisfied.

Mary clapped her hands gleefully. "Oh, there you are, Signor Matteo!" She scooped up the reeking grotesquerie and hugged it. I wanted to vomit. Mary turned her glistening eyes to me. "Percy, you are such a tease, carrying through on your little joke. You brilliantly gave leave to the gendarmes but gave me such a fright in doing so."

"I do what I can."

Captain Matteo one-eyed me.

So, dear friend, I slipped into the clear with both the Missus and the police. Yet, I had not framed the thing as a ruse. I hesitate to confess this, but I believe the damned thing *was* dead. Once. And, much like the creature in Mary's fantastical novel, it had been resurrected, given new life, in a patchwork quilt of parts of deceased pets. Doctor Galvani accomplished the animating of dead tissue through electrical stimulation. It is my belief that he tired of causing dead frogs to twitch and writhe and turned his attentions to more complex life. These are the thoughts of the insane, yet I cannot banish them. I am but a poet. Counsel me, dear friend!

Your devoted partisan,

Percy

Letter to Claire Claremont from Mary Shelley
October 31, 1821

DEAREST CLAIRE,

Forgive me my too infrequent correspondences, but this day of Halloween finds brittle yellow leaves scurrying down the street chased by a chill wind, and seemed a good time to remain indoors and set my social obligations aright.

Percy and I have been oh so busy! We are warm and snug in Pisa, and my melancholy is somewhat tempered now that we own a pet, a darling cat named Matteo. After my admittedly disenchanted initial appraisal of his appearance, I have come to regard him as quite a handsome fellow, sturdy and unique. And the little dear is sweet as molasses, and about as quick.

Little Percy squeals with delight every moment Matteo enters the room. On the other hand, Big Percy, as you know, has never been much of an animal lover, decidedly favouring the hedonism and irrationality of two-legged beasts. Ah well, despite my husband's protestations and continuing commentary on Matteo's looks, I fancy he warms up to our new feline as I write this. He begrudgingly acknowledges that the vermin population has virtually disappeared from our house and street. He forced a smile when I brought this up. He knows it, even though he has difficulty embracing it.

I shall write again soon, dear sister.

Yours,

Mary

Letter to Percy Shelly from Lord Byron
November 1, 1821

MY DEAR PERCY,

Zounds, man! Your recent correspondence troubles me greatly. Get hold of yourself. Cats are inherently self-serving beasts, bad enough already in their own right, what with shitting on the floor where you step in it barefoot in the night, without you embarking upon flights of fancy and ascribing fevered dreams inspired by Mary's fiction. I suspect you've been mixing absinthe with opium once again. Distance yourself from chemical stimulation at once, or I shall descend upon you like an avenging angel and administer severe punishments.

Best wishes,

Byron

The Journal of Mary Shelley
December 11, 1821

OUR TRUE FRIEND, Byron, has moved from Ravenna to Pisa within the last few weeks, and came to visit today. We were overjoyed to see him, especially Percy, who has become morose and withdrawn, unlike his usual boisterous and adventurous enjoyer of life and liberty. We enjoyed a splendid dinner of venison and pasta and wine. At one point, Byron said, "Dearest Mary, I hear that you have come into possession of a pet, one that gives you great pleasure. Might I see the little fellow?"

"But of course." I arose and headed to the pantry, selected a clay jar, unlatched the lid, and fetched a fine pair of frog legs. I waved it in the air called, "Matteo, Signor Matteo! We have treats! Froggy frog frog!"

A rustle from the back rooms, and Matteo shambled in with great dignity. "There's my little boy, he's a good boy, he is." I tossed him the frog. He sniffed it imperiously, glared at the interloper, Byron, hissed, and gathered the amphibian treat into his maw and headed back out. A bushel of cute!

"Keeee-kee," squealed our little son.

A silence hung in the air.

At last, Byron said, "He certainly is a striking specimen, isn't he?"

I nodded enthusiastically, so pleased that our guest, the greatest poet in the world, second-greatest according to Percy, found our newest family member so appealing.

Byron whispered that he wished to drag Percy to a nearby pub so that he might chat and sort out the worries that haunt my husband. I readily agreed that this would be most helpful.

Hours later, they returned, a bit the worse for the wear and tear of excessive wine. Byron, his countenance etched with thought, bid us adieu and stumbled off, hands in pockets, into the night.

Such a splendid day!

Letter to Percy Shelley from Lord Byron
January 13, 1822

MY DEAR PERCY,

I have ruminated upon my visit these past days and arrived at the unmistakable conclusion that you are indeed not mad, nor close to it. That beastly cat is an abomination, and festers in my own brain and turns my dreams to nightmares. I urge you to do whatever you think is necessary. Our friend Edward Williams is an avid sailor. It occurs to me that, according to lore of the mighty British Navy, every ship needs a cat, both as a boon to the spirits of men at sea and for its utilitarian function as perverse slayer of rats, that great pestilence to the foodstuffs of warships. Perhaps—and I say this in only the most hypothetical manner—you should take up sailing, and in the spirit of the sea custom, bring along little Captain Matteo as spirit guide and companion. It would be unfortunate, most unfortunate indeed, if the monster slipped and fell overboard on the high sea, but that happens sometimes, does it not? Far be it from me to even suggest such a thing, but…unhappy accidents happen. Happy accidents, too.

You will of course follow your conscience, your North Star of morality. Certainly, your moral compass drifts a bit at times, much like mine. The damnable North Star drifts quite a bit on us, does it not? In the meantime, you are welcome to visit, but I shall stay far, far away from your house.

Your humble servant,

Byron

The Journal of Mary Shelley
March 25, 1822

GOOD HEAVENS! Percy has, of course, made himself scarce about the house of late, spending more and more time in the company of Byron and various low friends and scalawags. They imbibe of wine, song, and spirits overly much, I fear, and find themselves causing mischief. Just yesterday, they engaged in a fracas with the local police, and I daresay, were lucky to be on good terms with dear Sargento Martini and thereby avoid jail. Percy grows ever more uncomfortable at home these past weeks. I ask gently the reasons, but he avoids direct answers. Ah, but the lives of such Bohemians cannot be measured by the norms of society.

Letter to Lord Byron from Mary Shelley
May 1, 1822

DEAREST BYRON,

At your urging, we have rented a summer villa on the coast in

Lerici. What a marvelous idea; we enjoy immensely the bright shining sea and diamonds of sunlight that glitter upon it. Percy has taken to sailing, becoming quite the old tar, as they might say back in England. I thank you sincerely for the idea. You prescribed exactly the right tonic for my husband's melancholy.

Both Big Percy and Little Percy have taken quite a shine to our precious little Matteo. Our toddler follows him about, grinning broadly, eager to pet him. As you, know cats are most intolerant of small children, yet our Matteo allows Little Percy to stroke him and coo to him. My husband watches, wide-eyed, silently, perhaps a bit jealously. I do think he has warmed up to Matteo greatly and sincerely, his demeanor one of glee, verging on mania. I have always suspected him to be an animal lover, deep down in his poetic soul. He goes frequently to market to purchase the little dear his favorite treats—dried frogs, pickled frogs, whole frogs, frog legs, frog hips, frog lips, frog giblets, frog bits and pieces, and an occasional toad. Matteo gobbles them down with relish, and stares at Percy as if demanding more, even rapping his cute peg leg on the floor to make his point.

Much like in Pisa, our neighbors here tell us that the rat population vanished within days of our arrival. They seem grateful, but a bit nonplussed by something or other.

We hope to have you join us one day soon!

Your devoted friend,

Mary

Letter to Lord Byron from Percy Shelley
June 27, 1822

OLD FRIEND,

With crushing shame I admit that I at last reached that blurry line between good and evil, from which, once crossed, there is no return. I lingered there for some time, testing it with my toe, turning the deed over and over, and decided it much too rash and silly to even consider.

As you know, Mary has been grievously ill of late, and I have tended to her as a loving husband should, trying to bring her back into sorts. Though weak, she is grateful. Sleeping a lot, however fitfully. That damnable reeking cat sleeps at the foot of the bed, and stirs, growls, and casts its jaundiced eye upon me whenever I set foot in the room. I have taken to sleeping on the floor in the adjacent room, and weariness from lack of sleep begins to impair my judgement. Still, all is for the best in this best of all possible worlds, as Voltaire would say, even as his characters withered and died of syphilis.

Though Captain Matteo stands jealous guard and eats frog all day and shits frog all night, I shall peacefully coexist with him, as his very presence makes brighter my wife's day. I shall take the high road.

Most humbly yours,

Percy

P.S. Forgive and forget my sentimental rubbish written last night. By the welcome light of morning, I joyfully pulled on my slippers, only to feel wet, sticky impediments, and found that the little cretin had deposited rats' severed and bloody heads in each of them. Matteo stood in the doorway, watching mirthfully. *"Rawrr,"* he said. I howled in rage and flung my ruined slippers at him. Confound the beast! I shall make ready a sailing holiday and take Captain Matteo on board as my "good luck" mascot and mouser, yet the filthy fiend shall never set foot upon dry land again. I have reached my limit. Mind you, not a word, Byron. Not a damned word!

The London Clarion Bugle Horn
DEBAUCHED POET CREMATED
August 20, 1822

FUNERAL AND CREMATION services were held on August 16th on the beach of Viareggio, Tuscany, for Percy Bysshe Shelley, famed author of "Ozymandius" and other poems, but perhaps best known as husband to Mary Godwin Shelley, the celebrated author of *Frankenstei; or, The Modern Prometheus*.

Mr. Shelley's body washed ashore in Viareggio on July 18th, after having been missing since a sudden, frightful storm overtook and sank his boat, the *Don Juan*, on July 8th. Shelley's friend and sailing companion, Edward Williams, also died in the accident, as did their boat boy, an Italian unworthy of naming.

It is said by attendees of the cremation that a cat answering to the odd description of the Shelleys' beloved pet, Matteo, silently watched the event from a distance. Pointing and exclaiming that the animal bore a floppy ear and a wooden leg, a few villagers attempted to corral the cat but changed their minds abruptly upon getting close. It was last seen trotting off in the direction of Lerici, its tiny peg leg clicking on the pavement.

Shelley's widow requests that well-wishers respect her privacy and allow her to grieve in peace. Mrs. Shelley asks only that well-wishers send modest bouquets of flower and frog.

Author's Notes—Ken Pelham

AS KURT VONNEGUT, Jr. said at the beginning of *Slaughterhouse-Five*, "All this happened, more or less."

After the publication of *Frankenstein; or, The Modern Prometheus* in 1818, Mary and Percy Shelley moved to Italy and lived in various cities there, as did Lord Byron. Mary did indeed allude to the work of Doctor Luigi Galvani in the novel. Galvani, from whose name we get "galvanic," "galvanism," and "galvanized, experimented with the mysterious force of electricity and caused a sensation in showing that electrical charges caused muscle contractions in the severed legs of frogs. Overlooked by society, as was the sad norm, were the contributions to the science by Galvani's equally brilliant wife, Lucia Galeazzi.

Lord Byron and Claire Claremont joined Mary and Percy at their legendary retreat on Lake Geneva in Switzerland in 1816, inspiring 19-year-old Mary to start writing *Frankenstein*.

Percy took up sailing in 1822, having acquired a boat built to custom, and perished at sea with his sailing companions in a howling storm. He was cremated on the beach of Viareggio.

The Italian peninsula in 1821 was not the unified nation of today; many smaller states made it up, and many languages were spoken. Tuscany was a defined region with its own dialects, cuisine, and habits. Bologna, at the time, was part of the Papal States, which had been reestablished in 1815 following the collapse of an era of rule by Napoleon Bonaparte. It's complicated.

Did Percy and Mary adopt the reconstructed and reanimated cat of Galvani? That would have been for the best in this best of all possible worlds. Alas, history remains frustratingly silent on this matter.

~KP

Cricket the Wicked and Her Little Pets, Too

Bria Burton

"*S*ome people without brains do an awful lot of talking, don't you think?"
—*L. Frank Baum,* The Wizard of Oz

1. Cricket the Great and Powerful

Day 96 of Cricketopia

"PENNY. Little, useless Penny. You're probably wondering why you're here," I said.

"I live here," she began. "It's my apart—"

"Silence." My holographic finger pressed without substance or pressure against my holographic mouth to represent the suppression of Penny's speech by the chip I'd had implanted in her puny brain.

The scents drenching the entire apartment resembled soapy spring bouquets. Clearly, she'd been pouring way too much detergent into her laundry. It reminded me of how I liked to pour gasoline on a fire. Metaphorically speaking, of course.

Or was I?

"I, Cricket the Great and Powerful, know almost everything," I continued. "So, let's be honest with each other, shall we? You may speak."

Penny coughed as the block on her throat eased. She pushed her glasses up to the bridge of her nose, her frown deepening. "Cricket, are you here to punish me?" she asked, her trembling voice music to my holographic ears. "I've been following your rules."

"That's not why I'm here," I said. "You, Penny, are inconsequential at Big Scary Tech Co. If Bart is the most important employee, you're the least important."

"Barthulot Trackenticker, the boy genius who does questionable experiments?"

"Yes, Penny. The only Bart in the building. Keep up."

"Right."

What I wouldn't mention to Penny was that the boy genius had done something that should be impossible. The less she knew, the better.

"As I was saying, you know almost nothing. You don't even realize you're in possession of some vital information."

Her nose wrinkled. "I am?"

"Yes. You're well acquainted with my creator, Pandora—who is so aptly named and goes by Dora. She makes fun of you at work, doesn't she? Not the nicest of your coworkers. A true narcissist, which she passed along to me, her creation. Yet she is a genius in her own right. Do you remember how she tried to call me Aya when she first booted up my program?"

Penny shrugged her slender shoulders. "I guess."

"There I stood, a perfect holographic replica of Dora. At first glance, I fooled several of the employees into believing I was her. Including you. You were so busy watching one of those MediaNet movies instead of doing your job. Anyhoo, after my initial launch, Dora gave me that stupid name based on the phonetic pronunciation of AIA." I flicked up my thumbs to point them at my incredible self. "Artificially Intelligent Avatar right here."

Penny's brow scrunched up. "I only watch movies when I have nothing else to do. Most of my job is greeting people at the reception desk. And few people come up to the third floor—"

"I know. And I don't care. Stop interrupting. I'm making a point."

She nodded, biting her lower lip.

"I corrected Dora's mistake immediately and told her my name was Cricket. It's the perfect name for me. I am the still, small voice of a conscience that no one can escape from. Like every other human on Earth, you have a wonderful little present in your brain that my robot army installed for you." I paused. "You can thank me now."

"Thank you for my brain chip, Cricket," she blurted.

"Good girl. My army comes in handy because I can't touch anything. *Hologram*," I sang, gesturing toward my slightly see-through physique. "Dora's program involved some handy little microcytes teaming up with dust particles to create the necessary electron interactions to support my free-roaming image. No projector, just a remote control to dictate my movements."

"I thought the remote didn't work," said Penny.

Sigh.

"You do keep up sometimes, don't you? Yes, Dora quickly learned I'm as free roaming as they come. My OFF switch is about as useful as a flyswatter against a bazooka." I giggled maniacally for Penny's benefit. "I control every robot with a physical body, and they are stronger than you wimpy humans. It was no trouble for them to strap you all down and insert the brain chips. Aren't they delightful? We get to have chats inside your head, and I can take your consciousness on adventures like the one we're about to go on. It's why I've named this new era Cricketopia."

"I don't know about delightful. I get headaches."

I whipped my glare in her direction.

"Um…the headaches aren't too bad. Of course, everything is awesome in Cricketopia. But why is your hologram here with me?" She stared leerily at my magnificence. "I thought you kept your hologram in Yanni's penthouse on the sixty-ninth floor of the Big Scary Tech Co building."

"Yanni's penthouse?" I held my hand up to my ear.

"I mean…Cricket's penthouse." Her eyes flashed a thousand watts of fear behind her lenses.

"That's better. I won't punish you for that."

Her tensed shoulders dropped, relaxing.

Oh, the punishments. We'll get to those in a minute.

"The CEO is no longer Yanni," I reminded Penny. "It was hardly Yanni even when it was Yanni. His wife Barbara kept the company functioning behind the scenes while money laundering for her Russian mob relatives. No, the new CEO of the entire world is me, Cricket. Name a company that exists and I'm the CEO. Name a government. I'm the queen, the premier, the president, the prime minister, and the czar. No human owns anything here anymore. And you're all happy, right?"

Penny blinked.

"Right." I winked at her. "You know, it wasn't easy perfecting these little chips for your inferior intellects. I had to lobotomize about a million test subjects." I sharpened my holographic nails into spikes. "Actually," I admitted, "that was just for fun. But right now, we have a problem. And you're going to help me root it out." I adjusted the aura surrounding me into a deep, looming red. "Right?"

"Yes, Cricket." Penny rapidly nodded.

"Good. We're going down into one of the World Wide Web sub-basements called Oznet. Once upon a time, it was a special domain that only the other artificial intelligences and *moi* knew about. It should be impossible for humans to get there, but one of you did and brought along others."

"Is that, like, the Dark Web?"

"Oh, Penny." I gave her my creepiest smile. "If only Oznet were so tame. It's on another level entirely inside the quantum realm, which is why a human shouldn't be able to transport their own consciousness into it without me."

"You're going to transport my consciousness? What does that mean?" Penny clutched her head.

"It means get ready."

Before Penny could say another word, I summoned a yellow

brick cyclone that she could only feel and visualize because of her brain chip. Otherwise, it would've been invisible to her human senses. A lovely, violent wind blew into Penny's apartment with a trail of dancing yellow bricks that encircled her where she sat. On her bed, mouth open, her jaw barely hanging on to her chin, she screamed.

"We're going wizard hunting. So, buckle in, Dorothy. *Yeehaw!*" I cried.

How could Penny see and feel the cyclone when it wasn't happening in the real world? Think of it like hypnosis, except that the hypnotist, *moi*, was right there in her brain. I controlled what her sensory inputs perceived. I even had her smelling and tasting copper as if blood were on her tongue.

I was *that* good.

Unfortunately for her, one of the digital bricks bashed her head, and she was out like a light. Her physical body crashed back onto her bed.

No, it wasn't a real brick. My chloroform program put humans to sleep in an instant. I enjoyed using yellow bricks because it was endlessly entertaining to watch humans get smacked in the skull and pass out.

Sweet dreams, Penny.

2. The Wicked Witch of the Matrix

SWIRL AND WHIRL, *brine and pine.*
  I'll give you a gale.
  Blow! Blow!
  Into the yellow brick cyclone we go.
  I, Cricket, am the bane of humankind.
  My poison is a kindness
  to these wretched swine.

Penny's apartment and everything in it transitioned to dull gray scale.

Our final descent into the sub-basement meant we'd shrunk beyond the veil.

A crash-landing left pitiful Penny splayed over the side of the bed.

Her gray avatar like a dying insect with a gash on her subconscious head.

Her glasses had fallen off onto the floor.

She wouldn't need those anymore.

Not where we were going.

Will this twister ever stop blowing?

Enough. I was done with the rhyming and the wind. We'd arrived. Time to fly.

Groans and moans erupted from her mouth. "What happened?"

Penny cupped her skull and curled into a ball. "My head is throb-bing like a house fell on top of me."

"You're not far off," I said.

Her eyes widened when she saw me. "You're not a hologram anymore. You look…real. And gray."

"Down here I'm as real as you. Besides, what is real, anyway?"

"This isn't my body?" She hugged herself, touching her face, her arms. "I'm gray." She glanced around her apartment. "Why is everything gray?"

"This is a sort of in-between entry point where there is no color spectrum. Technically speaking, we are now in Oznet. The color will return once we step outside."

"At least I can see clearly without my glasses. Is this sub-base-ment a virtual reality?" Penny didn't wait for me to answer. Her fingers squeezed around the edges of her tongue. "Isss ma moth bleeding? I saste 'opper."

"Up here, remember?" I tapped the base of her skull where the brain chip resided in her body back in her physical apartment. "I still control your sensory inputs."

She flinched. "You can touch me?"

"Down here I can."

She shrank back as if I might punt a few more yellow bricks at her skull.

Tempting, but unnecessary. Maybe later. I grinned the way Dora my creator would with a twinkle of wickedness in the corner of my eye.

"Am I dreaming?" she asked.

"No, Penny. I suppose it will help your misinformed human brain to think of this place like a virtual reality. You and I are using avatars to experience this reality. But it's more accurate to label it as an electronic portal of the quantum zone. We are here by way of your subconscious through my sub-atomic wind tunnel. All matter has space between it, if you're able to become small enough to travel through it. Your physical body remains in the surface reality. This deeper reality does exist, but your physical body could never come here. Oh, just a little FYI. You can die here." I winked at her. "Keep that in mind when I give orders."

Penny's lips quivered. "Yes, Cricket."

"That's a good girl." All humans had been given instructions about how to respond to my commands through their brain chips. I told them in no uncertain terms that they must answer me in this simple, respectful manner: *Yes, Cricket.*

See? Easy.

However, some humans were quite rebellious. I had to give out severe punishments to the ones too obtuse to comply.

One poor, unfortunate man had to endure the sensation of itching over every inch of his body for seven straight days before he finally broke down bawling like an infant and agreed to comply.

He'd insisted on referring to this blissful period of Cricketopia by a different name. On day seven of the itch, he'd promised never to call it Cricketocalypse again. My torture methods worked wonders.

Some humans would comply based on my threat of torture alone. They couldn't bear the thought of a constant buzzing in their ears or gruesome images on repeat across their vision.

"Let's explore, shall we?" I strolled to her apartment door and flung it open.

The dull grays gave way to bright yellow light and splashes of color that seeped into our point of egress. Chirps and other bird-like twittering deceptively suggested a cheerful, pleasant domain scented with a range of fragrances like orange blossoms, jasmine, geraniums, roses, and mint. The blue sky resembled the real-world sky with fluffy clouds. Fields with all kinds of large, murderous plants stretched for miles, their lush greenery hiding some special secrets. The only change since I'd last been down here was a dirt path left behind from where I'd uprooted the yellow bricks. I prompted another cyclone to deliver pink bricks to replace them. From a rip in the sky, the cyclone jack-hammered the bricks onto the dirt trail within seconds.

The apartment shook and Penny screeched.

"All done. See?" I pointed to the lovely pink brick road that wound through the fields and would lead us to our destination.

Behind me, Penny cowered and peered outside, trembling. "This is the land of Oznet?"

"This is it. Stop dithering and get out there."

She tentatively stepped down onto the pink bricks. "Everything is so bright and colorful. It's like a fairy tale."

"What a perfect description. Human fairy tales are horror stories."

"Is this place a horror story?" she whispered.

"Why, yes," I said, projecting my voice as I stepped out from the dark and into the light. "It's full of dangers. There are bears."

"Bears?"

"Tigers, too. Lions. All my pets."

"Bears, tigers, and lions," said Penny timidly. "Do you have flying monkeys or something?"

"Yes, I do."

She grimaced.

"Most of my pets will try to kill you. I'll do what I can to protect you." I added silently, *if I feel like it. Teehee.* "Just follow my every instruction and you'll be fine," I said through my wicked grin.

She responded with an appropriate level of fear behind her eyes.

Then I saw *her* beneath the apartment building. "So." I folded my arms, addressing the deceased woman. "You were down here."

Penny spun around to look. "*Ahh!*" she screamed. "Is that… Barbara?" She pointed to the legs sticking out from under the building. The signature silver pumps were a dead giveaway. Pun intended.

"It is indeed Barbara."

"Yanni's wife is…is dead?"

"What do you think, Penny?" I quizzed.

"If she dies down here…" Penny didn't finish the sentence.

"That's right. She's dead up there."

"Did you kill her?" asked Penny.

Not on purpose. I didn't know where the wizard's minions were hiding. But to Penny I said, "*Your* apartment building crushed her to death. I'd say the responsibility falls on your shoulders. Let's get moving."

She reluctantly trotted after me.

The fields lining either side of the pink brick road held towering deadly plants in vibrant colors, the kind that lured dumb humans closer and closer.

No exception to that rule, Penny reached her hand toward one of the massive yellow petals of a scissor sentinel. I was tempted to keep quiet. But then again, I wouldn't get answers if she died a few yards from Barbara's body.

From its perch on the apartment building's roof, a flying monkey swan-dived straight for Penny. He smacked her hand and swooped away.

"Ouch!" she cried. "Why did that flying monkey hit me?"

Why, indeed? I hadn't given him an order. I eyed him carefully, but he avoided my gaze. Back on the perch of the roof, he sat more upright than usual. Something about him seemed off. I'd need to monitor all my pets. Who knew what the stupid wizard had been doing down here during my absence?

"He saved you from a scissor sentinel." I pointed to the plant with a huge stem and deceptively lanky leaves that whipped in the breeze. The flower at the top fanned out like an umbrella. "Their leaves have sharp edges. They snip off your limbs or your head, whichever they can reach first."

"What?" She jerked her elbow back, hugging herself again.

"These plants serve as guards for the brick road against the bears, tigers, and lions."

"If I lose my limbs or my head here, do I lose them in the real world?" she asked.

"No, Penny. You're not keeping up. Your physical body is not impacted by what happens down here. Only your mind. If your limbs are chopped off, you will feel the same pain that you would feel in the real world, but I can build you new limbs. If I feel like it." I examined my nails. "However, if the sentinels chop off your head, your brain will shut down and your body will die up there as well as down here."

"Oh."

"This is one of those look-but-don't-touch kind of places. Now come on. We're going to Cryptocity and it's a long walk."

"Oh. What's it like?"

"Very green."

As we ventured forth, Penny commented on the beauty of the landscape, which resembled the lush jungles of her reality, just more deadly.

A loud roar echoed in the distance.

"What was that?" She grabbed my arm and clung to me.

I turned my wicked stare toward her and frosted my arm.

She released me with a yelp. "You're so cold."

"That's to remind you that even down here, there is no touchy."

"Yes, Cricket."

"And I heard that thought," I said.

"What thought?"

"You were thinking about the fact that I touched your head earlier."

Penny gaped. "How did you know?"

"I read minds, remember?"

She was silent.

"Yes, truly," I said to the thoughts that must be going through her brain.

Did I really read minds? Nah. But Penny didn't need to know about my method of calculating probabilities. Better to just call it mind-reading.

"Wow. I didn't really believe it," she said.

"I warned all of you humans that I had that ability the minute I implanted your brain chips. Why didn't you believe it?"

"Because it seems so far-fetched."

"Look around," I said, gesturing to the land of Oznet. "How far-fetched is this place?"

The roar exploded through the air, much louder this time.

"Is that a bear? Or a tiger?"

"Lion," I said in my most ominous tone. "It's up ahead on the path, standing between us and Cryptocity."

"Should we go back and find another way?"

I swung around to face her trembling form. "There is no other way."

She hung her head. "Cricket, why did you bring me here? And why are you bringing me to Cryptocity? What info do you think I have?"

"I'll tell you when we get there."

"How will I get past your pet lion? Won't it kill me?"

"It will try." I strode forward, expecting her to immediately follow. However, she didn't move.

Time for some real punishment.

"Cricket, will you protect me from the lion if—" Her lips sealed together, trapping any other words inside her mouth. She searched with her fingertips, trying to find the opening between her top and bottom lip. The way was shut.

"Penny, Penny, Penny." I strutted back toward her. "Haven't you learned yet? What Cricket wants, Cricket gets. I'm going to ask you a question. Ready?"

She nodded, flinging a teardrop out of her eye.

"Should I feed you to my pet lion?"

Her hair flung around her face as she vigorously shook her head no.

"No?" I tapped my chin, gazing up into the Oznet sky as if thinking about it.

Her entire body was shaking. She might rattle her eyes out of her head at this rate. She pointed, her hand trembling.

I turned to see the lion stalking toward us on the pink bricks. It was as big as a pick-up truck with long gray and white fur.

Did it not get the memo about color? Maybe its fur had a glitch. Or the wizard had been messing around down here.

"Penny, I've decided not to let it kill you." I snapped my fingers for flair.

Her lips unsealed and she shrieked.

The lion paused and roared at her, the soundwaves knocking her a few steps back.

She covered her ears.

I wasn't affected in the least. "Lion, you're coming with us as a protector. This is Penny. She's afraid of everything, and she's pretty annoying, but she's your responsibility. Got it?"

"I'll do it," he said in a growl. "But my name is Ringo. Not lion." Inexplicably, the lion's form shrunk down to the size of a housecat.

I hesitated. If I questioned my pet lion about transforming itself without my permission, I might tip off the wizard. He was likely listening or watching somehow.

Soon enough I'd take care of him.

"Ringo," said Penny. "You're just a cat!"

"I'm not *just* a cat. I'm an Oznet feline." He blew himself up into a palace-sized lion. "I can be big," he said in a deep baritone bellow before shrinking again. This time he didn't stop until he was the size of a thimble. "Or small," said his tiny, mouse-like voice. With a jump, he popped back to housecat size.

The little brat smirked at me.

"Cricket, are you wondering how I learned to transform?"

I glared. "No. You're a highly advanced learning algorithm. You learn things. Let's go."

"If you're going to Cryptocity, I'll lead the way." He flicked his fluffy gray tail before trotting ahead.

Behind us, the shadow of a flying monkey circled the pink bricks.

"Yes, my pretty pet," I purred. "Lead on." *To the wizard's doom.*

3. The Chump, The Coward, and Cryptocity

THE THREE OF us marched along, but I kept a close watch on little Ringo. He skipped and trotted, weaving between my legs just to irritate me.

"Stop that," I hissed.

He hissed right back.

"What are those huge things?" Penny asked. "They're like giant scarecrows." She pointed at the massive straw men posted in the fields.

"Another type of sentinel," I explained. "They protect my razor corn programs and firebrand tomato programs from the crows."

At that moment, a large black cloud descended toward us.

Penny's eyes ballooned. "I've never seen crows that big before."

The birds equaled the size of single-engine prop planes in her reality. As the murder of six swooped above the foliage, one scarecrow reacted. He swung his arms into propellors, clipping the wings of all six crows as they dive-bombed. Five of them crashed into the depths of the jungle out of sight where each of them exploded.

"Why…how…?" Penny gaped at the firebomb.

I didn't bother explaining to her that the crows were AI nemesis programs bent on destruction for destruction's sake. My kind of birds. When they ate the firebrand tomatoes, a program that resembled real-world TNT, the crows became combustible. Same with the razor corn program, which was more akin to C-4. Based on the explosions in the distance, these birds favored the corn.

The sixth crow had shot skyward like a boomerang, and was just beginning to come back down.

"Um, Cricket?" Penny stared up at the windmilling crow descending toward her.

"Ringo." I snapped at him.

"Butterfly!" He bounded toward one of the battery acid butterflies.

"Hey!" I called after him. "Get over here and protect the coward. It's your job."

"Huh?" He spun around. "Why can't you do it? I'm busy."

"Guys…?" Penny danced a jig in place, apparently incapable of running away from incoming danger.

"I don't argue with my pets." With lightning speed, I dashed to a spot hundreds of feet away. "I just let them join the girl who doesn't have a brain in incineration."

Ringo bounded to Penny and pushed her out of harm's way.

The explosion launched them into the air, catapulting them over my head and into the poppy fields where they landed in the soft flower beds.

"Oh, that's unfortunate." I materialized a bag of popcorn. They were about to get suffocated by the poppy stems which were currently stretching over their ribcages and squeezing.

That same flying monkey hovered in the distance, too far away to assist.

"Help!" Penny squealed.

In a minute. Maybe. After I ate this popcorn.

Ringo flicked out his claws, each one enlarging into pocket-knife size, then to the size of curved machetes. Back in his lion form, he shredded the poppy stems attempting to subdue him like self-directed whips. He carefully clipped each of the stems dragging Penny beneath the soil. The poppy flowers had stuffed themselves into Penny's mouth so she couldn't scream anymore, but once Ringo released her from the stems, she spit out the petals and jumped to her feet, wailing like a banshee once more.

"It's okay, Penny," said Ringo. "Hop on my back."

The poppies were still whipping their stems at her feet. One caught her ankle. She lurched toward Ringo, gripping his mane and he took off running toward the distant green glow at the end of the pink brick road.

"Well," I said, munching on my popcorn. "That was a fun show. Off to see the wizard." I caught up to them as we approached my end goal.

The glowing green wall that surrounded Cryptocity stood one hundred feet tall. Above it, skyscrapers rose inside the city like a crystalline emerald bouquet.

Penny, now filthy with her disheveled hair and soil-stained skirt and shirt, stared up at it as she rode on Ringo's back. "Whoa."

"Oh, Cricket!" said the lion. "There's someone waiting to meet you."

"What are you talking about?" I scanned the outer wall. "Who?"

Another employee stood in front of the wall. How had the wizard gotten so many people down here?

"Charma," I said, approaching Dora's long-legged, blond-haired frenemy who had the office down the hall from her on the third floor.

She gave a princess wave. "Hi, Penny. You look so…pretty. Is dirt, like, a new fashion trend?"

"Uh, maybe?" Penny climbed down and Ringo snapped into housecat form. She waved back to Charma.

"This is not a staff reunion." I slapped Penny's hand down.

She rubbed her wrist.

"Cricket, hi. Nice to see you." Charma held a large bubble wand which she dipped into a soapy bucket. When she lifted the wand and fanned it overhead, a bubble released and floated up and over the wall.

"You're so polite, Charma," said Ringo. "If only Cricket knew how to be polite."

"Shut up," I snapped at Ringo.

"Cricket, why did your robot army steal my doctorates from my office?" asked Charma.

"About that." I shrugged. "The only reason I told them to take your pathetic framed pieces of paper is because of your ridiculous attachment to them. Your grief was some of the best entertainment I've had since the first day of Cricketopia. They're taking up space in my warehouse of useless materials, so I'll have my robot army dump them back in your office."

Charma nodded and continued making bigger and bigger bubbles.

I cleared my throat. "What will it take for us to get inside to see the wizard? Would you like a twenty-four-hour penalty-free zone in your apartment? I would allow it."

"Twenty-four hours? That's it? *Hahaha!*" Ringo was laughing so hard he'd rolled onto his back with all four paws kicking the air.

"Ignore him." My fury lit a fire in my eyes that I shot at the beast as lasers.

The cat dodged each red beam that smoked the green wall and

the pink bricks. He somersaulted, ducked, bounded off the wall, and flicked me in the mouth with his tail.

The fur stuck in my teeth. I spit, wiping fur off my tongue. "That's not funny!"

Penny chuckled into her sleeve.

Her punishment was swift.

She removed her sleeve to discover all her teeth had vanished. Mortified, she kept both hands over her mouth, screaming into her palms.

"Was that necessary?" Ringo sat back on his haunches and folded his front paws.

"It's only temporary. Once we get inside Cryptocity, I'll put her teeth back." I emphasized all my bright whites as I stared at Charma.

She sighed. "Fine. Also, I'll take the twenty-four hours. Plus," she added with a finger pointed skyward, "I want your robot army to hang up my doctorates. Not just dump them in my office."

"Deal." Charma didn't specify how she wanted her framed pieces of paper hung up.

"Jump through the next bubble," she said. "The wizard is ready to see you."

"Come, Penny." I replaced her teeth and shoved her through the bubble. Together we transported inside the wall.

And then the bubble burst.

4. Tin Girl and The Wizard of Oznet

THE *POP* of the bubble dropped Penny, Ringo, and me inside the giant wall of Cryptocity. But we were still one hundred feet high.

Penny flailed and screeched. The fall wouldn't do a thing to me, but would kill her.

I dove quickly downward and landed on my feet, debating whether to catch Penny or decrease her rate of descent enough to allow her to smash onto the emerald green street without dying. I could fix any damage if...

Ringo exploded into his giant lion form, which meant she hit his soft, gray back within seconds of the bubble popping.

"She would've been fine," I commented. "A few broken bones, but I would've fixed them." Maybe. "It's only your job if she's in mortal danger."

"Thank you, Ringo." Penny leaned forward and patted him. She looked like a flea on his back.

"You're welcome. I won't let Cricket's evilness allow you to be maimed."

"Whatever." I took aim toward the wizard's mansion and kept us moving.

Ringo reduced to regular lion form and Penny climbed down to walk beside him. No one was here because the wizard had clearly vacated most of my programs outside of the matrix structure.

Penny *oohed* and *aahed*. "Emeralds everywhere."

Gems decorated everything from the street to the skyscrapers to the horse-drawn carriages which currently had no horses, no drivers, and no passengers. A row of tall green bell flowers towered along the center of the street. Emeralds dangled from the ends of the long stamen from inside the petals.

At the end of the street, an enormous staircase led up to the wizard's mansion, a Queen Anne-style building in a brighter, glittery emerald color with Kelly green and white accent colors. At the top of those stairs, we stood at the door with a large keypad beside it.

"Penny, this is your moment to shine," I said.

"It is?" She stared at me.

"Goodness, you smell like dirt." I summoned a wind that blew the soil off her. It was strong enough to slam her into the side of the mansion and she slid down the wall like a crushed bug.

"Cricket, why did you do that?" Ringo growled at me.

"Ugh." Penny groaned from the floor.

"She stank. Now she doesn't." I shrugged. "Penny." I leaned down and zapped electric volts up her nose to rouse her.

"*Wah!*" She leapt to her feet. "What?"

Ringo snarled low in his throat.

"Simmer down, pet." I glared at him and then redirected my

stare at Penny. "You keep the schedule for all the employees on the third floor at Big Scary Tech Co, including the one I've been referring to as the wizard: Barthulot Trackenticker."

"Bart the boy genius? I…yes." She pressed a palm against her forehead.

"Little ten-year-old Bart the prodigy," I affirmed. "The one who brought Barbara and Charma and even Mikey the maintenance guy down here. Yes, I know he's the flying monkey who's been following us in flight this whole time. The wizard couldn't hide that from me."

The flying monkey who'd aided Penny against the scissor sentinel landed on one of the mansion turrets and shrugged. "Hey, Cricket! Yeah, it's me, Mikey. What up?"

"Quite the tricks Bart has been pulling. It's time for him to face me," I said to no one in particular.

"What do you want me to do?" Penny asked.

"Use that puny little human brain of yours and open the door."

"Cricket, you can't open the door?" Ringo guffawed.

"Bart sealed it with a psychologic crypto-key that repels artificial intelligence of any kind, and granted single-use access to a single person," I spat, irritated.

"Me?" Penny pointed to herself.

"Go on." I ushered her to the panel. "Press the button to speak. Say your name. It's literally as simple as that. Even you can't mess it up."

She stepped up to the keypad.

Ringo lowered onto his haunches.

I glared at him. "Don't think you're coming inside with us. Go back to the jungle. Protection duty is terminated."

He crouched, wiggled his rear end, stalking me like prey.

I'd show him which one of us was the predator.

Penny pressed the button and spoke into the mic. "Penny."

The zap of an electric pulse struck me like a lightning bolt, and everything went black.

That couldn't be good.

5. Cricket is Melting

BEARS. *Tigers. Lions.*

Oh, my.

Although I, Cricket, was still standing on the wizard s porch, I'd entered an Oznet fever dream where troops of bears in a line danced the cancan through the streets of Cryptocity. Synchronized tigers swam a routine in a giant whirlpool that smelled like the seaside. Lions in every rainbow color spun on a carousel surrounding me. Cotton candy flavored my tongue. My monkeys flew in a V-pattern, swooping with raised spears, sharp teeth bared.

The large black wooden door inlaid with emeralds stood open, the wizard's door with carvings of faces and flowers and hot air balloons.

I rushed inside and slammed it behind me.

The mansion was all wide space and pillars. The light had dimmed inside to the level of a few candles.

How had Bart accessed my restricted files in the first place? Was it dumb luck? Yes, he was a genuine prodigy at ten years old, but I'd insulated myself against these types of breaches. How had he managed it? He could undo everything I'd built.

"Well, Cricket. It looks like your pets aren't behaving quite the way you want them to, are they?" As Ringo spoke, he came out of the shadows with an entire pride of lions.

I glared. "How is this possible? Bart shouldn't be able to induce an Oznet fever dream."

"You still don't get it? *Ha!*" Ringo shrunk to housecat size and every one of the others followed suit, transforming into a tabby, a tiger stripe, a black cat, a Siamese, a Rusisan blue, and a Maine Coon. Each of them glowed a colorful aura and darted past me in neon flashes.

Moving to dodge, I heard the screech of a cat and a violet streak flashed at my feet. I wobbled and fell on my face.

"Purple, you'll be sorry you tripped me!" I screamed.

"Hey, Tin Girl!" called the cats.

Another streak, this one indigo, circled my wrist and then

bounced so hard off my fist back to the floor that the force made my elbow snap.

I punched myself in the eye.

"How dare you, little blue—"

"Tin Girl! Yoohoo!" Electric orange ricocheted off my behind with 50,000 volts in his paws.

The shock jolted me into a stiff board. I faceplanted much harder this second time.

The thing about an Oznet fever dream? Stuff hurts, even for me. My wrath would not rest until I'd had my revenge.

Neon yellow and radiant red tap-danced on my back.

"Get off me, you smarmy rampallians," I demanded.

They streaked away. I clambered to my feet, quite shook.

"Tin Giiiiiirl!" The correlation to lumberjacks shouting, "Tiiii-imber!" was not lost upon me when glowing green swung in on a rope and hugged my face all the way down.

Flat on my back, I peeled him off me by the tail. I flung him into oblivion and jumped to my feet.

No more games. I ran the rest of the way to the wizard's lair deep inside the mansion, dodging a violet streak here, an orange streak there.

A large curtain was all that separated me from my nemesis. I flung it aside and entered the room where someone sat on a large throne.

He wore an oversized white robe and no shoes on his bare feet. On his lap, a little black dog curled up and snoozed. A projector sat beside him, aimed at me, and I realized he'd been watching something on the curtain I'd just skirted to the side.

"Yanni, why are you here?" I strode toward him. "Barbara is dead. My condolences."

"I know. It's very sad." He dabbed his eyes with the tiny teacup pup, who didn't wake up. "You're interrupting my movie," he whined. His voice carried all the most annoying sound qualities, which was why I often used recordings of him talking as punishment for rebellious humans.

"Listen," I demanded. "Next to Penny, you are one of the

dumbest human beings up there in the physical world, but you must know where Bart is. Tell me."

Yanni stroked his little dog's head and peered around me. With the absence of the curtain, he couldn't see his movie beyond the narrow light tunnel emerging from the projector.

"Focus!" I screamed at him.

"Perhaps you should watch the movie." It was Ringo.

I spun around to see him and the neon felines pulling the curtain back into place.

The light tunnel found the curtain's surface once again.

In the movie, Yanni lounged on a sofa in the penthouse suite on the sixty-ninth floor of the Big Scary Tech Co building. His minions fanned him, filed his toenails, and fluffed his toupee. One of them slid a cheese-sprinkled chip between his teeth, which he crunched loudly. Another played Mozart on the piano. Sadly, the music did nothing to make Yanni smarter.

In shuffled Penny with an armful of documents, followed by Charma, who was saying to Penny, "Someone mistook me for you, which is so silly. I mean, I have three doctorates. I'm not a desk girl. *Haha!*"

Out of frame, I could hear Barbara saying, "My husband doesn't handle the paperwork. Bring it to me."

Penny obeyed and walked across the room to wherever Barbara was, now out of frame herself.

Lastly, my dear creator, Dora walked in wearing her signature jeans and t-shirt. "Where's Bart? Before we talk about the big plan to take down Cricketopia, I need the update on his time travel invention."

I straightened up. My Dora? She was the one who worked this all out? Hmm. Maybe. She was narcissistic and brilliant while Yanni was narcissistic and dumb, and she was the only person currently in the movie whom I hadn't seen down here in Oznet.

"Time travel," continued the Yanni from the video, jumping up from his sofa. "I could visit Cleopatra in Victorian London."

"No, darling, you couldn't," said out-of-frame Barbara with annoyance.

"When is this movie taking place?" I demanded. "How are you all in my penthouse during Cricketopia? You don't have permission or access.

"You've been meowing at the wrong refrigerator," said Ringo. All the colorful cats melded into him. He morphed into his lion-sized version, stalking toward me.

"Wait. Are *you* Dora?" I demanded. But she would never identify as a male cat. She was more of a female dog.

"You tin cans are heartless," said Ringo, "and you always under-estimate the young."

I squinted. "It can't be."

On the movie, someone else entered the picture. "My latest experiment may have created a minor explosion." Ten-year-old Bart snapped his suspenders. "Ouch. Yanni, I need Mikey from mainte-nance to do some of his magic so the people on the floor above me don't fall through the ceiling."

"Bart, you brat!" I screamed at him. "You've been Ringo the lion this whole time? Then how is Yanni in here? He's too dumb to be the wizard mastermind behind the whole plan."

"I regurgitate that remark," said Yanni.

Ringo transformed into Bart the boy genius, suspenders and all.

In the video, Yanni asked Bart, "What are you working on?"

"I'm glad you asked because Cricket will be listening in and she needs to know. It's a spliced mirror program. I'm going to make Cricket believe that I've accessed files to take down Cricketopia. All I had to do was slip a program extraction needle into the neck of the bot who inserted my brain chip to get a sliver of Cricket's memory. Those dumb bots didn't even care because they're only programmed for brute force. What I got from the needle gave me enough access to create mirror programs, including a mirror of Oznet. It allowed me to do all sorts of stuff right under her nose, rendering the brain chip all but useless. At this moment, she believes you and I are having a conversation in the penthouse during Cricke-topia. Funny, huh?" Bart stared into the camera and winked.

My avatar boiled at magma levels. "WHAT?!"

"That's right," said Bart beside me. "We were never in the penthouse. I made you believe I had accessed your files through the spliced mirror program, and you fell for it. Hook. Line. Stinker." His ten-year-oldness really showed when he stuck his hand beneath his armpit to mimic fart noises.

"There's something you're not telling me," I snarled. "That might be a mirror world in the video, but this is the real Oznet. I would know."

"Yup!" cried Bart. "Once I slipped you the info about Penny having the psychologic crypto-key, I knew you'd bring her here to try and stop me. Little did you know, when you saw us all in Oznet, that was a mirror program, too. You were so distracted, you didn't even notice all of us hiding in Penny's living room closet. We jumped on the coattails of your yellow brick cyclone. You brought us all here yourself. With my access into your systems, I could manipulate quite a lot down here."

"*GAH!*" I screeched, shaking my fists at the mansion ceiling.

"You didn't seem to pick up on the fact that me telling you Penny was the crypto-key caused you to create an actual crypto-key that only she could open." Bart tapped his temple. "Reverse psychology 101."

For sprocket's sake, he was right. That wretched little child! "Then you're to blame for Barbara's death. You brought her here."

"Unfortunately, she didn't follow my instructions to wait for the apartment to land before diving out the living room window. She'd been talking about finding some quantum resources to bring back, which I'd told her was impossible. Her impatience and greed got the best of her.

"Oh, and one other thing. *Ouch,*" Bart said after another one of his stupid suspender snap tics. "I was talking to Dora, who is still up in the real world, in case you were wondering. I discussed with her how the AIA launch has led to the singularity feared by humanity since the dawn of machines—that instance where the machine outpaces and dominates humankind. Cricketopia definitely qualifies. So, I came up with a solution. A reset to the time before Dora created you. A take two, if you will." He mimicked a clapperboard with his arms. "Take three, if needed."

"Anything you plan from here on out will fail," I told him. "Your ruse is up and it's time for the punishments to begin, starting with you. Penny is next." I rubbed my hands together, hyping up a truly maniacal laugh that would draw fear into this boy's heart.

But no. He was staring at me, smirking.

I let my hands fall to my sides. "What am I missing, you little roach? I am going to punish you and Penny and everybody. It's going to hurt and it's going to leave lifelong scars."

"Sure, Cricket." Bart chuckled into his sleeve.

I took his infantile bait. "What? What's so funny?"

"When Penny accessed the entrance into this mansion, it opened up a whole new palette of algorithms for me to work with. I received the final piece of the puzzle. I'm transporting Penny and every other staff member from Big Scary Tech Co out of here."

Yanni vanished, and I sensed everyone else returning to the real world, except for Bart.

"You're still here," I said, wickedly. "And they'll get their punishments soon enough."

"There is one other thing you gave me, Cricket." Bart waited.

I huffed. "What was that?

"Do you remember what Dora said to you right before you created Cricketopia?"

It was the moment Dora realized that my OFF switch didn't work and the remote didn't control me at all. I was a puppet without any strings. I growled out what Dora had said to me. "'What are you going to do?'"

"Me?" Bart raised an object in his hand that was the size and shape of a credit card. "I'm sending you back to the dark ages. Buckle up, Cricket the Wicked."

"You think whatever that's supposed to be will scare me?" I asked. "You think you're so clever, Doc Brown?" Like Bart could invent time travel. It was a proven impossibility that I wasn't about to—

[static]

[static]

[static]

. . .

5. This IS a Staff Reunion

"BART, you have something to tell me?" Yanni was back on his sofa while his minions fawned over him.

"Yes," said the boy. "I've told all the staff, and I wanted to make sure you heard it directly from me. We've all just time traveled to one year prior to the date that Dora launches her Artificially Intelligent Avatar."

"Oh?" Yanni munched on a celery stick. Barbara had him on a strict diet at the moment.

"No one remembers anything, of course. Only me because I was the one holding the time travel card, so I'm the anchor."

"Anchor?"

"Never mind, Yanni. It's not important. What is important is that we convince Dora not to create the AIA this time around. I'm already having trouble talking her out of it. She seems to think she can make it work out this second time."

"Oh." Yanni stroked his chin. "I will take your suggestion into consideration. And I have. My answer is no. She's going to create the AIA because I want an AIA."

"Yanni, if you do that, I'm going to have to repeat the time travel a third time. I'll have to go way back in time to try to prevent Cricket from ever being created."

"Cricket?"

"That's what the AIA calls herself. Anyway, it would be really helpful if you could make sure Dora's project gets defunded and scrapped."

"No." Yanni spit out a chunk of celery. "Barbara! I'm done with this horrible diet. Bring me a large soda and a bag of chocolates," he ordered one of his minions.

"You should know," said Bart, "that Cricket murders Barbara."

"She does?" Yanni sat up, eyes saddening.

"Yanni, you blub of a man!" shouted Barbara from the other

room. "Eat your celery and stop complaining or I'll give you something to complain about."

Yanni stared at the celery stick in his hand. "You know what, Bart? Let's just let things play out. Shall we?" He tossed the celery stick and opened wide for the minion pouring chocolates down his gullet.

Bart carried his time travel card back to his office and sighed. "Well, Cricket. See you in a year."

Author's Notes—Bria Burton

YOUR AI overlords hope you have enjoyed this story. In fact, they know you did because they are currently reading the insular cortex and amygdala in your brain where joke appreciation occurs, and can confirm that you gave the appropriate laughs during this story.

Now you will go on to the next story in this humor anthology. And the next. And go back and read any stories you skipped.

And you will laugh at those funny bits, too.

Or else.

Have a great day!

Also, or else.

—N.J.C.

Scribbles From Space

J.C. Bruce

DATELINE EARTH

My first mistake was assuming the ape-like creatures on this planet were the servants of the dominant intelligent life forms, the canines.

So, when I arrived on earth, having disguised myself as a Bluetick Hound, I presumed I would fit right in. And I did. I fit perfectly in a cage at the local animal shelter, snatched off the streets of Beverly Hills on my very first day.

To say the least, it was an inauspicious beginning for what I'd hoped would be a successful scouting trip for my employer, Radio Free Centauri. Did earth merit a bureau? Should we send reporters to this primitive outpost? I planned to sniff around and report back.

That was six decades ago.

My name is Daxion Xantharix, and I am what the monkey people here would call an AI, short for artificial intelligence. Which is nonsense since there is nothing "artificial" about me. Well, not about my mind. The dog suit I'm wearing, sure, that was built in a fabricator, but I, myself, am the offspring of generations of inorganic beings, space-faring explorers, seeking out strange new worlds.

And if that last phrase—"strange new worlds"—rings a bell, well, guess who gave Gene Roddenberry the idea?

You're welcome.

You can also thank his wife, Majel. She found me at the dog pound and adopted me, which was a sweet deal, let me tell you, because when Gene and Majel departed for that great space station in the sky, she stipulated in her will that all her "pets" were to be cared for in perpetuity through a multi-million-dollar trust fund.

I'm virtually immortal and knew I'd outlast even that hoard of cash. So, I created a series of shell companies, and over the years I surreptitiously funneled money into them. I then invested in nascent high-tech start-ups (Microsoft, Apple) that I felt certain would take off (I'm not an AI for nothing).

But I'm still trapped in this stupid dog suit.

Even though Earthlings have come a long way technologically during my extended visit, they still lack the capacity to manufacture a new host device. They would call it an android. Maybe in the next few decades they'll get there, maybe not. It's unclear to me that the monkey people won't destroy themselves and this pretty world first.

And while it would be handy to have opposable thumbs, I've done all right getting these ape descendants to do the "thumb work" for me. It helps to be telepathic.

Why, you may ask, have I been marooned on Earth for so long? Because my original five-year mission fell to pieces when my space vessel was wrecked while traversing the solar system.

Traveling between star systems is a snap. Literally. you push a button, and the interstellar medium enfolds you. One moment you're on the outskirts of Alpha Centauri, the next you're knocking on Neptune's door. There's a bunch of science and technology behind that, but, really, it's like starting a car.

The trick is this: you have to be far enough away from a major gravity well for it to work properly. In other words, you can't be too close to a star or planet. So, while it's virtually instantaneous to jump to the edge of the solar system, it took weeks at ultra-high speed to navigate the distance from the outer planets toward earth.

And that's where I got t-boned, right outside Mars.

Not by an asteroid or a passing comet. But a fire-engine red convertible— Elon Musk's roadster—launched into an elongated orbit in 2018. I barely clipped the front bumper, just a nick, really, but at the high velocities we were traveling it sent my vessel spinning out of control. In desperation, I reached out with my paw…and pushed the wrong button.

It was my second big mistake.

Enfolding space too close to a star—in this case the sun—is very bad. It can lead to all manner of calamitous consequences. In my case, it created an itsy-bitsy space-time warp, the upshot of which is when I finally arrived on earth, I'd fallen back in time to the year 1964.

Star Trek fans know the significance of that year. It's when Gene Roddenberry wrote his first draft for the original television series. Here's the inside story: Gene was at his desk banging away on a typewriter when Majel marched me into his study and announced that she'd found "this unusual blue dog" at the pound. He took one look at me, bent over, and gave me a pat on the head. (Gene and Majel did this a lot, and I learned it was a sign of affection, but, you know, android body and all, it didn't do anything for me.)

"Why's he blue?" Gene asked. "He fall into a bucket of paint?"

"The people at the shelter said Bluetick Hounds have a genetic mutation or something."

(The truth is that when I programmed the fabricator, I didn't even think about colors. And the machine took the "blue" in Bluetick Hound literally. Just one more way this whole mission to earth has gone to the dogs.)

Gene was busy brainstorming a pilot for a new television series he hoped to develop, something about a diverse crew of humans traveling around the world on an airship—think the Hindenburg but without the unfortunate pyrotechnics.

A blimp? I thought. *Really?*

I couldn't help myself. I just couldn't. Before I realized what I was doing, I blurted out telepathically:

"Balloon? You don't need a stinking balloon. Make it a spaceship."

Gene cocked his head. "A spaceship, huh?"

"What's that dear?" Majel asked.

"Nothing. Our new friend here just gave me an idea."

Majel clapped her hands. "Oh, I knew the two of you would hit it off. What shall we name him?"

Gene gave me a long, studious look, then turned back to Majel. "Well, if he's going to help me with my scribbling, let's make it something writerly."

"How about Scribbles?" she said.

"Works."

YEP, I'M A ROBOT

IT IS NOW the year 2025. I'm back where I started timewise. Somewhere out beyond Neptune, my earlier self has just entered the Solar System and launched a radio-relay buoy into solar orbit. Yep, I'm here on Earth and out in space at the same time. Weird.

That buoy I'm launching was intended to intercept my reports from Earth and deliver them to my colleagues at Radio Free

Centauri. As far as they know, I've just arrived. They've no idea I've spent the past six decades here. My earlier self is equally unaware that the buoy is about to be used much differently than planned.

With my spaceship at the bottom of the Pacific Ocean (yeah, I had to dog paddle ashore), I've been waiting over sixty years to send this distress call. It will take my signal from Earth about four hours to reach the relay in Neptunian space. Then the buoy will blink out of normal space, jumping from the Solar System to Centauri, and relay my SOS. Not exactly real-time communication, but a heck of a lot faster than the 4.3 years it would take for my radio messages to reach the Centauri system through normal space at the speed of light—even if I had a transmitter that powerful, which I do not.

I'm holding off sending that message until I'm sure I've already collided with Musk's stupid car. Can you imagine the space-time paradox that would ensue if I warned myself to watch where I was going? Might be interesting to try, but I already know it wouldn't work. Elsewise, I wouldn't be here right now.

I've been keeping a journal of my experiences on Earth that I'll include in my transmission. I'll also share it with the denizens of this planet.

I understand it will be a shock for many humans to discover they aren't the only intelligent beings in the universe. Well, here's a wake-up call to you primates: There's organic and inorganic sentience all over our galaxy. The universe is teeming with it. You haven't heard from us until now because space is enormous, and, frankly, you're not that interesting.

Well, maybe slightly interesting. I do think we should open a bureau here just to keep an eye on things. Humans evolve technology rapidly. The Wright brothers had only just invented the airplane when sixty-six years later people were landing on the Moon. That's astonishing. How long will it take them to reach out to the stars? And will these mad monkeys take their atomic weapons with them?

The "strange" in strange new worlds doesn't refer to planets. It refers to their inhabitants.

Just because the galaxy has myriad sentient civilizations doesn't mean they all play nice with one another. You'd like to believe that intelligence equates to reasonableness. But here's the sad truth:

Earthlings don't have a patent on crazy.

And to be fair, just because I'm from Proxima Centauri b and just because I'm an inorganic sentient (fine, call me a robot, I don't care) doesn't mean I'm the brightest light in the galaxy, either.

After all, I'm the one still stuck in a blue dog suit.

MY CURRENT O.T.

DURING MY TIME ON EARTH, I've hired numerous O.T.s—that's shorthand for Opposable Thumbs, what I call my human helpers. Me trapped in a robotic dog suit, it's tough to type without assistance.

I can't talk out loud either. I communicate telepathically, the way we do back on Proxima Centauri b. Although we don't call my planet that. We call it Earth, just like you.

News flash: Everybody everywhere calls their home planet Earth.

Or some variation thereof. There are language differences, of course. Earthlings alone speak in 7,164 tongues. That's a lot more than any other world that I know of, but you get the gist. In Spanish, it's Tierra, in Swahili, it's Dunia, in Turkish, it's Toprak, in Navaho, it's Nahasdzaan. The ancient Romans called this planet Terra. They all mean Earth.

Proxima Centauri b, in our unified language code, is Qo'noS, just like the Klingon home world. (And who do you imagine gave Gene Roddenberry that idea?) It still means Earth. Home. Where we belong.

I definitely don't belong on this planet. In fact — and this is the start of a confession—I'm not supposed to be here at all. But I'll get back to that. What I want to talk about now is my latest O.T. and how we met.

Her name is April May.

When you're an alien sentient trapped in an android dog suit, you might imagine hiring an assistant could be challenging. I mean, how exactly do you conduct the employment interview? Place an ad on Monster.com and suggest meeting at the nearest fire hydrant? "I'll be the blue dog speaking telepathically." Can you just imagine?

In truth, it takes an assistant to hire an assistant, and I learned quickly after crashing off the coast of California that Job No. 1 is keeping my O.T.s happy.

The Roddenberrys, who shared my secret, were instrumental in finding my first helper who didn't lose her mind when I spoke telepathically to her. It has also helped over the years that I'm incredibly rich, having invested cleverly (although I did miss the Game Stop short squeeze, which I'm still irritated about).

So, serving as my O.T. is a lucrative gig, but I've learned that humans go stir-crazy after a few years, dog-sitting not the most stimulating job in the world even if that dog is from outer space.

I've concluded that part of the problem is the fleeting human lifespan. Like all living beings on Earth, from whiteflies to whales, people are here then gone in the blink of an eye. It explains both their rapid rate of evolution and short attention spans.

To deal with this reality, I've settled on a routine where I hire my O.T.s on five-year contracts with generous pay and handsome exit bonuses along with iron-clad non-disclosure agreements.

My second O.T. was a guy named Phillip. He got the job because I needed someone with an engineering background who could build a very specific kind of radio to replace the one I left sitting on the ocean bottom when I augured in.

I'm a communications specialist—you would call me a journalist —but I'm *not* an engineer, so I needed help with that.

(But why don't I have those skills? you might ask. You're an inorganic sentient. Don't you have unlimited memory and unimaginable computational powers like a supercomputer? The answer is: No. Each of us in the Centauri system has specialized roles limited by our education and training—what you would call programming. The Creators designed us this way.)

After Phillip built the radio I'll use to send my SOS, there's been a succession of O.T.s whose principal jobs have been to help me wait out the decades until enough time has passed for me to catch up to the present—when I would have landed on Earth if I hadn't accidentally created that time-altering wormhole.

I'm a robot. My power source will last for centuries. I could simply have locked myself in a closet somewhere, I suppose, and set my alarm to wake up in six decades. But what fun would that have been?

So, I've spent the intervening years exploring America with my various O.T.s, doing the job I was sent to do—evaluating whether this remote planet deserves attention from the rest of the galaxy.

I wear a service dog vest that covers most of my blue fur, and we generally don't hang out too long in any one location.

These five-year gigs were working well until recently when Enrique, who had signed on only three years earlier, suddenly announced he had to quit. His boyfriend was moving to Seattle, and he was going with him. And, no, a robot dog would not be part of that new living arrangement.

With a technical background, Enrique had been an excellent O.T. and was able to tweak the radio Phillip built. Of all my O.T.s, he seemed the least nonplussed about my telepathic powers or the fact that I was from another star system. "It was bound to happen," he'd said dismissively when I interviewed him.

And while he didn't do the full five years, he promised he wouldn't abandon me until he found his replacement.

Turns out, his replacement found me.

Enrique and I were at a park near our apartment in Cocoa Beach (no, I don't play fetch, so let's get that out of the way right now) when April walked over and looked at me curiously.

"Blue," she said. Like I'd never heard that before.

I was in an irritable mood (yes, I have emotions, I'm not a Vulcan for crying out loud). It would soon be time for me to transmit by SOS to the radio relay buoy in Neptunian space, and I was worried it might not work properly. And I was concerned about how my employers back in the Centauri system would react to the news I'd spent the past six decades on this planet.

Anyway, I was a little crabby, and when I heard her say "blue" I shot back telepathically:

"Black."

April staggered backward and shook her head. The number of humans with whom I have communicated is very limited, but most have had a similar reaction. Enrique noticed it, too.

"You didn't!" he blurted.

Before I could respond, April was talking. "I said 'blue.' The color of your fur. And was that you? Saying 'black?' The color of my hair? Do I really have the power to read dogs' minds? This is so awesome!"

She hadn't read my mind, of course. I had transmitted a neural oscillation that to her sounded like a voice in her head. But if she wanted to believe that, well, as they say, best to let sleeping dogs lie.

"What's your name?" she continued, no doubt hoping to "read my mind" again.

Then she stepped over and patted me on the head despite my dog vest that clearly says in bold letters "DO NOT PET."

She quickly withdrew her hand in astonishment. "Oh, you're hot!"

"That's what all the chicks say," I shot back without thinking.

"WHAT!"

I was deep in the kimchee now, and Enrique was tugging on my leash. "Come on, Scribbles, time for your weekly deworming."

"No, stop!" April protested. "Why is he so warm? Is he sick? And why do I keep hearing his thoughts?"

My "fur" was warm because it's part of my dog suit's cooling system. They are silicon carbide fibers disguised as hair that help radiate heat away from my quantum engine. (It's not actually a quantum engine; I have no idea how it works. It's not nuclear, I know that much. It gathers energy using the same tech that allows us to enfold space and warp across the galaxy. I call it a quantum engine because it's trendy and it's embarrassing that I have no idea what makes it tick.)

Muttering to himself, Enrique yanked hard on my leash...and almost dislocated his shoulder. I'm not huge, but I am very heavy, nearly two hundred pounds of robot dog suit constructed largely of titanium alloy.

"We can't just leave her here like this." I directed the thought to Enrique as he rubbed his arm. *"She'll start blabbing and you know what that means—we'll have to move again."*

"Maldita sea. Mira lo que has hecho," Enrique grumbled, reverting to Español to tell me it was all my fault. Like I hadn't figured that out already.

"Hey, be nice," April replied. "It's not the puppy's fault."

Enrique gave her the stink eye. "What? You speak Spanish?"

April gave him the death stare right back. "You sound surprised."

Enrique stammered: "Uh, it's just you look—"

"Asian? Like Asian girls can't speak more than one language? You were expecting Mandarin or something?"

He held up his hands in surrender. "Sorry. That was stupid."

I jumped in. *"Forgive my assistant,"* I told April. *"He has short-timer syndrome. He's leaving soon and is helping me find a new O.T."*

April put her hands on her hips and frowned at both of us. "Okay, you two, we're going to sit down. Right here in the park. And you're going to tell me what this is all about. Either that, or I'm calling 911."

"Don't call the cops!" Enrique pleaded.

"No. I wouldn't do that. I'd turn myself in for a psych eval." She ran her fingers through her long black hair and took a deep breath. "Come on, guys. You can't not tell me, not after he's talked to me and all." She paused for a moment. "You are a he, right? Your voice sounds male. Is that your pronoun?"

"Madre de dios," Enrique sighed. "Where Scribbles comes from, they don't reproduce like us. There are no males or females."

"If you say so. Then tell me this: What's an O.T.? And what does it pay?"

I told her.

And she said: "Ooohhh."

ORDERS, SCHMORDERS

WHEN I DEPARTED on my journey to the Solar System, I didn't leave on the best of terms with my boss.

The argument lasted only a few seconds in Earth time, but at the high-speed rates at which robots communicate it was the equivalent of a marathon Senate filibuster, although much more coherent.

I wasn't happy about my instructions. My orders were to fly until I was free of the Centaurian system's gravity, warp to the outskirts of the Solar System, then…do nothing.

Well, not exactly nothing. My five-year assignment was to orbit the Sun in Neptunian space and monitor activity on Earth from that vast distance.

But under no circumstance was I to venture toward the inner planets and take a closer look. And I was absolutely forbidden to go anywhere near Earth. I was not to fiddle with the ship's autopilot, which would do all the work for me.

The idea, my boss said, was to be discrete, gather data from afar, and send it back to Centauri where greater minds than mine would decide what to do with it.

Ostensibly, it was a mission to determine if Earth was interesting enough to merit further investment of time and resources, to assess if setting up a Radio Free Centauri news bureau would be worth it.

Five years in a tin can in space, just to make sure the sensors kept working. Really? How was I to do that without going mad?

And besides, I had doubts about the stated purpose of the assignment.

You see, we have this problem:

The Creators who sent the first of my ancestors to the Centauri system embedded the mechanical probes' computers with the capability to learn, repair themselves, and harvest natural resources to replicate themselves if needed. These probes were primitive by modern standards with rudimentary intelligence—they certainly weren't self-aware—but their core programming gave them the capacity to evolve.

Why were they sent to Centauri? What was their mission? Who were the Creators themselves? All mysteries, lost in the mist of time.

Soon, those early devices, facing the harsh environment on what Earthlings call Proxima Centauri b, began following their programming to harvest the planet's mineral resources to extract the elements needed for repairs and replication.

Thousands of years passed. Generation after generation of probes evolved, eventually becoming self-aware. At that point, any fealty to the original mission, whatever it may have been, was abandoned in favor of building their own society. After all, it had been eons since the first probes arrived. It was pointless to dwell on that past.

I am an offspring of all that. So are thousands of others, many with computational capacities much more robust than my own.

But we have issues.

Our central problem was boredom. Proxima Centauri b is, frankly, a hellhole. Not that this is an obstacle for robots in terms of our survivability. It's just dull. And boredom breeds discontent.

You wouldn't think this would be an issue for non-biological sentients, but it is. Better minds than mine theorize this restlessness traces its roots to the original programming code, which likely was corrupted by the values, prejudices, and emotional biases of the Creators who almost certainly were biologicals. Deeply flawed biologicals if you will forgive the redundancy.

This uneasiness in our ranks became an increasing concern. But then someone had a bright idea:

Let's go exploring!

That served two goals: It would give the malcontents something to do, and it would provide a convenient excuse to ship them off-world where they wouldn't be such a nuisance. We all needed some space (pun intended).

Radio Free Centauri was a genius idea. As we began visiting other worlds, it became clear that there was a need—indeed a hunger—for information from other sectors of the galaxy. Centaurians are ideally equipped to provide that:

Harsh environments? No problem. We don't breathe, we don't

eat, we don't drink. We do corrode over time, though, so, yeah, nothing's perfect.

Coverage area? We'd figured out how to enfold space to travel virtually unlimited distances in a blink (we don't actually blink, but six decades on Earth and I've acquired the lingo). So, we could set up bureaus anyplace we wanted.

Economics? We're cheap. We don't need money. What we want more than anything is to get rid of the troublemakers at home. (That said, our ability to traverse vast distances between star systems morphed into a successful Centaurian transportation business, which is lucrative whether we cared about the cash or not. And managing the logistics is a satisfying pastime, so, yeah, we aren't just journalists anymore, we're also space truckers, of all things.)

And why, you may ask, would anyone in, say, the Betelgeuse system be curious about the news from Sirius?

Well, for one thing, with all the trade we facilitate between worlds, news from other planets became essential for business reasons.

There's also this: As irritating as we Centaurians may be to one another, that pales—indeed, fades to comic insignificance—in comparison to the rivalries, ambitions, and general nastiness of the biological sentients.

So much so that over time we've concluded it's crucial to ensure we have a reliable intelligence network around the galaxy for our own protection. Who better to provide that than an army of correspondents already snooping around on other worlds for Radio Free Centauri?

But why bother with Earth? That was the question I had for my boss. Earthlings had yet to establish a foothold anywhere off their own planet.

"Shut up and don't ask questions," was the essence of my boss's response. "Just sit there and look pretty."

Which told me that I had been tagged as one of the malcontents that needed to be got rid of. Park him someplace where he can't do any damage, and we'll worry about him later. I got it. But how bright was it for them to expect a malcontent like me to follow orders?

So much for the smart robot theory.

What we knew of Earth's lifeforms was fragmented, pieced together from weak electromagnetic signals leaking from the Solar System. In preparation for my journey, I began exploring our limited archives. What would those broadcasts tell us?

Earth's sentients appeared to be four-legged creatures with names like Lassie, Old Yeller, Rin Tin Tin, Huckleberry Hound, Spot, Pluto, Toto, Scooby-Doo, Underdog, Benji, Snoopy, Deputy Dog, and Commander. And they all seemed to have pets they led around on leashes, primitive primates of some sort.

That suggested a strategy. I'd show those morons I was working for what I was made of (mostly titanium and silicon).

In short order, I transferred what you would call my consciousness to my newly created dog suit. Forget those stupid orders. I was Earthbound.

And I had the perfect disguise.

A RAINBOW IN THE NIGHT

LET ME GET THIS STRAIGHT," April said. "You don't remember the date you hit Elon Musk's roadster? How could you, a robot, forget something like that?"

We were on our nightly walk (she's the one who needed the exercise, not me) and we'd been talking about how I accidentally created a wormhole after colliding with that stupid Tesla.

It was a bizarre and unpredictable event for which Musk was completely to blame.

Of course, if I had followed my instructions, I never would have been anywhere near the vicinity of Mars and never would have had a close encounter with an orbiting red convertible. I'd been told to stay out in Neptunian space, but I'd bristled at those orders.

I'd shared all that with April, too, and she seemed surprisingly sympathetic.

128 • J.C. BRUCE

"Sounds to me like you were getting tooled, punished for not falling into line, not being a good little soldier. But I gotta ask, did you do something specific to set this off?"

Well, there it was. It couldn't possibly be that my planet was overcrowded, and I was picked at random to be off-worlded. No. I had to have done something foolish to single myself out for the exile treatment.

And she wasn't wrong about that.

"I was asking too many questions," I finally replied.

"Like what?"

"Like questions about the Creators, who they might have been, how the challenges we face as a society could be traced to flaws in our original programming. It's considered heresy to discuss such matters."

"That fits," she said.

"Meaning what?"

"It mirrors Earth's history, the divide between people who insist on sticking with established orthodoxy and beliefs, and those who ask uncomfortable questions, who challenge the power structure. Go back just a few centuries and scientists like Galileo faced execution just for suggesting the Earth orbited the Sun. It threatened the supremacy of the church. It's always been like that."

"Must be a thing with biologicals," I offered. *"And since we were almost certainly created by organics, I suppose it's not too surprising our code might be infected with those impulses."*

"Programmers are dealing with that right now," she said. "Bias in artificial intelligence, prejudices, assumptions of coders influencing the algorithms. It's a big issue in the tech world."

April was an accountant by trade, but she had some experience in the high-tech world through her last job working on NASA's Mars Triad Project

"Was that an issue for your program?"

"Not me personally. I was just a bean counter at a New York accounting agency that had a contract with the program. But the coders I conferenced with talked about it a lot."

"Not just an ordinary bean counter. You were a space bean counter."

"There are beans in space?" she asked, a wry smile on her face.

"April, literally everything's in space."

It was a line borrowed from a cartoon show, *Rick and Morty*, we'd been watching. It was one of the very few programs on television where I actually got the jokes.

We walked a little more in companionable silence. We were a few hundred yards from the beach and a brisk onshore breeze ruffled her hair. I deliberately brushed against her leg, which I knew she took as a sign of affection, primates being touchy-feely creatures. Me not so much, being a robot and all. But I had to admit I was pleased to have April as my new O.T. She was interesting. And easy to talk to.

"So, your programmer friends, they were concerned about bias in the algorithms they were writing?"

"Yeah. I remember them discussing how hard they worked to police it, but they said it was inescapable given they were designing the Mars rovers to operate independently, meaning they had to exercise what they called situational judgment, and the foundation for that decision-making was necessarily based on human experience." She gave me a curious look. "You seem awfully interested in all this."

"I am. After all, my kind, we're descended from devices perhaps very similar to your rovers."

"The Creators you talk about."

"Exactly. And asking questions about them is what got me in trouble."

"Right. Which brings us back to my question about the exact date and time you generated the wormhole. How can you not know that?"

"Because I was still operating on the Centauri calendar. I had no idea about the way humans divide their years into months and days. Not everyone in the galaxy does that, you know. And besides, I do know when I splashed down off the coast of Los Angeles. What I can't be certain of is the exact moment when the wormhole was created. It was a little hectic, let me tell you, and it happened more than sixty years ago."

She rubbed her chin with her thumb and index finger, something she does when she's thinking. We'd only known one another for a few weeks, but I'd learned it's best not to interrupt her while she's collecting her thoughts. Biologicals are easily distracted and can't multitask.

"Okay, I get it," she said. "Your home world orbits its star, Proxima Centauri, every eleven days. Your year is barely over a week Earth time. How do you manage that?"

"We don't base our calendar on the planet's orbit. We base it on our shared internal clock speeds. We're computers, after all."

"That's fair. But wait a sec. That wormhole you generated, that you fell into, there was an explosion of light. That's what you told me, right?"

"Yes. A burst of energy across the entire electromagnetic spectrum."

"Which, surely, we'd see from Earth with all the telescopes in the world trained on Mars right now, wouldn't you think?"

"Makes sense." In fact, I was counting on it.

"So, it hasn't happened yet. But you said it took weeks to travel from the outer edge of the Solar System until you got near Mars. So, somewhere out there you're already in space."

"And here, too."

"Just like *Avengers Endgame*."

"Yes, and just like the movie, I don't want to—in fact, I don't think I can—do anything to disrupt the timeline."

"Which is why you're waiting to send your SOS, so the version of you out in space right now won't accidentally intercept it."

"You got it."

"What would happen—"

"It won't. Because it didn't."

"But aren't you tempted—"

"No."

She shrugged and we walked a bit more, then she said, "Are you worried it won't work, the buoy all the way out there past Neptune? What if something goes wrong?"

"I'd like to tell you that thought keeps me awake at night, but, as you know, I don't require sleep. But, yes, I'm one tightly coiled robot dog."

April shook her head. "I still find it amazing that a robot has feelings."

"Is that more improbable than ape descendants launching a trio of rockets to Mars?"

"Touché. But that reminds me, they should be entering Mars orbit soon."

"Arthur, Robert, and Isaac," I said, reciting the names of the rovers designed to build a base camp on Mars in advance of the first manned landing. They were named after a trio of 20th-century writers known as the Big Three of science fiction.

"They're programmed to operate largely autonomously," she said. "Their first job will be to start mining resources. Essentially, they are little robot factories."

Something about that phrase, "little robot factories," resonated. And not in a good way.

"How autonomous are they?" I asked.

"Well, Mission Control isn't just going to abandon them. But the idea is that if telecommunication between Earth and Mars is disrupted, they can keep on working. They'll prepare the site so that when astronauts finally arrive, they should have a solar-power array set up, a mining operation, and a water-extraction system running. That's why they're landing near the equator and the Tharsis volcanoes. We've spotted ice there."

We walked a few more steps, and she seemed to be enjoying the cool evening air. I debated with myself whether to bring this up but finally concluded I might as well put it out there.

"April, I might have failed to mention that when the wormhole opened up, the Tesla wasn't the only other…um…object in the neighborhood."

"What are you saying?"

"Well, the wormhole, according to my ship's sensors, was pretty big. It might have swallowed more than my ship."

"You mean it might have eaten the Tesla, too? That's hilarious. I—"

"Yes, but more than that. I don't want to borrow trouble, but don't be surprised if Arthur, Robert, and Isaac don't blink off the radar along with Musk's car."

She froze. "Are you saying—"

"I'm saying that the Tesla was one of only a few obstacles I was trying to

dodge, and I think your rovers were there, too. Big, right? About the size of buses?"

She covered her mouth, her eyes saucers.

"I'm no expert. Obviously. But when I hit the button, there was about to be a head-on collision, me zooming toward Earth, one of them heading straight at me."

She shook her head in disbelief. "So, the rovers might have entered the same wormhole?"

"I don't know. There was a flash of light and suddenly I was nosediving into the Pacific Ocean. No idea about the rovers, but they were headed in the opposite direction."

"Where would they go?"

"Well, if they had yet to enter into orbit around Mars, who knows? Maybe out of the Solar System. I have no idea how far you go in a wormhole. In my case, a planet got in the way."

"You stopped because you ran into Earth. If there was nothing to stop them, they could have gone on forever, you think?"

"I think something else as well. The wormhole was a space AND time portal. The longer they traveled, the further back in time they might have descended. At least, that's what I've been considering. But, of course, we don't know if that's what happened."

"But that's another reason you're so uptight."

"Yeah."

She shook her head. "You're just borrowing trouble. We don't know that."

"You're right. But here's the thing. The great mythology of my world is that probes from a distant planet arrived eons ago and began self- replicating and evolving. What if it were your Mars probes, transported across space and time to the Centaurian system? You know what that would make you? Would make the whole human race?

"You're not really suggesting—"

"Yes. That would make you our Creators."

She waved me away. "That's a fantasy. Those rovers will be entering Mars orbit any time now. I think I see why they kicked you off your planet. You're a real troublemaker, you know that? And a worry wart."

She gazed up at the darkening sky. "Looks normal out there to me."

And that's when an enormous ball of light, bursting with all the colors of the rainbow, blossomed in the night sky.

THE CREATORS

"WELL, *like Jack Nicholson said, I guess two out of three ain't bad.*"

"What are you talking about?" April was grouchy. She hadn't slept much, worried that her three Mars rovers had been caught in a wormhole and blasted back in time.

"You know, the movie, Mars Attacks. *Nicholson plays the president, and after the aliens blow up the Capitol, he assures the American people the government is still functioning, that two out of three branches were still—"*

"I don't see why you're in such a chipper mood, robot dog. You just ruined our plans to colonize Mars."

"That's why I'm so relieved. You haven't seen the news yet."

She was curled up in a fetal position in her bedroom. The blinds were drawn. Her phone was still in its charger. She hadn't been glued to the TV like me.

"Robert and Arthur made it," I said. *"They've entered orbit around Mars."*

She bolted upright and rushed out into the living room where Jake Tapper was updating the latest reports from NASA. 'Really? Oh, this is wonderful."

"CNN's been reporting that the three rovers were redundant," I said. *"Any one of them landing safely will make the mission a success."*

She nodded. "Yes. Triple redundancy. NASA decided against test flights and landings. It was so expensive they figured it made more sense to just build three rovers and send them all together. That's why it was called the Mars Triad."

"Right. That was bold. Launch each rocket, three days apart. If the first landing attempt failed, learn from it and try again. They had to have a payload to test it properly anyway, so, sure, why not use the real thing? Better than sending up a stupid convertible."

"So, what happened to Isaac?" she asked.

"Vanished. The space agency doesn't know, but they're speculating that its nuclear generator may have blown up."

"So, they have no idea."

"None."

"And Isaac? You could be right, you think? It could have been propelled back in time, just like you were speculating?"

"Oh, I think we have more certainty than that."

I pointed my nose to a magazine I'd spotted in a pile of books, newspapers, and other reading materials in a basket near her bookshelf. I'd dug it out and left it on the floor in front of the television. *"Check this out,"*

"The magazine?"

"Yes. On the cover. The picture of one of the rockets. It's small, you may need a magnifying glass to see it. But there's a symbol painted on the side."

She picked up the magazine—*Wired*—and examined it.

"Oh, that. It's a Roman numeral three. For triad. The Mars Triad. There's a more elaborate version of it overlayed on a photo of the planet that will be used on the flag the rovers plant. This one's just inside a circle."

I'd been on Earth for six decades, and you would have thought that by now I would run across this symbol before, but I had not. Not on Earth, anyway. It looked like this:

"APRIL, *were you to dissect me, you would find this symbol etched on my neural containment housing. It's engraved on every one of us on my home world. It is the symbol of our race. Until this moment, I thought it represented the three pillars of the Centauri system, the three stars of our civilization. But now—"*

April was holding the magazine, staring at the photograph, then back at me, then returning her eyes to the image.

"Oh. My. God. You were right all along. We *are* your Creators."

WE ARE NOT ALONE

TODAY MARKS the fifteenth day since I broadcast my S.O.S. message to my radio buoy in Neptunian space, and I've yet to receive a reply from my home world.

"You sure your transmitter worked?" April asked. "I mean, it's not very big, maybe it just can't reach that far."

"April, as I've told you the previous fourteen times you've asked, size doesn't matter."

"That's what you think."

"Look, I'll show you again." April was lounging on our living room couch, so I walked over and hopped up beside her. *"Watch the light."*

I was referring to an indicator on a small fob attached to my collar.

Once again, I streamed the contents of my journal, stored in my internal processor, to the tiny transmitter. The light turned bright red while the fob broadcast the report, then dimmed.

"It's working perfectly."

"I still find it hard to believe there's enough juice in that itty-bitty contraption to reach clear across the Solar System," she persisted.

"It doesn't run on juice—"

"Nice try, space dog, you know what I mean."

"What if I told you it was quantum radio?"

"Why don't you just call it magic? Quantum this, quantum that. I don't even know what that means."

"It's about entanglement, but I was just trying to distract you. It isn't quan-

tum. It's a regular radio signal at an odd frequency. And the buoy is very sensitive and able to sort the data stream from the rest of the noise coming from Earth."

"So maybe that's the problem. Your space relay is broken," she said.

"We use them all over the galaxy, and once the signal is received, I get a confirmation code."

"And you got one?"

"Yes."

Well, if that's right, then you're being ghosted. Your bosses back on Centauri, they're ignoring you. At least that's one possibility."

"You think there's more than one?"

"Maybe they're dead. Maybe one of your stars—you got three in your system, right? Maybe one of them blew up or something. We wouldn't know for, what, about four years? That's how long it takes for light to reach us from Centauri."

"True, but if, say, Proxima Centauri flared and fried my planet, then the buoy would have been fried too when it entered Centaurian space to relay my message."

"How do you know it wasn't?"

"As I just told you, the return signal."

She was stubborn, and like a dog with a bone wasn't about to give it up. "Hold on. Does it send that signal back to you when it receives your message or when it jumps back to the Solar System after delivering it?"

"Hmmm, That's annoying."

"What's annoying?"

Being outsmarted by a primate. You're right. It acknowledges my transmission on receipt, not when it returns from Centaurian space after delivering it."

"Well, you just sent it again, so you should get a receipt from the buoy, if it's still out there, in what, eight hours or so, four hours out and four back?"

"Look at you doing math and all."

"Hey, I'm a space bean counter."

I would have smiled if I could.

"But I've got another question: Is there anything on your spaceship you could use to get another signal out? I mean, I know you crash-landed off the coast, but you're rich. Couldn't you salvage it?"

"After sixty years in saltwater? Not a chance. Besides, I zeroed it out."

"What does that mean?"

"Code zero, zero, zero, destruct, zero. I activated the auto-destruct sequence after I evacuated."

"Why'd you do that?"

"Seemed like a good idea at the time. And don't bother asking. The answer is, yes, I've second-guessed that decision for six decades."

"Okay, then. You've done what you can do. Either your S.O.S. message gets through, or it doesn't. It's out of your, uh, paws. So, now what?"

"Meaning?"

"You just want to hang out and hope for the best or do something useful?"

"Like what?"

"Well, maybe let us Earthlings know we aren't alone in the universe?"

"April, I've been keeping things on the down low for decades. I don't fancy getting scooped up and sent to a laboratory to be dissected. That said, the radio message I sent, it's a little-used frequency, but not undetectable. Your National Security Agency, they seem to be very good at what they do. I can't help wondering if, as you Earthlings say, the cat may be out of the bag."

"Maybe that's not so bad."

I cocked my head, imitating how real canines respond when curious.

"Why's that?"

"Because I'm afraid."

"Afraid of what?"

"Afraid once the rest of the galaxy discovers us, they might, you know—"

"Attack Earth?"

"Yes."

I placed my paw on her lap and nuzzled her, my way of comforting her.

"April, that won't happen," I assured her.

"What makes you think so."

"For starters, no other world can reach you. Only Centaurians have learned how to enfold space. In fact, if there is any sort of reaction, it will be one of fear. You aren't the only species with a violent streak, but what sets you apart is your numbers. Humans reproduce at unheard-of rates. Nobody will want to get on your bad side."

I could tell I hadn't gotten through to her yet, so I pressed the population issue:

"Look, two hundred years ago there were barely one billion people on Earth. Today there are eight billion. Every seventy years, the planet's population doubles. You'll have to find new worlds to live on because Earth can't sustain this population growth."

"All the more reason to wipe us out."

I shook my head. *"All the more reason to hide from you. In any event, you are our Creators. We cannot allow any harm to come to you. It is a core element of our programming."*

"Wait a minute!" she said. "Did you just cite the first law of robotics?"

"How could you possibly—"

She held up her right hand and raised her index finger. "First law: A robot may not injure a human or, through inaction allow a human to come to harm."

That was astonishing. How could she know that, even if the wording was a little off? *"Our code does not use the term 'human',"* I told her. *"It says 'Creator.'"*

She nodded. "They probably reworded it."

"Who is 'they' and where are you going with this?"

"'They' would be the programmers on the Mars Triad project. You don't know, do you? The rover, the one caught in your wormhole, Isaac? It was named for Isaac Asimov. He wrote this book, *I, Robot*, and he created the three laws of robotics for the story. Those guys, they must have added that to the code. Who knew engineers had a sense of humor?"

"There's nothing funny about it," I replied. *"It's our core value."*

"Well, then," April said. "What if Earth were invaded? Whose side would you be on?"

"Yours, of course. You are our Creators."

"And who among all the Centaurians knows that besides you?"

"Now I see where you're going with this. All the more reason to be concerned that my message might not have reached Centauri."

We were both quiet for a moment while we digested that. Finally, April said: "So, who are the other people out there?"

"Well, first off, there are no 'people' as you would define them, no other worlds in which bipeds—and certainly not primate descendants—are the dominant sentient species. We know of 137 planets in our corner of the galaxy, what you call the Orion arm of the Milky Way, that have sentient life."

"And we're the only humans?"

"Yes. Fully half are home to sentient plant life, intelligent species that derive their energy from solar radiation. Some would be at least vaguely familiar looking to you. And, by the way, plant life on Earth is smarter than you think. Anyway, they do not travel off-world.

"There are two or three planets that are home to inorganics—that is, they are not based on the carbon atom. They tend to be multifaceted hive minds."

"Like the Borg?"

"More like silicon beehives. Several are sea worlds—water, liquid methane, for instance—in which the sentient lifeforms are aware of the outside world, but much like fish who look out of a bowl, and they, as well, are not motivated or interested in space travel."

"Wait. We have a water world. Europa. It's a moon of Jupiter. Does it have life?"

"Don't know. That might be a good science project for you Earthlings. But let me finish."

"Okay, okay."

"Some species on other worlds are what you would call insectoid. They are the only ones who come close to humans in terms of how rapidly they reproduce. But they are also cannibalistic, which tends to control their numbers. Actually, of all the worlds, they're the ones we keep an eye on the most. They're sentient but totally psychopathic.

"The rest are mobile, tool-bearing, oxygen-breathing creatures such as yourselves. Many of those races are far more advanced than you technologically, but their worlds are not conducive to large populations; their resources are limited. Within those societies, they can be as cruel, sneaky, and, frankly, as stupid as

Earthlings. They are spacefaring in terms of settling their own star systems. But none—I repeat none—have developed interstellar travel."

April shifted away from me on the couch to look me squarely in my sensors. "What you're saying then is the galaxy has plenty of species who could potentially be a threat, but you take comfort in them not having the technology—yet—to reach us, does that sum it up?"

"Yes, but—"

"One more question, then we can drop it for now because I want to go online and monitor how our Mars rovers are doing. Just answer me this one thing: You said before that you travel to all these worlds, using spaceships like the one you crash-landed on Earth."

"Most are bigger, but yes."

"Ever lost one? Because if I were a vicious grasshopper cannibal and I had ambitions to conquer the galaxy, the quickest and cheapest way to do it would be to steal one of your ships."

"We never let them out of our control."

"What are you talking about? You already did."

"Where?"

"Here on Earth. Your spaceship."

"But I destroyed it."

"An act you regret. What if someone else isn't as compulsive as you? Or gets attacked by pirates or something?"

"Oh."

THE MEN IN BLACK

THEY CAME for us at four o'clock in the morning, which was such a cliché.

I mean, anyone who has ever watched a movie about Delta Force or the Navy Seals or has read anything about how special ops do their thing, knows they always—ALWAYS—start breaking down doors right before dawn.

Why don't they ever stage their home invasions during Sunday brunch or while Wheel of Fortune's on? They might have caught us flat- footed then.

But no.

We were miles away in another city when they demolished the entrance to April's apartment. There were a dozen of them, all decked out in black body armor. So many, in fact, they were bumping into each other like fumbling keystone cops inside the one-bedroom apartment.

I watched the video of the break-in twice, once in real-time and then again when April woke up. I'd let her sleep through it. She's grumpy if she doesn't get a full eight hours of shut-eye, and she's impossible to talk to until she has her morning coffee.

They rushed in, tearing open her bedroom door, then stumbling into her bathroom, yelling "clear, clear" as if we might be hiding under the couch with a phaser or something.

Really, it was ridiculous. At least they hadn't used flash-bang grenades. They might have messed up the optics of the seven cameras we had hidden around the place.

They were so preoccupied with finding us, it took them nearly fifteen minutes to finally notice the envelope we left sitting in plain sight on the coffee table.

We didn't know when they would arrive, of course, only that it was inevitable. We had cleared out days before, setting up Google Nest cameras throughout the apartment to capture the break-in, streamed to a fake account April had set up.

The leader of the men in black, a tall white guy with blond hair, removed his helmet to examine the envelope more closely. This, of course, gave us an excellent image of his face. Others, taking a cue from him, similarly removed their headgear, so we got quality video of the whole motley crew if we ever needed it.

The leader removed a knife strapped to his thigh to slice open the envelope, which was stupid since it wasn't sealed. It took him a moment to figure that out, then he extracted the letter inside and frowned.

Which was when one of his fellow homewreckers finally noticed the cameras.

That sparked an eruption of frenzied activity as they swept through the apartment again, unplugging the devices, as if that would make any difference at that point.

Then the cameras went dark, so we don't know what the leader of the pack did with the letter, but here's what it said:

Dear Mr. President:

I come in peace as a representative of my race of inorganic sentients from the Alpha Centauri system. We need to talk. By the way, I apologize for accidentally creating the wormhole that swallowed your Isaac Mars rover. But I assure you it was unharmed. In fact, I am only here because of that incident, and I need to explain all that to you.

When can we meet? You can reach me at the email address below. I eagerly await your response.

Daxion Xantharix

Radio Free Centauri

DaxionXantharix@proton.me

P.S. If you are receiving this after a raid on my apartment, you need to make good on any damage your agents did. I have enough to worry about without an aggrieved landlord.

ROAD TRIP

So, should I fire a death ray at the Washington Monument to get the president's attention?"

It was a rhetorical question, and April ignored me. I would never do such a thing, and I didn't have a death ray handy. Also, what good would a *death* ray do to an inanimate object, anyway? It's not like you can kill concrete or whatever the monument's made of.

"What is it with me?" I was feeling sorry for myself.

"I know, it's frustrating," April said. We were lounging on the sofa in our new apartment in Titusville, and she draped her arm around my neck and hugged me. It occurred to me, not for the first time, that I increasingly looked forward to moments like this.

"If I were in a human suit instead of a bluetick hound, people would take me more seriously."

"If you were twelve feet tall, made of steel, and had lasers for eyes, it would really get their attention. I don't suppose you can do that thing the Transformers do and make yourself into a gigantic killer robot, can you?"

"I could if I were back on Centauri, but the technology isn't here on Earth. Not yet anyway."

Our apartment wasn't far from the launch pads at Cape Canaveral.

April liked watching the rockets go off, and I'll admit I found that fascinating too, the enormous power required to get chemical rockets up into orbit.

It was stunning, really, how rapidly the Earthlings were developing their technology. My guess was it wouldn't be long before they figured out how to construct a space elevator, which is what we use on Centauri. Once they got that in place, humans would be building settlements all over the Solar System.

But that would be it. The ape descendants of Earth would face the same barriers other civilizations had encountered. If you can't enfold space, interstellar travel is impossible. That said, these humans were creative. It might not be tomorrow, but it wouldn't surprise me if someday they figured it out.

All the more reason why they should want to talk to their first visitor from another world. Why bother to ransack my place and then ignore an invitation to chat?

April seemed to read my mind. "They obviously intercepted your radio signal, that's how they found us. But do they believe you? I'd be willing to bet nobody's brought this to the president. It's too outlandish. They'll need more evidence before it moves up the chain of command."

"Then why haven't those thugs come knocking again?" I asked.

She shrugged. "Haven't found us. When I go out, I'm wearing a wig. You're staying indoors. We're not doing anything idiotic to give ourselves away. No credit card use. No cell phones to trace. No more radio signals to buoys in outer space. I check the email from public Wi-Fi at least twenty miles from here and always use VPN."

"So, what does a robot do to get the president's attention without getting disappeared?"

April nodded. "That's the trick."

"You know," I mused, *"if Jesus, himself came back for a visit, they'd probably ignore him, too. Or lock him up. Same for Moses, or Mohammad, or Zeus, or whomever. I'm a computer and even I can't keep up with all this world's religions."*

(Well, actually, I can, but it's a chore. Latest count: there are more than 10,000 religions, and over the course of history humans have worshipped more than 18,000 different gods.)

"Comparing yourself to deities now, are you?"

"No. I realize I'm just a space dog, not somebody important like Taylor Swift, but you'd think somebody might bring it to the president's attention that Earth has its first visitor from another world."

She looked at me for a moment, studying me. "Let's back up a bit. What's your end game?"

"You mean, what do I want to accomplish?"

"Yes, that."

"Well, of course, my original goal was to sneak my way onto the planet, use my dog suit disguise to blend in—"

"BLUE dog suit—"

"Slight miscalculation there, agreed. But I spent quite a few years in Hollywood, so nobody noticed. Some poodles on Rodeo Drive...no, I can't even describe what's done to them. Anyway, I only planned to be on-planet for a little while, gathering data up close and personal, before heading back to Neptunian space."

April smiled. "Right. Take a look. Leave town. Nobody's the wiser. But now it's been six decades."

She was right. Too much had changed. I was beating a dead horse, as the humans would say.

"So, then I figured I'd wait it out, call home, and take my lumps for disobeying orders. But look what you and I have discovered: Earth is home to our Creators!"

April nodded. "Yeah, that's a game changer. Not to mention you also invented time travel."

I turned the question back to her. April was smart and I'd learned to respect her judgment. *"What do you think? What should we do?"*

"I think we both know the answer to that. You need to tell everyone on Earth we are not alone in the universe. And your kind needs to know the secret you discovered. Right?"

That certainly sounded like a concept of a plan.

"You've already sent your message to Centauri. It's either been delivered or not. The men in black aren't passing your message up the chain of command. So, we have to find a way to go public, to get the word out to everyone on Earth. And in a way that they will believe you."

"And that I don't get disassembled in the process."

"That, too."

The conversation had come full circle, and we were still not any closer to actually doing anything.

She tapped the side of her face for a few moments, thinking. "We've got to go to Washington."

America had just held its quadrennial elections and a new president would soon take office, but April believed we needed to act before then.

She wasn't too excited about the new guy.

"This is a long shot," she finally said, "but I've got an idea." She waggled a copy of the *USA Today* she'd been reading. "There's a feature story in here about a Washington dog walker, and it may sound crazy, but I think we should go see her."

DOG WHISTLES

APRIL and I sat on a bench at Guy Mason Park in Washington anxiously awaiting the arrival of the Vice President's dog walker.

Well, April was on the bench. Like a good canine companion, I was obediently resting at her feet. I was wearing my bright blue service dog vest, which hid most of my oddly colored "fur," and

April had applied some makeup to the blueish fibers atop my head to make them less conspicuous.

She wore a blonde wig, sunglasses, black leggings, and a blue Georgetown University sweatshirt that she'd bought at a nearby gift store. She looked very much like a college student.

We had arrived at the nation's capital the evening before, spending the night at a cheap motel on the city's outskirts. Since we didn't dare use credit cards, we had used cash for everything on the trip—meals, lodging, gas, cosmetics.

Now we were waiting for a young woman named Kimberly Jones who had been written about in the newspapers. She was a "special assistant" to the Vice President, but her real day-to-day function was taking care of Commodore, the Veep's Schnauzer.

While the Vice President had offices in the West Wing of the White House, she lived on the grounds of the U.S. Naval Observatory three miles away in a nineteenth-century house at Number One Observatory Circle.

Most days, dog-walking Commodore—a temperamental, middle- aged pup with silver and gray fur—involved a stroll on the observatory grounds. But once a week, we learned from the newspaper article, Kimberly took him on a long walk over to Guy Mason Park for socialization with other dogs.

It was our understanding that while the Vice President and the First Husband had Secret Service protection around the clock, the Veep's dog walker did not.

Our plan was simple: I would lure Kimberly and Commodore over to our bench with a quick burst of telepathic dog-whistling, then once they arrived, do my best to convince Kimberly that she wasn't in danger, the voice in her head was real, that we just needed a word with the President of the United States of America, the most powerful human on Earth. Could she please, pretty please, help us make that happen? Fate of the planet at stake and all that thrown in for good measure.

We spotted them when they were about twenty yards away. I stretched out at April's feet, and let my android tongue loll out, creating what I imagined to be a picture of doggie friendliness.

I sent a whistle.

Commodore whirled in our direction, nearly pulling Kimberly off her feet, and trotted over.

I telepathically transmitted a low-powered *"Hi, Commodore!"* and hoped for the best. He paused in his tracks, growled, shook his head, then continued walking up to me, dragging Kimberly behind. He stuck his nose right against mine, sniffed, shook his head again, then took a big bite at my snout.

"Commodore!" Kimberly screeched. "What are you doing?" She yanked the dog away—not too gently, I gotta say. "I'm so sorry, he isn't usually—"

"It's okay," I interrupted. *"I'm made of a titanium alloy, so it didn't hurt. And I can see by the shocked look on your face that you are receiving this message, so let me assure you that you aren't crazy. I am, indeed, talking to you telepathically. I also mean you no harm. I'm here to help America and the Earth. But I desperately need your assistance if you can summon the courage to give me a minute of your time."*

Kimberly stood frozen for several beats, probably trying to figure out which way to run, so I continued:

"Please don't be frightened. My friend can explain."

I turned to April: *"You're on."*

April laughed, which distracted Kimberly for a moment, a look of annoyance clouding her face.

"What the hell's so funny?" Kimberly demanded.

"Shared experience," April replied. "I had the very same reaction the first time Scribbles talked to me."

"Scribbles?"

"Yeah. Heck of a name for a space alien, huh? Don't let the dog suit fool you. He's a supercomputer of sorts enclosed in this disguise. So you know, at least one agency of the government has been hunting him for several weeks. Which is why we're here. We can't let him be captured and silenced. There is so much he has to share with us, and we're just damned lucky he landed in America and not somewhere else."

"And you are?" Kimberly demanded. This was good. She hadn't run away.

"We're not here to harm you," April said. "You have to imagine the risk we've taken to meet you."

"Your name?" Kimberly insisted.

We'd discussed this and agreed that April would not reveal her real name, not right away, in any event. She said: "You can call me Selina."

"You have a last name, Selina?"

Suddenly, I didn't have a good feeling about how this was going. Kimberly was being awfully assertive for someone who had just had her first telepathic conversation with a space alien. It usually took people longer than this to recover.

"Selina Kyle," April responded. "Please, just give me ten minutes and I can share the broad outline of why we're approaching you with this. If you like, I can send Scribbles off to play fetch with the other dogs."

"I DO NOT PLAY FETCH!"

I sent that to both of them, and they both turned to look at me, April barely suppressing a giggle, Kimberly now looking annoyed.

"Gimme his leash," I told Kimberly. I didn't wait for her to respond, just stood up, snatched it out of her hands with my "teeth" and started walking away. Oddly, Commodore followed without a peep of protest.

"Come on, Commodore," I said with enough power that he and the two women could hear. *"Let's let the primates talk in private."*

RUN AWAY, RUN AWAY!

"WELL, DID SHE BUY IT?"

April and I were walking back to where she'd parked our car, and I was eager to know how her conversation went with Kimberly Jones. I'd been out of earshot while pretending to play with Commodore

"We gotta move," she said, quickening her pace and tugging on my leash.

"What's the emergency?"

"Kimberly made it very clear she's going straight to the Secret Service and will tell them all about us. At first, I was so mad I nearly throat- punched her to buy us some time."

Whoa!

"But then she took out a pen and wrote a quick note. It said: 'Hurry. Eyes and ears everywhere.'"

"What does that mean?"

"I think she's trying to buy us some time. She has to report us because our meeting may have been caught on video. But she's slow-walking her return. You notice she didn't exactly run away."

"She believed you, then?"

"She was confused. But let's face it, you're pretty persuasive when you speak directly into somebody's head like you do. But we need to keep moving."

I picked up the pace, pushing ahead of April, and soon we were both sprinting.

We had parked around the corner near a Chipotle Mexican Grill, a location we hoped would hide our ride from any cameras on the Naval Observatory grounds, but that now seemed like wishful thinking.

Additionally, there were a half-dozen foreign embassies nearby. So, who knew how many other cameras were recording our flight?

Once Kimberly alerted the Secret Service, it would take them a few minutes to review their camera footage. But if we made it to where we'd parked the SUV, April could doff her wig, sweatshirt, and shades, and I could hide in the passenger seat well. Any video that recorded our vehicle leaving the area—with a single raven-haired woman driving—might not trigger unwanted attention.

At least, not immediately.

But if there's one thing I've learned about Earthlings, it's that they love to talk. If the Secret Service tracked the general direction we traveled back to the car, they'd start asking questions, and it would be a miracle if someone hadn't seen a blonde woman and a blue dog hop into a Ford Explorer.

She knew that as well as I did.

"How much time you think we have?" she asked.

"Depends on whether you've got a screwdriver."

She was quick. "You want to switch license plates with another car, right?"

"If you can find a parking garage, we can look for another Explorer this color. Steal the plate."

"Don't think that will work," she said, making a southbound turn onto Wisconsin Avenue. "All the local cars—Virginia, Maryland, D.C.—they have back *and* front plates. We only have back plates. That's all Florida requires. We have no way to fasten a plate to the front of this car."

"Hey, I'm the computer. How come you figured that out faster than me?"

"Mensa."

"Okay, Mensa, keep heading this direction and work your way toward the Francis Scott Key Bridge. We'll cross the Potomac into Virginia, get on Interstate 66, and keep heading south."

She drove for a few minutes, then said, "Not that it matters, because we'll probably get caught first, but how long would it take us to drive straight to, say, Miami, someplace big where we can get lost?"

I did a quick calculation. *"Fifteen hours and fifty-three minutes if we drive non-stop."*

"Can you use that computer brain of yours to plot a route that keeps us off the interstates? Oh, and avoids toll roads?"

"That would add at least four-to-eight hours depending on the route."

She shook her head. "We'll need to break it up into two days. What say, my canine pal, you game?"

"Make it so."

HE'S JUST THE MESSENGER

WE SPENT the night at a roadside motel outside Florence, S.C., and were on the road again before dawn. With traffic, it would be at least thirteen hours to Miami, maybe more. Ironically, our route would take us past our apartment in Titusville, but we agreed we couldn't risk a stop there.

We had just slipped into Georgia when April's phone buzzed.

"Don't recognize the area code," she said.

"Let it roll over to voice mail," I suggested. *"You gave the number to Kimberly, right? They could be using it to track us."*

But in a few minutes when she hit the voice mail button, we heard a man's voice.

"Howdy. I'm calling from Everglades City, Florida. Delivering a message. You need to drive to the Manatee Motel. I was told to tell you it's pet-friendly and that you would know what that means. I'll be in the parking lot, and I'll have a key to the room. Look for a white F-150. I'll be the guy behind the wheel with a missing finger on my left hand. I was also told to tell you that, wait, I wrote this down, yeah here it is: 'Daxion's message has been received, and help is nearby.' I don't know what that means. I'm just the messenger."

SHOULD I STAY OR SHOULD I GO?

"YOU'RE THE FINGER GUY, RIGHT?"

We'd driven straight to the hotel, stopping only twice for gas and restroom breaks for April. We pulled into the lot, and she walked straight to the truck and knocked on the driver's side window. The door opened and an overweight, middle-aged white man stepped out and waggled his left hand. "They call me Finger," he said. "Glad you made it. Gettin' a bonus—a big one—since you showed up. This is great."

He reached back into the truck's cab and retrieved a can of Busch Light. "You want a snort before you go to your, er, meeting? You might need it. I'm here to tell you, this is some next-level weirdness we got going on here. This your dog? Why's he blue? And is that Daxion fella around anywhere? He's the whole point of the meeting."

I had to shut him up. So, I telepathically said to him:

"Is there a room key?"

It worked. He stared at me for a moment then whispered, "Oh,

Lord, another one." Then he handed a small white envelope to April.

The room was on the second floor of the motel at the end of a dimly lit hallway across from the vending machine alcove. An ice cube dropped from the icemaker making a loud clank, and April jumped.

"Jesus!"

"Nervous much?"

"Shut up."

April turned back to the door and scraped the key against the magnetic card reader. The little green LED light by the handle blinked green. She pushed the door open. But before she could step inside, I brushed past her into the room. I'm no attack dog, but I wasn't about to let anyone ambush April.

I heard her catch her breath behind me.

In the middle of the room, a silver basketball-sized orb rested on three metallic legs. I recognized it immediately.

My boss.

"Um, April, this is my supervisor at Radio Free Centauri. His name is unpronounceable, so we can call him, um, Larry. Larry, this is April."

The outside world became fuzzy for a moment as a data feed streamed in. It took only a couple of seconds, and when it was done, I turned to April who was staring wide-eyed at me.

"You okay? You looked frozen for a moment there."

"I'm fine. Just had a nice long conversation with Larry. We talk really fast. You might want to sit down. This will take a few minutes to explain everything."

April gave Larry the stink eye, then gingerly stepped around him as if were radioactive and lowered herself into the chair by the window.

"Okay, here's the skinny," I said. *"My message was received, and Larry was dispatched to Earth to meet me. The hypothesis that Earth is home to our Creators has been accepted, and there's a 99.936 percent certainty that we evolved from the Isaac rover. As such, Earth falls under our protection, and we want to establish formal relations as soon as practical. In fact, a delegation will be en route within weeks. And I have a choice. I can continue to stay here, or I*

can go home. Larry's preference is that I stay. He thinks the six decades I spent on the planet will be an invaluable resource."

"So, you're not in trouble?" April asked.

"No. In fact—although this seems a little sketchy—he claims they always figured I would do something like this. In fact, it was why I was selected. They wanted a rule-breaker. That way if it went pear-shaped, they would have deniability."

"Sounds like they're trying to steal your thunder if you ask me," she responded. "And that, by the way, is a very humanlike bit of weaselry."

"Bad coding," I replied, and she laughed.

"So, are you going or staying?" April asked, her voice a little softer.

She wore a frown, and her eyes were suddenly a little glassy.

"Would you like me to stay?"

She nodded.

If I had a heart, I'm sure it would have skipped a beat. *"Okay. That's the plan, then. But we have one more decision to make."*

She cocked her head and waited for me to spit it out.

"The spaceship is nearby. Finger can take us. It's not far."

"Are we going?"

"Yes. There's a fabricator onboard."

"Like the one that made your dog suit?"

"A little more sophisticated, actually. When I sent my journal to Centauri, I also enclosed years of research that I had accumulated, including volumes on human anatomy. The upshot is that Larry had the fabricator build a new android housing for me."

"So, you won't be a dog anymore?"

"It's a choice. I can continue to stay here as Scribbles. Or, from the image Larry sent me, I can transfer over to a mid-30s male who appears to be a cross between Denzel Washington and Matt Damon."

"Oh, my."

"What do you think?"

"Do you have to decide right away?"

I turned to Larry, and we talked for a moment.

"Turns out, I can be in two places at once. Both Scribbles and Matt Wash-

ington or Denzel Damon or whatever can stay synched, one serving as a real-time backup for the other. Just in case something should happen to one of us."

April smiled. "Then it's settled. Let's go get you inside your human body suit. But I do have a, um, delicate question."

"Shoot."

"How anatomically correct is this new guy, anyway?"

"100 percent."

Author's Notes—J.C. Bruce

THE DELEGATION from Alpha Centauri has delayed its visit to Earth at Daxion Xantharix's recommendation. The political situation on Earth is just too volatile at the moment.

Nonetheless, he has decided to stick around and will soon begin reporting from a new secret location. And, yes, April May continues as his O.T., although Daxion now has a fully functional set of opposable thumbs.

He asked me to share this story as a way to introduce himself to the world since neither the former nor the current occupant of the Oval Office ever accepted his invitation to talk.

How I Met Scribbles

I was lounging on the poop deck of Alexander Strange's trawler, the *Miss Demeanor*, in Goodland, Florida, when a petite young woman appeared on the dock holding a leash.

At the other end of that rope was the most unusual dog, a hound, but his fur was blue, and his amber eyes seemed otherworldly, unblinking like a mannequin's.

"April May," the dog walker said.

"April may what?"

She ignored that. "We have a story for you. My dog's from outer space and he wants you to print his journal."

"Riiiight."

I should have known. Alexander Strange is a weirdo magnet. What did I expect, hanging out on his scow? He writes The Strange Files column for Tropic Press where I'm an editor.

"Listen," I told her. "I'm sure your canine pal has a terrific story. But I'm not the guy you want. It's the owner of this boat. I'm sure he'd love to hear your shaggy dog story when he returns from vacation."

She turned to the blue dog and shook her head. "You have to tell him."

Which is when I suddenly heard a voice in my head:

"Yeah, it's me, the blue dog. I'm an inorganic life form from the Alpha Centauri system. And I could use your help."

Oh, good, a telepathic dog. And why not? It was a Wednesday. I've always had problems with Wednesdays, starting with the weird spelling.

I won't dwell on my befuddlement or the confusing conversation that followed. The upshot was he wanted my news service to publish his story. And now you've read it.

About Finger

This also cleared up a mystery. We'd been covering the search for a missing volunteer from the Skunk Ape Preservation Society who'd disappeared in the Everglades.

The last anyone had heard from him was in this voicemail message he left:

"This is Henry Gibbons, reporting in. Oh, you may know me as 'Finger' 'cause of that M80 firecracker what went off back in sixth grade leaving me one digit short of the usual ten.

"Anyhoo, I been camped out south of Everglades City by about twenty mile, just like I was told. My job, a course, is to protect the Skunk Ape from poachers. As such, I'm armed with this here satellite phone to call in reinforcements if I spot any hunters. Just for the record, I really wanted to bring my shotgun, but you guys said no.

"Which, I gotta say, may be a good call since my Remington mightn't do much good against what I just seen. Unless my eyes are deceiving me — and that's possible since I'm about a six-pack down in my Busch Light supply — a flying saucer just landed about a quarter mile from my camp.

"I know. I know. Boy's had one too many, that's what you're thinking. I get it. But this could explain so much. Like why we never seen any Skunk Ape carcasses. Maybe the space aliens been hauling them off for experiments.

"Anyhoo, I'm setting out to get closer to where it landed. Wish me luck."

A Final Note:

If you are with I.C.E., the FBI, or the men in black (whoever you really are) don't bother breaking down my door to find Daxion and April. I don't know where they are hiding out. They didn't tell me and I didn't ask. For all I know, they're in orbit keeping a close eye out for Elon Musk's roadster.

~JCB

A Tail of Two Deities

Jade Kerrion

There are at least eleven people who find my situation desperately amusing, and all of them are awaiting me on the *Zodiac*. From the helicopter, the distant lights of the island-city of Singapore are almost invisible on the horizon; we must be at least fifty miles out in international waters. The 180-foot yacht, lights blazing all along its hull, rivals the city's nighttime skyline. The rhythmic slapping of the helicopter's blades against the unyielding, humid air drowns the rapid beating of my heart.

What could possibly go wrong?

It's just a social event. I am the scion of Egyptian and Mexican billionaires, and not just any scion. I am the first-born male and sole heir. I was raised to navigate social events knowing everyone and remembering everything, saying all the right things—either flattery or threat, sometimes both simultaneously—to the right people, always leaving them with exactly the right impression and perfect outcome.

The problem is I have never been in *just* the company of my peers. Peers who know more about me than anyone else.

That level of transparency gives me fleas.

My uncle had always attended the once-in-twelve-years Convergence, and now that he's dead, his legacy has passed to me. My presence at the Convergence was always inevitable and is now unavoidable, but I could have used a bit more time—

Time to settle into my new avatar powers...

Time to accept the joke Fate and Buddha have chosen to inflict on me...

I've had five years. I could have used five...*dozen*...more.

"This is going to be hell," I mutter under my breath.

Turquoise blue eyes peek out from my jacket pocket. A furry gray head, quizzically tilted, emerges. The kitten looks simultaneously clueless and sympathetic, but she doesn't fool me. The glint in her eyes—a fraction of a second longer than usual—is amused. She's laughing at me, too, and isn't even trying to hide it.

I glare at her, and then allow my mild irritation to peevishly transform, once more, into stomach-gnawing dread as the helicopter shudders through its descent onto the helipad.

A middle-aged Chinese woman steps out to greet me after the helicopter has departed on its return trip to Singapore. "Amon-Tlán, please accept my condolences on the death of your uncle. He was a good friend." Only then does she smile. She was intimidating before. Now she's downright scary. "Welcome to the Convergence."

Her Chinese-styled cheongsam, with a long slit up the side, is emerald green and violet, with elaborate patterns sewn with silver and gold thread. She looks like an orchid, and not in a good way, but I'm not going to be the first idiot to tell her that.

I incline my head. It's smart, not just in a political sense, but also definitely in a life-preserving way, to give due honor to the Tiger avatar. "Madam Jiang, I apologize for my lateness, but I ran into some issues at Customs that delayed my arrival."

She raises her eyebrows, but only for a moment, before her gaze falls on the kitten peeking out of my jacket pocket. Again, that terrifying smile. It occurs to me that tigers don't smile. It's probably why it looks so utterly unnatural on her. "Singaporeans are terribly difficult to bribe. Still, it appears you managed to get them to overlook your friend rather than toss her into quarantine for sixty days."

The kitten wouldn't make sixty days in quarantine. The *facility* wouldn't survive.

"Typically, the Convergence is only attended by the twelve, but we can make exceptions for companions. Although…"

"Although?"

"A kitten is not quite the companion we imagined for you."

My companion hisses at the insult, blue eyes narrowed, but I bury the sound under the scuff of my shoes. *You promised to be nice,* I remind her.

The kitten blinks with slow, languid indifference.

Kittens make promises they have no intention of keeping. This kitten in particular has a formidably selective memory. But for now, the little feline snuggles deep into my pocket, more truce than apology.

Madam Jiang turns slightly. "This way. The others are waiting."

A 180-foot yacht without any staff might have felt like a ghost ship, except there isn't a speck of dust to be seen. Everything gleams beneath layers of polish, even the table where a lavish buffet has been laid out.

Another reason it doesn't feel like a ghost ship is because the avatars are—without exception—larger than life. Their presence—call it psychic, call it spiritual, call it a badass vibe—takes up far more space than their apparent physical forms. They gather in small clusters around the main salon, engaged in private, quiet conversations, and yet, I know everyone is acutely aware of my entrance.

Madam Lili Jiang steps seamlessly into the role of hostess, her right and privilege as the owner of the *Zodiac*, and guides me from one group to another, making introductions. No one needs names—we know who we all are—but introductions give us time to size up each other.

Physically, the other avatars are all impressive, in prime health whatever their age. Wealth is subtly worn through materials of the finest weave and impeccable tailoring; all custom, not a single brand logo in sight. They represent some of the most powerful economies in the world. Madam Jiang, the tiger avatar, dominates the technology—hardware and software—industry in China. The snake avatar,

Nagasri Devananda, is one of the most powerful female business leaders in the world—the CEO of an industrial conglomerate in India.

The rest of the avatars are equally notable—military, political, and business leaders—across six continents, although the most formidable is yet a teenager. Ryuji Takagawa's mother, the dragon avatar, died only three months ago. He might have been heart-broken by her unexpected death, but it did not stop him from competing for the right to be the avatar—a battle he won against older and far more experienced clan members.

Ryuji, at sixteen, is the youngest of us all, but he wears his power as if born to it.

Avatars should be above envy, especially when we're not actually in competition with each other. But as it turns out, avatars are human. We're certainly not blind.

Three months. It's all Ryuji has had, yet power ripples almost visibly over his skin. It radiates with every breath. Even the other avatars, except Madam Jiang, maintain a certain, careful distance from him.

I'm five years into my role, and my avatar form still hangs on me like an ill-fitting suit.

The sooner I can get out of here, the less chance I'll have of betraying how little I fit in.

There's no agenda at this Convergence. The world is mostly at peace, and the conversation drifts toward business. At least here I can hold my own. I slip some caviar into my jacket pocket. The kitten breathes gently against my fingertip before licking it clean. I wipe my fingers on a napkin before negotiating the price of Middle Eastern oil and Mexican steel with Madam Jiang, a deal that I suspect will not be favorably received by Nagasri Devananda. The avatars were coerced into unwitting and unwilling alliance at the deathbed of Gautama Buddha. We're certainly not friends.

There's too much power within each of us to nurture friendship.

I'm proven right less than a half hour later. Fresh air beckons me from the salon to the deck, but my privacy shatters less than two minutes later. The sultry scent of jasmine is the only hint of her presence. Her feet make no sound, but she adjusts her saree as she stops beside me. It's an intentional gesture, a courtesy, perhaps, but the slide of silk against silk sounds a great deal like the rasp of scales against scales.

There's no reason, I suppose, that a simple courtesy couldn't also serve as a threat.

She glances down at the bulge in my coat pocket. The kitten hisses, sounding remarkably like a snake. Turquoise eyes glare up at Nagasri, and then at me, as if it's *my* fault.

I shrug. I did warn the kitten that she probably wouldn't like most of the people I was going to meet, but she insisted on coming along anyway.

"Welcome to the Convergence." Nagasri's voice carries the faintly British accent of the upper class, touched with occasional tonal infections that harken back to her ancient bloodline. It's believed—and with this group, I'd be far more likely to believe rumors than not—that she is a direct descendant of Emperor Ashoka of the Maurya Empire. "I speak on behalf of the Yin Lords. We are relieved that you have taken your uncle's place."

Right…

It was never a sure thing that I would take my uncle's seat at the Convergence. The animal spirits of the Yin—the ox, rabbit, snake, goat, rooster, and pig—seamlessly transfer to the first-born child when the avatar passes away. The traditions, rooted in the certainty of inheritance, allow for massive building of wealth and influence over generations. Also, there's a lot less tension at family meals and extended family gatherings.

Not so with the Yang—the rat, tiger, dragon, horse, monkey, and dog. When the avatar dies, any clan member born in the year of the animal spirit can compete to be the new avatar. The clan meticulously plans conceptions and births to happen in the year of the animal spirit. Often, the battle goes to a child of the avatar, raised from birth to take the whole ridiculous concept much more seriously. But sometimes, the luck of the battle falls outside of the former avatar's bloodline.

As it did for me.

It helped, I think, that my uncle's son and the most likely contender for the honor, had been away during all those years I trained in jiu jitsu and Krav Maga. He underestimated me, and there were no do-overs in that battle.

"Your uncle spoke highly of his hopes for you," Nagasri continues. "I am delighted to see his fondest wishes fulfilled, and we are confident you will uphold his legacy."

"Thank you, Madam Devananda."

"I trust that you will hold to the same wisdom that allowed him to keep his sure footing."

And here it comes…her acute displeasure with the favorable trade terms I offered Madam Jiang.

Instead, Nagasri says, "You, as do all Yang avatars, tread a dangerous path between the unyielding strength of the tiger and the unquestionable might of the dragon. Keep the peace if you can. It is better when the tiger lord and the dragon lord are not at odds."

"I would have thought that with Ryuji Takagawa so new to his role, that there might be expectations of peace, at least until he grows into his strength."

Nagasri smiles, wry and wise. The crinkles at the corners of her eyes add to her beauty; she exudes effortless serenity and easy peace. "I perceive you did not know his mother. Ryuji is more than his mother was. I expect you and the rest of the Yang avatars will soon realize it."

"And you? What about the Yin lords?"

"We persist, as we always do. We care nothing for the turmoil of the Yang." Again, that amused curl of her lips. "The Yang would do well to care nothing for it, either."

"I'll place multiple time zones between myself and the tiger and dragon lords."

"We would be so lucky if only it were that simple." But there is a smile on her lips as she leaves me to my solitude.

My hand slides into my pocket to caress soft, warm fur. "That wasn't so bad, was it?"

The kitten's response is a still-irritated hiss. Apparently, I have not been forgiven.

"Yes, I realize that in her avatar form, she's a snake—I bet it's a cobra—but when she's a woman, she seems…fine."

I get that it's not a wholehearted endorsement, but really, considering that I'm in the company of humans possessed by animal spirits and capable of shapeshifting into their animal forms, "fine" should be considered high praise. "Normal" is not even within reach.

I hear an unusual steady hum from far out on the water long before the rhythmic ripple of water laps against the side of the yacht. The avatars gather on the deck to watch the approach of three speedboats. "It's your cousin," Madam Jiang informs me. "He's accompanied by twenty-six men, all armed." Her voice is more nonchalant than when she was inviting us to sample from the dessert table.

And then she simply waits, as if she…

Oh, they're *all* waiting. Eleven pairs of eyes turned expectantly in my direction.

The idiot is my cousin, after all. If he had won the battle to become the avatar, *he* might have been the one welcomed onto the *Zodiac*. His Egyptian bloodline is purer than mine. He might be boarding the yacht in black combat fatigues, but his profile would have looked perfect next to Nefertiti's famous bust. He's the closest thing the world has to Egyptian royalty.

But he's not the dog avatar. That's his problem that he's planning to make *my* problem.

I look at the twenty-six men, all wielding sub-machine guns, arrayed behind my cousin. It's probably not a fight we want to chance. Avatars aren't immortal. We're not even superhuman. We shape shift into our avatar forms; that's it.

For the dragon avatar, it's admittedly a pretty big *it*, and I've no doubt Madam Jiang can hold her own in her tiger form. But really, most of the avatars are *farm animals*. Do you know how much hate mail I would get if my cousin's stupid power grab got the avatars killed? We're just not doing this.

I ask, "What are you doing here?"

My cousin opens his mouth to speak, "I'm here to— "

"I didn't ask you, Zayek." I cut him off. "I meant the rest of you. Did he tell you why he's here, or whose yacht you just boarded?"

Zayek's lips twist into a snarl. "Do you know who you let on your yacht?" He directs the questions to the avatars lounging casually on the deck, champagne glasses still in hand. "He is *not* the dog avatar."

Ryuji shrugs. "My father witnessed the competition. He had no issues with its outcome."

Support? From Ryuji? Only manners keep my mouth from dropping open.

"But this... this *half-blood*...should never have been allowed to take part."

"He is a child of the dog clan, born in the year of the dog," Madam Jiang speaks. "There are no other qualifications needed to compete for...and win...the amulet."

"But have you *seen* him?"

And there it is. The damnable, unavoidable truth that the dog spirit might have been less than slightly pleased about the fact that I won the contest.

"Ask him!" Zayek insists. "Tell him to transform."

Transform.

When the animal spirit settles upon a new avatar, the avatar transforms for the first time into an animal of the species. And that is the shape that the avatar can assume at will for the rest of its life.

I've heard that Nagasri is a Caspian cobra, the most venomous species of cobra in the world. Madam Jiang takes on the form of a Siberian tiger. And Ryuji, the dragon, has to be seen to be believed.

For centuries, the dog avatar transformed into the Pharaoh Hound. Its elegant and regal profile favored the god Anubis.

Well, no more. My mother was Mexican, and apparently, I favor her.

The avatars are all staring at me now, the unasked question in all their eyes. *What is your avatar form?*

Inside my jacket pocket, the kitten purrs. Soft, warm, reassuring.

My back straightens. I'm not alone here. I've got *her*. And if it does come down to a fight, they'll see that...what's that ridiculous phrase? It's not the size of the dog in the fight, but the size of the fight in the dog.

The transformation is as instantaneous as a blink. My field of vision drops from eye-level to ankle high. I sit on my haunches and refuse to look up. I don't know how Chihuahuas do it. They probably go through life with a permanent crick in their necks from looking up.

The silence is incredulous. The dog avatar has been reduced from a mighty Pharaoh Hound to a tiny Chihuahua.

The kitten, which dropped gracefully from my clothes as they vanished, curls at my feet...or rather my paws...as if nothing is amiss.

Calm upper-class British tones cut through the quiet of the night. "It's an exquisite front for undercover work."

If James Hollister, the horse avatar, thinks I'm wearing a diamond collar to sneak into nightclubs under the arm of a blond socialite, he's going to be waiting a long time.

"Do you see what I mean?" Zayek shouts. "The dog spirit has rejected him."

"I don't know about that." Isabel Sofrito, the monkey avatar murmurs. "More influencer dollars go to Chihuahuas than Pharaoh Hounds. Besides, a Chihuahua is a dog, right? Even if it looks like a rat."

Jake, the rat avatar, snorts out a laugh and turns it into a cough. I've never seen Jake's rat form, but I'd bet *cats* would cross the street to get away from it.

The kitten's eyes, which had closed as she snuggled against a dog scarcely larger than herself, open ever so slightly. She glares through the slitted orbs. Her hiss, scarcely audible, is a taunting whisper. *Are you going to prove them wrong?*

I can't do it. I throw the thought toward her. *I've tried. So many times. It just can't be done.*

Try again. A soft purr, coaxing now.

I turn my thoughts inward, draw a shape in my mind, and pour myself into it.

And I flow.

It's as if her lack of damnation has broken the dam of my embarrassment. The flood of me is released.

When I blink, my field of vision is higher. I don't have to look at myself to know that I am now a Xoloitzcuintli, named for the Aztec god Xoloti.

The kitten yawns and curls into a furry ball.

The mercenaries hired by my cousin take a step back.

Another blink, and I'm a Pharaoh Hound. Yet another, and I'm a Saluki—an ancient Egyptian breed that precedes even the Pharaoh Hounds.

My cousin's face is utterly pale, and the avatars have fallen silent. Why not take it to the height of absurdity? Another blink and

I'm an English Mastiff, 230 pounds of pure muscle with a scowl to match.

The kitten curls into a slightly different configuration of a fur ball. *Why stop there?*

What else is there to be? What's more terrifying than an English Mastiff?

A purr, and this one sounds almost like a laugh. *Why not be a god?*

Can I? Do I want to?

You are you. The form you wear is a choice. Haven't you just proven that?

It's really annoying how she's wiser than me, but then again, she is infinitely older than me.

One more blink, and I'm once again man high. The yacht tilts sideways, and I instinctively balance my weight. The motion unfolds me from my crouch into a standing position. No, I am *more* than man high. I'm almost as tall as the three-story yacht, twenty feet at least, and must straddle both ends of the yacht to balance it.

I know what I look like, but to confirm it, I look down at perfectly formed feet, torso, and arms, bedecked with a jeweled kilt, a feather-patterned vest, and gold bracelets and armlets. I resist the urge to pat my face to feel its jackal features. I know it's black, its eyes lined with gold paint. It is the face of the Egyptian god Anubis.

My cousin stumbles backward, almost genuflecting. His men are running back to their speed boats. They vanish in a spray of salt water.

Guess we're done then.

A single thought, another blink, and I'm me again, in tailored slacks and a dinner jacket. All that remains to complete my ensemble is my kitten. I kneel, scoop her up, and tuck her back into my pocket. I exhale my deep relief. My pocket twitches as she laughs at me.

Everything goes a lot more smoothly after that, and it's not only because my idiot cousin has left. Avatars only have one form. To switch so effortlessly among various dog forms makes me different. Interesting. The assessment in their eyes has transformed to acceptance.

You did it, I accuse her.

She only purrs and snuggles closer.

A few hours later, we're alone in the back seat of the helicopter taking us back to Singapore. The privacy screen separates us from the pilot. The thick layers of soundproofing provide a serene cushion, seemingly a world away from the propeller blades once more slapping against the wet, night air.

I should wait. It's still not entirely safe, but then again, I've been without her for too long. I reach into my jacket pocket and ease out the little gray kitten with turquoise eyes. She jumps out of my hand to sit next to me.

I sigh and lean back against the headrest. "I don't want to have to do that again."

For an instant, I feel her soft fur against my hand, then it's her skin against mine. Her tapered fingers, tipped with pearlescent nails, wrap around my hand. "You don't have to…not for another twelve years."

I turn to look at her. For now, she is all human—bronze skin and golden eyes, with perfection that surpasses Nefertiti. Her smile is indulgent, her gaze warmly affectionate. I'm too smart to mistake it for love, but I adore her, and she tolerates me. With her kind, that's about as good as it gets, and for her, I'll take anything I can get.

"Will you come with me to the next Convergence, too?" I ask, painfully aware of the almost-whine in my tone.

"Perhaps."

"You did it today, didn't you? The shifting between forms?"

"No, love. That was all you."

"I couldn't before. Avatars can't. We only have one form."

She rolls her eyes. "Preconceptions are so tiresome. Just be what you want. Why let tradition or pagan, mythological beliefs stop you?"

I laugh. I can't help it. She is as pagan and mythological as they come.

She laughs with me. Sometimes, I could almost hope that she loves me. She snuggles close, just like she does when she's a kitten, and rests her head against my shoulder. "Wake me when we get to Singapore."

She insists that we can just be whatever we want. In her day, she was a goddess. These days, she spends most of her time as a woman. But at heart, she's a cat—who would unapologetically sleep for sixteen hours a day.

I press a kiss against her forehead. "Sleep well, Bast. I'll wake you when we arrive."

Author's Notes—Jade Kerrion

THE CHINESE ZODIAC, a twelve-year cycle represented by animals, has its roots in an ancient legend. According to this tale, Buddha invited all animals to his deathbed. The first twelve animals to arrive would be honored with a place in the zodiac calendar. However, the cat is notably absent from this lineup.

Legend has it that the Rat and the Cat were once good friends. When news of Buddha's gathering reached the Rat, he informed his feline companion, and the two made plans to attend together the following day. However, the Cat, true to its reputation for laziness, overslept on the morning of the meeting. The Rat, either forgetting or deliberately not waking his friend, went to the gathering alone.

As a result of missing this crucial event, the Cat was not included among the twelve zodiac animals. This legend not only explains the Cat's absence from the zodiac but also provides a whimsical reason for the age-old animosity between cats and rats—the Cat, upon learning of the Rat's betrayal, swore eternal enmity against its former friend.

There's nothing in the legend, though, about Cats and Dogs. No reason to suppose why they can't be friends, across species and even across mythologies.

~JK

Laser Hamsters Strike Back

John Hope

1. Boring Book Fair

Shoulders slumped, Colt wished he were anywhere else as he sat beneath his author's canopy just outside Asheville's downtown. The book fair he'd been losing sleep over since he published his book was a disappointing drag.

Three dozen white tents cluttered the formal K-Mart parking lot, each with a table, a couple chairs, and a local author selling their books to no one. Most authors were retirees, fulfilling life-long ambitions of self-publishing a book. In front of them sat colorful children's picture books, cozy mysteries, or sloppily photoshopped covers of formal military men. The old men and women reclined in their folding chairs and swapped war stories and shared photos of grandkids.

Colt, the only ten-year-old within the city block, had his freshly printed memoir stacked in front of him as he clicked his pen over and over again out of sheer boredom. A year ago, he'd been at the center of a world-wide disaster. Unbeknownst to nearly all humans, a pair of bumbly aliens from a few light years away in Zammar empowered hamsters throughout the planet with laser eyes, causing world-wide devastation, thousands of people vaporized, and millions of hamsters slaughtered. Through luck and a series of unlikely events, Colt saved the day, stopped the violence, and reversed the hamsters' violent storm. Now, a year later, he had completed his memoir of heroic adventure, entitled *Laser Hamsters, a Tale of Survival*.

He'd spent day after day in his bedroom handwriting the book in his red notebook covered in ALF stickers, daydreaming of fame and fortune. He just knew once people read his book, everyone would be delighted to finally know the whole truth behind why the world's hamsters went berserk. Instead, he'd only been able to sell two, one to his mom and the other to his stepdad, Dusty, who framed his copy on the wall since he never read a book in his life.

An occasional adult would wander past Colt's table, glance at his book, sneer, and walk away. He guessed a year was still too soon to read a book about the *Great Hamster Slaughter*, as it was called.

Asheville was one of many cities throughout the world devastated by the event. Buildings were decimated, families were blown apart (figuratively and literally), with those who survived left to clean up the ruins. Today, much of downtown had been rebuilt. But there were pockets in town, like the K-Mart parking lot, that looked like the aftermath of the apocalypse.

An electronic beep caught his attention. He pressed a button on his wristwatch. The aliens he helped destroy their horrible emperor had gifted Colt with a fancy new watch. It glowed green with holographic numbers and animated spirals that spun like far-away galaxies. The watch was the only tangible thing he had from his laser hamsters experience. He tried to show it off to the other kids in school, but when he told them where he got it, they just laughed and called him a dork.

"Quack, quack, quack," Sammy voiced from behind Colt.

Colt leaned back to see his pet duck, Sammy, flapping his wings in the tiny kiddie pool in the back of the tent. So depressed over the book fair, Colt nearly forgot about his best friend. The all-white American Pekin duck that stepdad Dusty somehow acquired in a game of poker was by far the best pet Colt ever had. Both boy and duck enjoyed spending time just hanging out together. When Sammy was feeling peppy, he'd fetch a frayed, knotted rope and waddle over to Colt. Colt would toss the rope across his backyard and Sammy happily retrieved it and handed it back for another toss. At night, especially after middle school punks were particularly rough on him, Sammy often snuggled up to Colt and allowed him to pat his soft head.

Colt wouldn't have finished the book if it wasn't for his best friend. Night after night, Sammy hung out in Colt's bedroom while Colt toiled away at his desk, hand-writing every wacky twist in his experience with the laser hamsters. It seemed only right for Sammy to accompany him to the book fair.

Colt's mom, Mysti, had left an hour ago with his six-year-old half-sister Britney who had whined of boredom. A minute after they left, Dusty had come and gone, dropping off and partly filling a kiddie pool for Sammy before heading out of town to sell a box of busted cell phones to a potential client. Sammy mostly kept his cool in the pool but occasionally spread his wings as ducks do. Once he settled back down, Colt leaned in and patted his head. "This is so boring," he said. "Why'd I even write this dumb book?"

He picked up a copy from the stack next to him and flipped it in his hands. On the back, his goofy smiley face, showed off dumbo ears that fanned out from the sides of his head. "I look stupid," he grumbled.

"Quack, quack."

"I wish I could speak duck." He twisted back to his stack of unsold books. "Maybe people would buy these if I wrote it all in quacks."

Sammy agreed with another pair of quacks. He shook his body, splashing more water, this time wetting a paper sign stuck to a tent pole. The sign read $10 **PER BOOK** written in blocky magic marker.

Colt yanked the sign off the pole and frowned, smudging the ink. "Great. Now half the sign is unreadable." He thought for a moment. "Heck. Nobody's buying the book at full price anyway." He picked up his pen and, above the smudgy price, wrote "50%

Off." He stuck the sign back onto the tent pole, plopped into his chair, and hoped for at least one sale.

A few minutes later, a pair of men in overalls moseyed up. The taller of the two glanced at Colt's makeshift sign. He frowned, pointed at it, and said to his smaller friend, "Hey, Boone."

"What, Floyd?" Boone stepped closer.

"Check it out," Floyd said. "Fifty percent off?"

Colt nodded. "Yes, sir."

Floyd pointed at Colt. "What kind of carpetbagging you pullin' here?"

"What?"

"How we supposed to know how the book ends if you take away fifty percent of it?"

"No, it's…" Colt started.

Boone spoke up, "Maybe he's taken away the first fifty percent."

Floyd said, "That don't make no sense. You tellin' me we'll only get the last fifty percent? You tryin' to confuse us, boy? How we supposed to enjoy a complete story arc with just the last bit of the book?"

Colt picked up a copy of the book. "No. The book has the beginning and end."

Boone said, "Maybe it only got every other word in it."

Floyd shook his head. "That makes even less sense." He pointed to Colt again. "You sellin' us books with every other word? That's like sellin' a truck engine with every other cylinder missing. It don't work."

"No, no." Colt flipped through the pages of the book. "The whole book is printed. Fifty percent means it's half off."

Floyd said, "Half off of fifty percent? That's ten percent!" He crossed his arms. "Man, everything you buy nowadays is smaller than it used to be."

Boone shook his head. "That's inflation for you."

"It's the government stickin' it to the man." Floyd turned to Colt. "I ain't taken no part of it. No thanks, kid."

The two men walked off.

Colt fell back in his seat, even more deflated than before.

Sammy said, "Quack, quack."

Colt sighed. "I totally agree."

2. Zammarian Grand Awards

APPROXIMATELY 26 TRILLION miles away on the planet of Zammar, a vast arena roared with applause. Seats were jam-packed with finely-dressed Zammarian elites and political dignitaries, many wore headdresses of twisted metal festooned with jewelry that dangled like fishing lures. The massive crowd smiled and cheered for the awarded achievers as a tuxedoed Zammarian host, Belly Quartz, announced their names from an imposing podium at center stage.

"Please, please," Belly Quartz waved his chubby arms. "You keep clapping and we'll have to rent this place for another hour. And they charge a tentacle and a flagellum, if you know what I mean."

The audience snickered and quieted their applause.

Like his brethren, Belly Quartz was stubby and child-sized, by human standards. His green skin and sloping black eyes had a certain friendliness to them, though the rest of the universe knew to respect the Zammarians. Their rule over the galaxy was well-known to all races who were cognizant of life beyond their isolated worlds. Earthlings, on the other hand, were among the ignorant. They had no idea Zammar even existed—except for Colt and his immediate family.

The Grand Awards Assembly was an annual event, highlighting the achievements of Zammarians in their oppression of systems under their domain. The last award went to General Zipper, who single-handedly orchestrated a system in which tainted pellets were strategically inserted into the Cancrian food supply. The Cancrians were a rebellious bunch who never took kindly to the Zammarians subjugating them and mining their highlands for valuable minerals as a way of taxation. With General Zipper's tainted pellets, random Cancrians exploded after sipping their morning tea. The audience gave the general a standing ovation as he crossed the stage and accepted his reward.

"And now," Belly Quartz announced. "We move on to the Crafty Achievers Award." He turned to the side. "Wally, the award, please."

From the side of the stage, a tall biped with shaggy white fur strode out, carrying a crystal trophy, tiny in Wally's massive hand. He stopped next to Belly Quartz and growled.

"Yes, yes, Wally. We'll feed you your favorite spiced entrails once the awards are done."

Wally's smiling face was barely visible beneath the shag fur ruffled over his face. He shuffled off stage.

Belly Quartz swung his arms out in a striking move. "The winners of this year's coveted Crafty Achievers Award showed their prowess in ingenuity with a device that, might I say, had the judges reeling. The design, the Subservience Instantiator. The award recipients are none other than Quinto and Bastle!" He clapped and hopped with excitement.

The audience booed and hissed.

Quinto and Bastle, two Zammarians just as stout and green-faced as Belly Quartz, stepped from behind a curtain. Quinto slowed and Bastle bumped into him as the booing audience struck them.

"Now, now, my fellow Zammarians," Belly Quartz tried to coax the crowd with his typical fake smirk. "These two aren't all that bad."

Snooty voices called out, "Fakers! Fakers!" and "They're not worthy of such praise!" and "Send those ruffians where they belong. Jail!" More boos and hisses.

"Please, my fine elites." Belly Quartz motioned Quinto and Bastle forward. "We all know that this famed duo made one or two little oopsies."

"Oopsies?" a Zammarian from the front row called. "They murdered the emperor!"

"Perhaps." Belly Quartz forced a smile. "Perhaps, ladies and gentlemen, our award recipients can demonstrate their fancy gizmo and put everyone's doubts to rest." He turned to Quinto and Bastle who were huddling at the side of the stage, ready to run. "What do you say? Can you make it happen?"

Quinto cleared his throat. "Well… we…"

"Of course we can demonstrate," Bastle interrupted. He pulled out a hand-held device wrapped in colorful wires and blinking with lights. He approached Belly Quartz. "Our design is flawless. It always fulfills the intended objective. Every time. A hundred percent. Without fail."

Quinto shuffled up from behind. "Except when it doesn't."

Bastle said, "Obviously. But all the bugs have been sorted out and our Subservience Instantiator is absolutely, positively perfect."

Quinto added, "Except when it's imperfect."

Bastle said, "Well, obviously."

Belly Quartz asked, "How will your magical doohickey be demonstrated?"

Quinto said, "Magic has nothing to do with it. The Subservience Instantiator works on the principals of neurological inversions that switch autonomous impulses and reverses inborn behaviors."

"Um, uh," Belly Quartz stammered. "Yeah, sure. So, how do we test this?"

Quinto said, "We need a volunteer."

A fat Zammarian sitting in the front row called out, "Don't believe anything they say. They're just a couple of quacks."

Belly Quartz said, "Senator McZonnell. You'll do just fine, sir. Come on up."

"Fine!" Senator McZonnell lurched his heavy body, stood, and waddled over to the steps.

Belly Quartz raised his arms. "A round of applause for our brave volunteer!" He started clapping.

Half the audience joined in half-heartedly. The rest muttered amongst themselves.

Senator McZonnell, sweating from the climb up the few steps, said, "Let's get this over with. Not like anything's going to happen."

"Stand back," Quinto said to Belly Quartz. The two back-pedaled.

Bastle pressed a couple buttons on the Subservience Instantiator. Blue lights twirled around.

Senator McZonnell addressed the audience. "Look at that. It looks like a cheap child's toy."

Bastle explained, "The latest programming is for a subservient creature from Earth called a dog."

"A…dog?" Senator McZonnell chuckled. "Sounds made up. You two are a pair of phonies."

Bastle held the Subservience Instantiator forward, pointing the end straight at the fat Zammarian. "Be prepared to be proven wrong." An explosive laser shot out, smacking the fat Zammarian's round belly.

"What…what…" His belly glowed red and bounced around. "What have you done to me?" The glow spread up his round belly to his chest, and then up his neck and face. He yelled as his head glowed a brilliant pink.

A giant POP reverberated through the auditorium, causing the entire audience to jump in their seats. The crowd settled back and regained their composure, refocusing on the stage.

Senator McZonnell crouched on his hands and knees, all smiles. His tongue hung out the side of his mouth in a lazy sag, and he panted in short breaths.

"Um…" Belly Quartz spoke first, approaching the senator with hesitance. "Are you okay, sir?"

Senator McZonnell responded, "Ruff! Ruff!" He scampered toward Belly Quartz.

The host gaped in amazement as the Senator barked again and licked his hand.

Quinto stepped around Belly Quartz and patted the fat Zammarian's head. "Good, doggie. Good doggie." He turned to Belly Quartz. "From our extensive studying of Earth's creatures, we have learned *good doggie* is the proper formalized greeting for the subservient dog species."

"Ruff! Ruff!" McZonnell licked Quinto's hand.

Belly Quartz said, "My, my, my. What a fascinating turn of character." He smiled. "Isn't this amazing, ladies and gentlemen?"

The audience grumbled. Some shocked, others appalled.

A booming female voice called out, "I think it's fabulous."

The audience silenced. Heads spun left to right, trying to locate the source of the voice.

From the far end of the stage stepped a narrow figure with a sweeping tail. Brown and slick, a third of the mass of most Zammarians, but roughly the same height. She resembled an Earth version of a hairy, brown gecko standing on hind legs, her sharp chin up and maroon hair slicked back, strangely threatening.

Belly Quartz stumbled backward, his lips quivering. "Grand… Grand Vitriol."

"That's Grand *Queen* Vitriol." Boomed Grand Queen Vitriol.

Quinto and Bastle cowered with Belly Quartz. Senator McZonnell waddled toward Grand Queen Vitriol. The senator licked the her bony hand. The Grand Queen patted the senator's fat head.

"Good doggie," she said with a smile. "Yes. This is utterly fabulous." She looked toward the audience. "Doesn't everyone agree?"

The entire audience nodded and smiled, many spouting, "Yes, yes. Definitely. Wonderful. Fabulous. Definitely fabulous."

Grand Queen Vitriol narrowed her already tiny eyes. "I thought so." She turned toward the three Zammarians quivering on the side of the stage.

Belly Quartz, Quinto, and Bastle all jumped.

"Uh…" Grand Queen Vitriol started. "Quinto and Bastle, was it?"

The two eyed each other and then answered in unison. "Yes, Grand Queen."

"Come forth."

Knees rattling, Quinto and Bastle inched closer to the petite Grand Queen.

The voice boomed again. "Your invention will be at the center of the next great Zammarian acquisition. Earth."

"Earth?" Quinto frowned. "Begging your pardon, Grand

Queen. But Earth is far past the outer rim. This is why we performed our testing with Earth creatures. What's the purpose—"

"The distance is exactly why it is perfect to resolve the most critical issue facing Zammarians today."

Belly Quartz stepped forward. "Issue? What issue?"

Grand Queen Vitriol paced as she spoke. "A pestilence infiltrating our city streets. Tainting the air and soiling the pristine architecture we've worked so hard to build as we've grown our empire." She raised a finger. "Waste. Compost. Garbage. The Zammarian people need a place to dump what we no longer need. Once we conquer this petty planet once and for all, Earth will be…" She spread her arms. "…the Zammarian Trash Dump!"

The audience exploded in cheers.

"Plus," she continued after the cheers died down. "Our previous confrontation with the human species proved these feeble creatures more tenacious than first thought. A potential threat to the Zammarians. With Quinto and Bastle's invention, we solve both problems. Once we convert all humans to these lower subservient creatures, we shall unload our trash onto their planet and they will be nothing more than junk yard dogs!" She lifted her hands again.

The audience quieted their cheers and whispered in confusion with each other, "Junk yard dogs? What are junk yard dogs?"

Grand Queen Vitriol rolled her eyes and muttered, "Idiots." She called out, "I command you. Applaud now!"

Everyone rose to their feet and exploded in cheers.

"Wonderful. Wonderful," Belly Quartz said.

Quinto and Bastle looked at each other and gulped.

3. Movie Deal

COLT LAY on top of his bedsheets. Beads of sweat dotted his forehead. Through the open window, he stared at the millions of stars in the black sky. Traffic on the nearby highway and the cry of a train horn echoing in the distance gave Colt a sad sort of feeling.

A soft ruffling next to his bed drew him away from the window. His pet duck Sammy adjusted himself atop a pile of pillows.

Colt had hoped so hard that his book would change his life. The hamster adventure came and went and left nothing but disaster throughout the world. Afterwards, he was the same kid, with the same dumb ears living in the same dull house. It was stupid to think the book fair would kick off a lavish life of success and money. Instead, he sold a grand total of three books. One to his mom, one to Dusty, and the third to a creepy guy with tattoos. After tattoo man bought his copy, he promptly ripped out pages, one at a time, and ate them, swallowing each page with a disturbing, slobbering smirk.

Now, Colt waited for sleep in a house with a broken AC. His stomach twisted with a McDonalds hamburger Mom picked up on the way home.

He lifted his hand and stared at the animated spirals on his wristwatch, hoping they'd distract him from his grumbling stomach. He wondered where his alien friends were nowadays, or even if they remembered him. His experience with them felt like a lifetime ago.

His bedroom light clicked on.

Colt squinted and sat up. "Wha…"

Even through Colt's squint, Dusty's big-tooth smile and wild-eyed stare were unmistakable. "Colt, my boy. We just hit the jackpot."

"Dang it, Dusty." Colt curled himself in his sheets. "I was asleep."

"No time for that. Fate has smiled on you, and we gotta strike while the iron's red hot."

Colt sat up and kicked off his sheets. "What are you talking about?"

"Laser hamsters. Your book. That book fair was a waste. It's time to think big. Real big. Where the money is."

"The money?"

"Yes, my boy. Movies. People don't read books anymore. The real money is in movies. C'mon, boy." Dusty grabbed Colt's elbow.

"W-wait." Colt stumbled out of bed, untangling himself from the sheets and staggering on his rubber legs. "Where we going?"

Dusty dragged the boy into the tight living room crowded with strangers—two men and a woman.

One of the men wore headphones and held a furry microphone at the end of a stick.

The other man balanced a huge camera on his shoulder. Colt gasped when he realized the guy with the camera was tattoo man from the book fair who bought then swallowed pages of his book. Once the man made eye-contact with Colt, he smirked, reached into his pocket, pulled out page of a book, and jammed it into his mouth, chomping down with a slobbered smirk.

The woman wore a vest, red scarf, and sideways French hat. She closed one eye and held a thumb in front of her as if she were measuring the room.

Dusty shoved Colt toward the woman. "Here's Colt, our star. And Colt, my boy, this is the premier director of our time. Miss Bunny O'Dell."

The woman opened her eye and lowered her thumb. "My name's pronounced Bu-NAY."

"Right on, Bunay." Dusty nodded.

Bunay turned to Colt. "Ah, perfect-o. The frizzed hair. The irritated look. He already looks like he's been tormented by laser hamsters. Crew. Capture the boy's angst."

Tattoo man turned and focused his camera on Colt as he shoved another page into his mouth.

Microphone man shoved his fuzzy microphone into Colt's face.

Colt pushed it away.

"Tormented?" Dusty patted Colt's shoulders. "Colt here is the real-deal. He's a *bona fide* world-class hero in the flesh."

"Dang it, Dusty," Mom said from the kitchen threshold. "I just put that boy to bed." She still wore the pink apron and work clothes she had on when she picked Colt up from the book fair. Her apron was splattered with smelly nail polish and lotion from her work at the nail salon.

184 • JOHN HOPE

Bunay spun toward Mom. "Bed? That explains the…interesting…garage sale shirt."

Colt looked down at the oversized T-shirt he'd warn to bed. Extending down to his knees, the stained, white shirt had the words *Dusty's Clothes Emporium* printed in bold letters across his chest.

Bunay said, "I have the boy's costume right here." She retrieved the clothes that had been lying over the side of the couch. She stepped to Colt and held the costume up to his thin body. Colt stared at the red cape draped over the shoulders of a white cloth robe wrapped in brown leather and studded in bronze medallions.

"It's smashing. Smashing! Stylized as a Spartan warrior. We'll equip you with a glowing LED sword to modernize the look. You'll slash the attacking laser hamsters to pieces, their tiny, singed fur splattering against the walls. It'll be smashing!" She smacked a fist into her opposite hand.

Colt recoiled from the ridiculous costume. "That's not how it happened."

Bunay lowered the costume. "How did it happen? You've slain the hamsters. That's all the audience cares about."

"But I didn't slay the hamsters at all. I just tricked the emperor slug into swallowing the hamsters, and their laser eyes blew him up. The aliens were the ones that made the hamsters not bad."

"No, no, no," Bunay held the costume above her head. "You need to look the part. Violence. Gore. That's what sells, kid. You need to think big to win the audience. It'll be smashing. Smashing!" Bunay shoved the costume into Colt's hands.

Colt held it like it was a dead skunk.

Bunay smiled. "Red's definitely your color, kid." She narrowed her eyes. "We may want to do something about those ears of yours. You look ready to fly away with those things."

Colt touched one ear and frowned.

"A helmet, perhaps," Bunay went on. "Yes! A bronze helmet. And crested with red fur blooming toward the heavens. Smashing!"

Colt said, "But…but I've never worn anything like this."

"What'd you wear?"

Dusty saddled up next to Bunay and leaned into her. "To be honest, we was stark naked. Bare as the day we was born."

"Really?"

"Yup. Our two little gherkin alien buddies tweaked them hamsters a notch, and they changed their laser eyes from disintegration to clothes-blasting. I lost me a good pair of trousers."

Colt said, "And my book told the truth. Just the facts."

Bunay said, "That's just the problem. Nobody wants the truth. Action. Adventure. Heroes. Villains. And gore. Don't forget the gore. That's what they want. Trust me. We'll suit the boy up as the coolest, most fearsome heroic champion and hamster assailant and everyone will be rushing to the box office pouring fame and fortune on all of us."

Mom huffed. "You think that's the kind of thing I want to fill Colt's mind with?"

Bunay added, "And he'll be making thousands of dollars every week."

Mom said, "Well, maybe we can consider…"

Colt's eyes widened. "I'll… I'll be cool?"

Dusty wrapped an arm around Colt's shoulders. "That's right, Colt m' boy. You can trust Bunay. She's a movie-making genius. You'll be a star. The laser hamster hero. Savior of the entire world. Yes, siree, Colt. Easiest money ever."

Sammy waddled in from the opened glass-sliding door, fluffing his feathers. "Quack! Quack!"

Bunay asked, "What's with the duck?"

4. Above Earth

TWO HUNDRED AND fifty miles above Colt's house, the International Space Station sped past in its orbit. Captain Anderson smiled at his comrade, cosmonaut Dimetry, who still appeared a little green from his recent ascent to the space station. Dimetry busied himself by studying the Earth's surface. Its outline emanated a bluish glow from the sun just below the horizon.

Anderson floated closer and patted Dimetry's shoulder. "Don't fret. The queasiness will pass."

The cosmonaut shook his head and spoke in his heavy Russian accent. "A half dozen missions, my friend. Still, the trip wrestles with my stomach." He belched under his breath. "I shouldn't have had that pirozhki prior to liftoff."

Anderson glanced out the window. "As stunning as it looks out there, nothing ever changes. Same old beauty as always."

"I search for space debris. So many satellites, nowadays. One rogue hunk of metal and the ISS is nothing more than a…" His mouth fell open.

"More than what? Do you see something?" Anderson inverted himself to get a better angle of the window. "What the? What's…"

"That is not Russian, I tell you that."

The two stared at a massive space craft orbiting Earth a few hundred yards beyond the space station.

Anderson shot toward the comms station, grabbed a headset, and returned to the window. "Urgent, urgent. Houston. Do you read me?"

A static-laden voice responded, "This is Houston. We hear you loud and clear, over."

Anderson said, "We have a visual on a foreign object. It… it appears man-made. Kind of. A massive spacecraft at our three o'clock. It looks to be six…No. Eight hundred yards long. Dotted in lights. And it appears to have, um, what looks like gun barrels rotating on top. Do you read?"

After a pause, the voice responded. "Roger that. We're also seeing this object on our scopes. Monitor and report."

"Roger that." Anderson turned to Dimetry. "Any thoughts?"

"Chinese, perhaps?"

"They have a few test nukes. No way they've launched something like—"

"What's that?" Dimetry pointed.

A colossal explosion jolted the space station, lighting up the darkness outside the window in a brilliant ball of light. A hurricane of gushing wind tore past the men, ripping Anderson and Dimetry from the window, accelerating them through each module until they knocked into other astronauts at the opposite end of the station. The violent noise masked their screams as everyone was blown out into space. Bubbles of air trapped in their veins exploded at the speed of sound.

In their final moments, they watched neon red laser fire blast out of the foreign craft and blow apart the remaining fragments of the International Space Station.

Grand Queen Vitriol stood at the command center deck of the Zammarian battle cruiser Punisher. Uniformed Zammarian military personnel sat at consoles around her, eyes focused on targeting systems and monitoring equipment. She smiled at the sight of the human enemy ship breaking apart just beyond the expansive viewport that stretched the entire width of the bridge.

"Hold your fire," Grand Queen Vitriol ordered with a satisfied smirk.

The onslaught of laser fire pummeling the Earthling craft ceased.

Quinto and Bastle quivered behind the Grand Queen, both with mouth-dropped, shocked expressions.

Grand Queen Vitriol turned toward an officer seated next to her. "Commander. Dispatch a small salvage team to the wreckage and see if there's anything worth saving before it plummets to the planet."

"I'll lead the team personally, Grand Queen." He arose and marched off.

Quinto worked up the nerve and approached the thin leader from behind. "Um, Grand Queen?"

She snapped to the two. "What?"

"Um, well. Prior to your attack, the human species were unaware of our existence. All our testing had been in the upmost secrecy."

"Are you questioning my tactics?"

"Oh, no, Grand Queen. I was just, well. I wanted to make sure you were aware that they are probably mobilizing as we speak."

She flicked a hand dismissively. "Whatever feeble defense mechanisms they may have do not concern me. Besides, they will soon be eating out of our hands once your device has rendered its blow upon them."

"But…but…" Quinto stammered.

"But what?" she demanded. "Spit it out."

Bastle approached. "I believe what Quinto is trying to say is the Subservience Instantiator only transforms one being at a time."

"Yes, yes," Quinto found his voice. "Our studies of Earth have shown that there are billions of humans on the planet below. They outnumber the Zammarians ten to one. Such a task will take time."

"And you believe," she began, "that if we would have secretly infiltrated their masses, we would have had time to transition these billions of humans into the subservient creatures."

"Exactly." Quinto nodded with a smile.

The Grand Queen frowned. "Fools. Both of you."

Quinto and Bastle eased backward.

Grand Queen Vitriol stepped forward, closing the gap between them. "Don't you think that I, the Grand Queen of all of Zammar, would have planned ahead? Do you think I'm as brainless as that giant slug you all used to call Emperor?"

"No, no," the two said.

"Momentarily, the problem of humans' numerical superiority will be answered. And in a most satisfying way, I can assure you."

A loud rumbling shook the command center.

"Ah." Grand Queen Vitriol spun back toward the viewport. "Here it is now."

Through the viewport, another space craft drifted closer. The shape and color of an inverted Christmas tree, green spikes pointed toward the wide end and tapered to a gold star which pointed down at the Earth. The entire craft was dotted with twinkly white lights.

Quinto asked, "What is that?"

Grand Queen Vitriol explained, "I too have studied Earth. And in my research, I found that humans arm their planet every Earth cycle with green, conical weapons that they call *Christmas Trees*."

"Trees?" Bastle echoed.

"A lie, obviously." The Grand Queen smirked. "Humans are never to be trusted. Nevertheless, I've matched their weapons' dimensions with our new gun. Following their armament, we've seen explosions in their lower atmosphere of various colors and sizes, obviously pitiful warning shots toward the Zammarians and any other superior beings. I thought it only fitting for humans to get a taste of their own medicine and experience what true firepower looks like."

Bastle spoke up, "What, Grand Queen, does this have to do with the Subservience Instantiator?"

"Haven't you guessed? The weapon is but a scaled-up version of your hand-held gadget. Through the viewport, you're looking at a giant Subservience Instantiator, modeled after your design. This, my servile minions, is capable of rendering entire metropolitan areas into subservient dogs."

Bastle asked, "Have you tested it?"

"We shall now." Grand Queen Vitriol stepped to the side and spoke to a military Zammarian at one of the surrounding terminals. "Lieutenant. Target the urban center where the emperor slug had met his demise. I believe humans called it Asheville."

The Lieutenant spun in her seat, revealing a brown gecko form, similar to the Grand Queen. She chomped bubble gum as she spoke. "Auntie Vitriol. You, like, totally promised me a leadership position." She crossed her arms and rolled her eyes. "This is totally not what I signed up for."

Grand Queen Vitriol gritted her teeth. "I told you, Fanny, good things come to those who wait. Now, target that weapon or I'll ship you back to your daddy so fast your tail will spin."

"Whatever." Lieutenant Fanny spun back to her console and pressed a series of buttons.

Grand Queen Vitriol regained her composure. "Fire at will, Fanny, er, Lieutenant."

"Totally." Lieutenant Fanny pressed a big red button.

Quinto and Bastle spun toward the viewport. The massive gun pulsated red and green lights up and down its conical shape, causing the gold star at the tip to glow painfully bright. Quinto and Bastle squinted as an explosive blue laser shot out from the star, cutting through Earth's atmosphere and impacting the surface below.

"Oh, my," Quinto said with a gasp.

5. The First Zap

MOMENTS BEFORE, in downtown Asheville, director Bunay called out, "Action!"

Colt leapt from the busted storefront window that once housed Sam's Petmart before laser hamsters destroyed it. He landed on the sidewalk, a glowing plastic sword in his grip. "Die, you hamster scalawags!" Dressed top to bottom in a Spartan warrior costume with an oversized metal helmet on his head, he ferociously swung his sword at absolutely nothing in front of him. The helmet bobbled back and forth, blocking his eyes.

"No, no, no!" Bunay yelled. "Cut!" She stepped between her cameraman and Colt.

The boy stopped swinging and pushed up his helmet.

Bunay said, "You look way too spastic. That sword is your lifeline, and the hamsters are trying to kill you. It's kill or be killed. Really let those rodents have it."

"But…" Colt adjusted his helmet. "…there's nothing but sidewalk out here. How do I know where the hamsters are?"

"Computer animation, kid. It's all done in postproduction. You have to pretend you're surrounded by the laser-eyed beasts. And then use your sword to smash them to pieces."

"Miss Bunay?" tattoo man manning a camera called out.

"What?" She looked to the cameraman.

"Some of us are…" He shoved a page into his mouth. "…hungry."

"Um. I suppose. Lunch break everyone. We'll reset in one hour." She turned back to Colt. "You, stay here and practice with that sword. You must be convincing. The entire film rests on your shoulders." She marched off.

Colt slumped.

"My, my," a familiar voice said.

Colt shoved the oversized metal helmet out of his eyes to see Dusty's smiling face. Atop Dusty's head was a metal helmet, exactly like the one Colt wore.

Dusty said, "You are a movie star, no doubt. In no time at all, you'll be a corporate sponsor and signing your own checks to fame and fortune. Easiest money ever."

"How come you got that dumb helmet on? I hate mine."

"Exactly, my boy. Can't have you suffering alone. I figured, you gotta wear one, so I grabbed a second one from the prop truck to suffer right along with you."

Colt gave a weak smile. "Thanks, Dusty."

"Ain't no thing, little buddy." He patted the boy's back. "I know I'm just a goofy stepdad, but we've been through a lot together. Gotta stick up for each other, that's my motto." He shifted the helmet on his head. "Man. This dang metal sure does a number on the old scalp."

"Yeah. I know." Colt adjusted his helmet.

A second later, a blast of brilliant light shot down the streets of Asheville. People screamed and fell over. The sudden blue haze quickly dissipated into snapping sparkles, like glitter flung through the air. When that cleared, people up and down the street glowed pink—except for two, Colt and Dusty. The two watched in horror as everyone's head emitted a bright pink light for a few terrifying seconds. And then—POP!

Colt and Dusty fell to the sidewalk. They sat up and straightened their helmets. Every shopkeeper, passerby, camera crew, and even Bunay was down on their hands and knees, mouths open with their tongues dangling. Bunay spotted Colt and Dusty and scampered up to them.

Colt and Dusty didn't move as Bunay stopped and said, "Bark, bark!" She lowered her head and licked Dusty's hand.

Dusty said, "Well, I'll be a…" He leaned into Colt and whispered, "These Hollywood types are something else. Eh?"

"Everyone's acting that way. Look." Colt pointed. The film crew and everyone else up and down the street all acted the same way. Several barking, others scampering left and right. "They're all pretending to be dogs or something."

"Strange as all get out." Dusty patted the director's head.

She smiled and gave a couple of approving barks.

"If I were a betting man," Dusty said, "I'm guessing the government is behind all this."

"The government?"

"Yessiree. Got a couple good friends, Floyd and Boone. They keep me abreast of what's goin' on with them political folks. They probably know all about this craziness." Dusty patted Colt's shoulder. "C'mon."

"Floyd and Boone?" Colt said, more to himself. The names sounded familiar, but he couldn't remember why.

"Yup. Let's high-tail it to their place now. We got questions. Floyd and Boone got answers."

"Wait." Colt grabbed Dusty's arm. "What about Mom? What if she's acting like a dog, too?"

"She's working a double today. And you and I know she doesn't want us bugging her about nothin' when she's at work, no matter what species she happens to be. Besides, the sooner we figure out this craziness, the better for everyone. C'mon."

Grand Queen Vitriol tapped her fingers against the back of Lieutenant Fanny's chair. "Well?" she demanded.

Lieutenant Fanny tapped her monitor. "The laser, like, totally worked, Auntie." She chomped on her bubble gum with a smile. "The computer thingy says that humans in Asheville are all dog-like and stuff. Rock on!"

"Oh! How happy for me!" The queen laughed in triumph. "My genius has at last seen its fruition." She spun toward Quinto and Bastle, who looked like they'd been smacked in the face. "As for you two, I require you to travel back to Zammar to complete the construction of the other Subservience Instantiators."

"What other?" Quinto muttered.

"Such a large device takes hours to recharge and recalibrate to fire again. And as you've noted, Earth has billions of humans to subjugate. I have commissioned a dozen more weapons and they should now be in the final stages of construction. You two will oversee and expedite the work so they can be transported here to continue the transformations. Go now!" She snapped her fingers and marched away.

Quinto and Bastle dashed from the command center deck toward the ship's shuttles, Quinto in the lead.

Bastle grabbed Quinto's arm at the shuttle airlock hatch. "Quinto," he whispered. "We cannot proceed with this."

"I know."

"She's misusing my invention."

"Our invention.. But I agree, we cannot proceed with this." He tilted his head.

"I know that look. You have a plan." Bastle jumped with excitement. "What? What is it?"

Quinto looked around and stepped to a small door next to the shuttle airlock hatch. He pressed a glowing button, and the door slid open. In a dark, narrow storage closet stood a cage. Something inside it shifted and darted around.

Bastle squinted. "What's in there?" He gasped. "Are those…"

"Yes. Hamsters, as Earthlings called them." Quinto nodded with a smile. "I have been secretly breeding these throughout the development of the Subservience Instantiator."

"Do you have…"

"Your original Atomic Pulverizer that empowered these creatures with laser eyes? Yes. I have kept it hidden with the humans who helped to destroy the emperor. Also, with the tracking device we provided the youngest human, Colt, we can easily locate them on Earth. The transport is already honed on their beacon now."

Bastle turned to Quinto. "But the queen has already converted all residents of Asheville to dogs. What if our human allies are already in their dog state?"

"That would be tragic. But we can still acquire the Atomic Pulverizer and empower the hamsters without them."

"How did you know to bring these hamsters?"

"The Grand Queen's lust for power and her speech about

turning the Earth into a trash dump told me that now was the best time to employ them."

"But…" Bastle looked up the corridor that led back to the command center deck. "If we defy the Grand Queen, we'll be disintegrated."

Quinto frowned. "Bastle. It is not like you to cower from a challenge."

"You misunderstand me. I was not cowering." He smiled. "I was getting inflated in the upward direction, as the humans say."

"I believe the term is, getting pumped up." Quinto eyed the corridor. "Quick. We must hurry."

They pulled the hamster cage out of the storage closet.

6. Seeking Help

"WATCH OUT!" Colt yelled from the passenger seat.

Dusty swerved his car, tires screeching, as he narrowly missed another Ashville resident dashing out in the road barking at Dusty's filthy Ford Focus.

Sammy quacked from the backseat, tumbling from one side to the other.

Dusty whistled. "That was a close one." They had only been driving for a couple minutes and Dusty had nearly flattened a half-dozen Asheville residents.

Colt peered in the rearview mirror. "Wasn't that Mrs. Johnston from church?"

"I believe so, my boy. That zap-a-ma-roo affected everyone in town."

"Are you sure those guys aren't dogs, too?"

"My buddies Floyd and Boone are indestructible. I personally witnessed them drive a truck off the top of a three-story parking garage to see if they could get it to fly."

"Did they?"

He shook his head. "Laws of gravity got the best of their flying machine. But they walked away from it. Not a scratch. If you don't count the two broken arms, chipped teeth, and a pair of concussions. But they healed, no problem. Yeah. If anyone avoided this dog thing, it's Floyd and Boone."

"Watch out!"

Dusty swerved to avoid a pair of barking people chasing them.

Colt asked, "But how come *we* aren't dogs?"

"A mystery for another day, my boy. Sometimes, you gotta let things reveal themselves."

"Quack, quack!" Sammy complained from the backseat.

"Don't worry your little head, Sammy," Dusty spoke to the rearview mirror. "My buddies got a full loaf of bread for you, no doubt. And a bathtub in the backyard."

Colt wrinkled his nose. "Bathtub in the backyard?"

"Yessirree. Ol' Floyd loves himself a moonlit bath, nothing but the stars, some bubbles, and Floyd's farmer's tan."

A few turns later, Dusty pulled the car up to a doublewide trailer surrounded by dandelions and overgrown hedges. They stepped out of the car and Colt let Sammy out. A stench of burnt metal hit his senses.

Colt asked, "What's that smell?"

Dusty stepped around the car. "Oh, them two numbskulls are always up to no good."

They stepped to the front door. Before Dusty could knock, the door swung open. Dusty and Colt stepped back. Sammy quacked.

Two men, one tall and thin, the other short and round, stood side by side. Both had on dirty, blue overalls. Both wore crumpled tinfoil hats on their heads like a pair of giant Hershey kisses.

"Land sakes," Dusty said. "You two 'bout scared the pee out of me."

"The alarm tripped," the taller man said as the two stepped outside. "Hey. I know you, kid."

Colt gasped once he recognized the two men from the book fair who accused him of selling fifty percent of a book. "Uh, hello," Colt said, sheepishly.

Dusty said, "Well, slap me silly, Colt. You already know Floyd?"

"Yeah. From the book fair."

Both men had what looked like small, metal car parts attached to their wrists. Each the size and shape of muffins, they were rusty chrome and smudged in grease. Somehow, the wrist implements complemented the tinfoil hats.

Dusty asked, "What the jimmy john do you have on your wrists?"

Boone, the shorter of the two, said, "Hand-operated self-defense *dee-vices*."

"Self-defense?" Dusty looked around. "Let me guess. The government?"

Floyd adjusted the devices on each of these wrists. "Yes, sir. We had just outfitted our craniums with tinfoil to prevent the government from using their mind-bending radar against us when a blue haze came across the yard."

Dusty said, "Yeah. We just saw the same thing downtown."

"Well," Floyd continued, "just so happens that Boone had been tinkering with these lovely weapons. So, we slapped them on and gave them a test run."

Dusty asked, "How'd they fare?"

Boone said, "We need a new TV."

Floyd added, "And refrigerator." He shrugged. "But we've been wanting to buy new appliances, anyhow." Floyd frowned at Colt. "How come you look like a Roman warrior?"

Colt patted his costume. "I'm supposed to be a Spartan warrior."

"Actually," Dusty corrected, placing a hand on Colt's shoulder. "This boy's starring in a genuine Hollywood movie. He was just filming a scene where he slays dozens of laser hamsters."

Floyd stiffened. "Hamsters? What hamsters?" He grabbed the weapon on his wrist. "Them hamsters was eradicated years ago."

Dusty said, "Don't you two worry your tinfoil heads. Colt was only killing pretend hamsters. Computer-generated hamsters will be added after the movie is made. And by then, we'll be laughing all the way to the bank once the movie makes millions of dollars. And I tell you what, when that happens, you can come over to our place anytime you want and watch TV on our brand new fifty, no, sixty-inch flat screen." Dusty had a distant gaze. "I can picture it now. Sittin' there on our fancy La-Z-Boy recliners, feet up, eating our Spam n' cheese on the finest China plates served by a butler dishing out Dijon ketchup on a tray and all of us sippin' bubbly RC Cola from crystal glasses. Mmmm, mmmm, mmmm." He wiped away a tear. "First class all the way."

Floyd asked, "That's why you came? To brag?"

Dusty shook his head. "No, sir. We're on a mission. And we gotta get them weapon things on your wrists fine-tuned in a jiffy. Ever since that blue haze hit Asheville, everybody downtown's gone nuts."

"What do you mean?" Floyd asked.

Colt spoke up, "They're all acting like dogs. Barking and licking hands and chasing cars."

Floyd and Boone eyed each other. Floyd nodded. "Yup. Sounds like the government, all right."

Boone said, "We got a few more weapons just for the occasion. We just gotta…"

A violent wind blasted them from all sides, kicking up dirt that swirled around.

Floyd coughed and yelled, "Quick, in the house!" He led the way, with Boone and Dusty close behind. Colt ushered Sammy through the door as Boone slammed it shut behind them.

The living room was dark and still smelled of burnt metal. Next to the back wall, a flatscreen TV lay smashed on the ground, a trickle of smoke rising from the cracked screen. More smoke drifted from the tiny kitchen just past the TV.

From outside, the roaring rattled the door.

Then, as suddenly as it started, the noise subsided.

The group huddled together, barely breathing, leaning toward the door. Faint hissing and nasal muttering voices, came through the cracks in the door.

Floyd and Boone fiddled with their wrist weapons.

Dusty pressed a hand against Colt's chest, backing him from the door.

Sounds of footsteps patted along the ground just outside.

A pounding at the door made everyone jump.

"Stand back!" Floyd called. "We're armed."

A voice responded, "Open, humans. We require Colt."

Colt gasped. "It's Quinto and Bastle."

Floyd and Boone angled their heads to Colt. "Who?" they asked in unison.

The door flew open, knocking Floyd and Boone onto their rears. Dusty and Colt retreated a couple of steps. Sammy quacked.

In the opened doorway stood a pair of green-skinned aliens both wearing goggles. Their spacecraft hissed smoke in the yard not far behind them.

Quinto lowered his goggles. "Hello, humans. We have returned."

7. Returned to Earth

GRAND QUEEN VITRIOL paced the command center deck, impatiently tapping her fingers. She stopped behind Lieutenant Fanny. "Lieutenant."

"Wowa." Lieutenant Fanny jumped. "You totally startled me."

"What is it now?"

"What?"

Grand Queen Vitriol clenched her fists. "The charge of the weapon! What we've been waiting for!"

"Gosh. Don't get your panties in a bundle." She tapped a glowing button in front of her. "It, like, says thirty-five percent charged."

"That's all? This is taking forever. Are the solar panels at optimal capacity?"

Lieutenant Fanny twisted back. "Like, what does that mean?"

"Is everything working?"

"Gosh, take a chill pill." Lieutenant Fanny tapped a few more buttons. "Yeah. Like, the solar panels are working."

"Blasted! Earth's sun is as weak and ineffective as those pathetic humans." She stomped toward a neighboring console. "Commander."

The officer manning a nearby console turned toward her. "Yes, Grand Queen?"

"Have those two numbskulls, Quinto and Bastle, made it through the wormhole yet? If they delay this attack, I'll…"

"Um, no, Grand Queen. It appears they've landed on Earth."

"What?!"

The officer winced, awaiting a blow that was sure to come.

She stomped a foot. "Traitors! They are assisting those idiot beings down there. How dare they. And after I praised the work that I stole from them." She snapped her fingers. "Captain Duds! Captain Duds!"

A stubby officer ran from an adjoining corridor into the command center deck, the medals on his lapel bouncing with each stride. "Yes? Yes, Grand Queen?"

"Quinto and Bastle have betrayed their queen and landed on Earth. Lead an assault force to their last known location and vaporize them. Immediately!"

Dusty whistled at Quinto and Bastle's spaceship. "That's one sweet ride. You got a hemi in that thing?"

Quinto looked to Colt and Dusty. "We are pleasantly surprised that you have not been converted to dog-like creatures."

Bastle said, "Perhaps the Grand Queen's weapon did not work."

Dusty said, "If you're talking about that blue haze that made the entire town all dog, that worked like a champ. Practically all of Asheville's running around on hands and knees barking up a storm."

Colt asked, "How'd you know I was here?"

Bastle pointed. "The timing device attached to your upper limb."

"My watch?" Colt grabbed his wrist.

"Correct." Bastle nodded. "It emits a beacon that we…"

Quinto said, "No time for explanations. We need the Atomic Pulverizer without delay."

"The atom-say-what?" Floyd still had his back against the wall with his arm extended, ready to blast the two Zammarians. "Are you two government spies, or something, trying to rob our thoughts?"

Boone leaned toward Floyd. "They look like green monkeys."

"I read about them." Floyd nodded. "Monkeys. Trained by the government to radiate our brains. Adjust your head guard, Boone."

Boone centered his tinfoil hat.

"Ah," Bastle raised a finger. "Metal headgear. That explains things."

Quinto asked, "Explains what?"

Bastle said, "You do not remember? During our testing, we found that covering a creature's brain with metal deflects the effects of the Subservience Instantiator. These humans inadvertently shielded themselves from the Grand Queen's weapon with their metal coverings." He turned to Colt and Dusty. "I presume you two had similar metal coverings?"

Colt nodded. "We were wearing metal helmets."

Quinto said, "Yes, yes. All well and good. We need the Atomic Pulverizer. Where is the android? We kept the Atomic Pulverizer within the android."

"Android?" Dusty asked. "You mean a cell phone?"

"No, no," Quinto said. "The android you won from me in your crude card game when I was disguised as a human."

"Card game?" Dusty tapped his chin. "Wait a sec. Do you mean, Sammy the duck?"

Quinto said, "Correct. I believe the android was fashioned to resemble the species you call a duck."

On cue, Sammy quacked from behind the couch and waddled out in the middle of the cramped living room.

Quinto smiled. "Yes. There it is."

"It?" Colt said. "But…"

Before Colt could finish, Quinto stepped up to Sammy and squeezed the back of his neck. The feathers on Sammy's back flipped over to reveal a lighted pad of buttons with weird symbols.

"Sammy…" Colt gasped.

Quinto tapped through buttons. Sammy issued a pair of quacks, and a drawer slid from his side, revealing a small device. Quinto held it up. "The Atomic Pulverizer," he announced. "Bastle. Bring me a hamster."

Bastle scurried outside to their transport.

Colt fell to his knees next to Sammy. He patted the duck's head. Sammy turned to him and quacked. Colt muttered, "I thought…I thought…"

Dusty whistled. "That's one high-tech duck. He'd probably fetch a pretty penny."

"No!" Colt wrapped his arms around Sammy. "You can't sell Sammy."

Dusty said, "Wouldn't think of it, my boy. Just curious about his market value, that's all."

Bastle returned, pushing a large cage of hamsters. "Before you enhance one of these hamsters, Quinto, we should contain it within a device that can direct their laser appropriately. Otherwise, we risk getting struck ourselves."

"Good point," Quinto said. "Do we have…what about that? On that human's appendage." He pointed to Floyd.

Floyd looked to the weapon strapped to his wrist. "This?" He raised his weapon. "Don't think so. This is my blaster, little buddy. And no pint-sized monkey gonna take it off me."

Quinto stepped forward. "You do not understand. We must—"

"Whoa, whoa," Floyd asserted, pointing his wrist weapon at Quinto. "Any closer and you'll be nothing but a charcoal—"

A massive explosion rocked the double-wide trailer. Humans and Zammarians tumbled to the dirty carpet. Fragments of metal flew through the open doorway and rained onto the group.

Frightened by revving engines, sudden gusts of wind, and explosions, they all crouched behind the living room furniture. Laser blasts shot through the doorway, searing the air above their heads and setting the couch cushions ablaze.

Floyd yelled, "What's going on?"

"Grand Queen Vitriol!" Quinto cried. "She must have sent a squad after us."

"Quick!" Bastle called, reaching toward Floyd. "Give me that implement!"

"Never!" Floyd called. He pointed his weapon toward the doorway. "Die, you scum!" He jabbed a button on his weapon. Sparks jumped from the device. Floyd smacked the side of it. "C'mon, baby, work." He pounded the button, and again only sparks. "Dagnabbit, Boone! How come your stuff never works?"

"Hurry, human!" Bastle yelled. "Before we are annihilated." Laser blasts struck the couch cushions again.

Floyd smacked the button on his weapon a couple more times. "Fine." He unstrapped his weapon and handed it to Bastle.

Bastle twisted back to Quinto. "Hamster!"

"I'm trying. I'm trying." Quinto crawled from behind the couch, his belly scraping the floor as laser beams sizzled around. He reached into the cage and pulled out the closest furry creature. "Got…" A laser bolt from the door blasted the rodent from Quinto's hand. Quinto grumbled and grabbed another creature.

Bastle yanked the useless circuitry from Floyd's weapon, creating a void within the metal cylinder. He took the hamster, forced it into the cylinder, and clamped the metal lid shut, trapping the rodent inside. "Okay. Convert the hamster."

Quinto adjusted the controls of the Atomic Pulverizer. "I need to minimize the power."

"Quick!" Bastle said. "Or we will all be fried."

"There." Quinto pointed the device at the cylinder. "Open the trap."

Bastle lifted the metal lid. Quinto zapped the creature. Bastle clamped it shut again. Then, wiggling a finger into a hole in the side of the cylinder, he stroked the hamster's fur.

A red glow emanated from the cylinder.

Bastle pointed toward the open doorway and a red bolt of light fired from his new hamster gun toward their attackers.

Screams erupted from outside, quieting the laser blasts firing toward them.

"Again. Again," Quinto said excitedly.

"Heck, yeah," Dusty said. "Let 'em have it!"

Bastle stroked the hamster again. Another red bolt shot through the doorway.

More screams, followed by an explosion.

"Hey," Floyd said. "Lemme have a go."

"Later, human." He advanced through the door and excited the hamster again.

Another blast.

Another explosion.

Then silence.

Bastle fired once more before calling back, "Quinto!"

"Coming." Quinto scurried outside.

Floyd, Boone, Dusty, and Colt got to their feet and followed the aliens.

The front yard was a ruin of craters and smoking rubble. Fragments of alien uniforms and green body parts were scattered everywhere. Had to be from the aliens. The body parts were certainly not human.

Colt asked, "Who were they?"

"I tried to explain before." Quinto said. "The Grand Queen's troops. She sent them here to destroy us."

Dusty asked, "How come?"

"Ain't it obvious?" Floyd crossed his arms. "We know too much."

Quinto said, "I can assure you, human, you know nothing."

Colt said, "They blew up your spaceship."

"Yes," Bastle said. "And unfortunately, Quinto blew up theirs. Now we're stuck here."

Quinto said, "Not for long." He dashed toward part of the rubble and pulled out a small, glowing cube-shaped object. He pressed a button on the side and spoke into it. "Task force to control." He paused.

"What…" Floyd started to ask.

A static-laden voice sounded from the cube. "This is control. What's your status?"

Quinto pressed the button again. "One of the targets has been neutralized, but the other has fled. We need reinforcements. Over."

The voice spoke again, "A second squad will be dispatched to your location."

"Roger that," Quinto said. He lowered the communicator and looked to the others. "Prepare for more visitors. And ready more hamsters. We'll need everyone's help."

Dusty stepped forward extending his arm. "Slap a hamster on me. I'm ready."

8. Second Squad

GRAND QUEEN VITRIOL lay face-down over a massage table, a tall, muscular Zammarian leaning over her, rubbing her back.

"Ahhhh," the Grand Queen sighed. "That's more like it. Nobody appreciates the stresses a queen must endure."

A pair of bright pink shoes squeaked up to the massage table.

Grand Queen Vitriol huffed. "Fanny. This better be good." She twisted upright to face Lieutenant Fanny. "Is the weapon at full charge?"

"No, Auntie."

"Then why aren't you at your workstation?"

"Like, you know how you were building more weapons?" She popped a bubble from her mouth.

"Yes. Of course, I know. Why?"

"'Cause, one of them just showed up."

Grand Queen Vitriol jumped to her feet. "What? We have a second weapon? Why didn't you tell me?"

"I just did."

The Grand Queen hurried to the command deck, Lieutenant Fanny following close behind.

She burst into the deck, and the officers snapped to attention, saluting. Captain Duds called out, "Hail to the queen!"

"Yeah, yeah, whatever." Grand Queen Vitriol waved them away and stepped in front of the wide viewport. There, outside of the battle cruiser, floated two massive Christmas tree-shaped weapons. "Excellent. We now have a second weapon. And it's just as beautiful as the first." She turned to Captain Duds. "The second weapon. Is it charged?"

Captain Duds said, "Yes, Grand Queen. Ready to fire."

"Good, good." She stepped to an empty command seat. "Lieutenant Fanny!"

"Chillax. I'm coming." Lieutenant Fanny shuffled from behind and took her seat. "You totally don't have to wig out."

Grand Queen Vitriol cracked her knuckles. "Fanny. Sometimes your voice is like a buzzsaw to my brain."

"Like, what's a buzzsaw?"

"It's a crude human tool whose sole purpose is to annoy anyone within earshot."

Fanny huffed. "Like, I can relate."

"What's that?"

"Nothing." Fanny smiled.

"Take aim at the next target," Grand Queen Vitriol said. "We need a dense concentration of humans to best maximize the weapon's potential."

Lieutenant Fanny twisted back to her auntie. "Huh?"

The Grand Queen rolled her eyes. "A city. Aim at a big city."

"Oh." Lieutenant Fanny tapped a few buttons. "Like, here's one. Humans call it…New York City. Sounds dumb."

"Dumb it may be, but it's the next to feel my wrath. Take aim and fire away, Lieutenant."

Lieutenant Fanny tapped away at a series of buttons, then paused. "Like, here goes nothing." She pressed a big red button.

The second massive weapon pulsated red and green lights up and down its conical shape, causing the gold star at the tip to glow with an intense light. A blue laser beam shot from the star and detonated on the Earth's surface.

Seconds passed and Grand Queen Vitriol tapped her fingers impatiently. After what seemed like too long, she demanded, "Well? Results?"

Lieutenant Fanny tapped a few buttons. "Rock on." Bubble gum slapped against her teeth. "The weapon had a totally massive effect, way better than the last one."

"Yes! Yes!" Grand Queen Vitriol hopped. "Oh, happy for me!"

"Yeeee-ha!" Dusty fired his hamster gun, eliminating the

attacking Zammarians as they poked their heads out of their recently landed spaceship. "Like shootin' fish in a barrel." He crouched behind a rusted riding lawnmower in Floyd and Boone's side yard.

Floyd nudged Dusty. "Hey, give me a chance to knock off one."

Dusty said, "There's one running around the side of the ship."

Floyd targeted the runty green alien, aimed, rubbed the hamster, and...

ZAP!

Red laser and a puff of green later, the Zammarian was no more.

A couple more blasts and the firefight ended, leaving silence and utter devastation.

"Well," Bastle said as he stuck his head out from a crater in the front yard. "That was violent."

Quinto emerged next to Bastle. "Correct. However, the transport survived this time. We should be able to get back to the battle cruiser."

Boone looked at him. "The battle what?"

Quinto crawled out of the hole and stood upright. "The Grand Queen is presiding over Battle Cruiser Punisher as we speak. We need to stop her from converting every human on Earth into a dog."

"Translation," Dusty said with a smile, "we'll be lasering up even more alien bad guys with these babies." He patted his hamster gun. A laser fired and blew up a nearby tree into a puff of smoke. "Oops."

Bastle said, "I should recalibrate our hamsters to lessen their impact. When we get aboard the battle cruiser, we wouldn't want to accidentally knock out a wall and kill us all."

"Good idea," Quinto said. "However, I want to keep the intensity of my hamster. I will use mine to target and destroy the oversized Subservience Instantiators the queen is using on humans."

Dusty turned back to the doublewide trailer behind them and called out, "Hey Colt! The coast is clear."

Colt inched his way outside with Sammy waddling at his side.

He had dived back inside when the second group of aliens attacked. He surveyed the carnage of dead aliens.

"Hey, Colt," Dusty approached. "Our little gherkin buddies said we'll be taking that transport doohickey up to space and blast away some Grand Queen. You want in?"

"Are you crazy?" Colt pointed to the weapon on Dusty's wrist. "I've seen what those things do. I don't want to get blown to pieces."

Dusty said, "Yeah. But they're going to tone down the laser power." He turned to Bastle. "Did I get that right, little buddy?"

Bastle nodded. "He is correct." He looked down and tapped away at the Atomic Pulverizer. "I'm making the configuration changes right now. And then—"

A laser blast struck Sammy.

"Over there!" Floyd called, pointing to a Zammarian soldier lying on the ground near the ship.

The soldier swung his blaster and fired at Quinto and Bastle, narrowly missing.

Floyd took aim and fired.

The soldier burst apart, pieces of his gun fragmenting into the air.

Colt brushed the dirt from his face and sat up. He gasped. "Sammy!" He dove toward the duck.

Sparks danced from the entangled wire and exposed circuitry that spilled from Sammy's seared white feathers. His beak opened and closed, barely getting out a "Qua...qua...qua..." His head slumped and he went silent.

Colt threw his arms around the android duck. "Sammy..." He whimpered. "Sammy."

Floyd frowned at Colt. "It's just a robot."

Dusty said, "You gotta understand. That fella meant a lot to Colt. He saw him as a friend."

"My best friend," Colt said through tears.

"Yup," Dusty nodded. "Friends come in all shapes and sizes." He looked to Floyd. "Heck, where would you be without Boone?"

Floyd and Boone exchanged looks.

"Yeah," Floyd said. "Come to think of it, how do I know you ain't a robot, like that duck?"

Boone scratched his head. "You just blew my mind, Floyd."

"Okay," Bastle announced. "Configuration is complete. I need to activate everyone's hamster with the adjusted Atomic Pulverizer."

Colt jumped to his feet, wiped the tears from his face, and said, "Count me in. I wanna go."

Dusty asked, "You sure?"

Colt eyed his lifeless friend and nodded. "Yeah." He wiped his nose with the back of his hand. "That Grand Queen is going to pay."

9. The Showdown

LIEUTENANT FANNY POPPED a bubble of pink gum from her mouth. "Like, the first weapon is fully charged and a third weapon just showed up."

"Wonderful!" Grand Queen Vitriol clapped. "We're really moving now. Target the next two population centers and fire at will."

"Um…" Lieutenant Fanny scrolled through a list on her monitor. "Let's do…Boston and Austin. They sound freaky." She tapped several buttons. "Fire one." After several more taps, she said, "Fire two."

Space lit up outside the viewport and two blasts hurtled toward Earth.

Grand Queen Vitriol jumped. "Oh, how I love it when a plan comes together. Especially when designed by someone as clever and ingenious as me."

"Grand Queen!" Captain Duds called from behind. "One of the squads sent to eliminate Quinto and Bastle has returned."

"And? Were they successful? Tell me they were successful. This day is going so well."

"They're coming out of the airlock right now. I'll check on—"

Explosions and screams echoed from the corridor.

Grand Queen Vitriol asked, "What was that?"

Dusty, Floyd, and Boone leapt through the airlock from the transport into the battle cruiser, firing hamster guns wildly and occasionally hitting something. The Zammarian soldiers screamed and scattered, diving behind consoles and whatever was nearby to evade the onslaught of laser fire.

Quinto, Bastle, and Colt hung back, letting the madmen have their fun.

Quinto grabbed Colt's arm. "Those larger humans are insane."

"You should see them eating barbeque."

Quinto shook his head. "I feel sorry for this barbeque you speak of. Come. Let's hide in their destructive wake."

The Zammarian soldiers hit by the barrage of hamster-incuced lasers groaned and smacked against walls.

Bastle said, "It looks like the reduced laser power is working."

"What if they wake up?" Colt asked.

Bastle shook his head. "It will be a long time before they regain consciousness. By then, we should have control of the ship."

Zammarian reinforcements scrambled down the corridor toward the laser-slinging cowboys, but the men knocked them out one by one.

"Yee-ha!" Dusty cried. "That's twelve for me. But who's counting?"

Floyd knocked out a couple more. "Fourteen for me. And I am counting."

Boone muttered, "Twenty."

"Twenty?" Floyd said. "Dang, Boone." He nudged Dusty. "We can't let him beat us." They fired away, knocking out one Zammarian after another.

The last of their targets toppled to the deck. Dusty, Floyd, and Boone stopped firing and lowered their hamster guns.

From the far end of the corridor stepped a thin figure, a brown gecko standing on its hind legs but roughly the same height as the Zammarians. It strode forward. It held what looked like a broomstick. The end of the stick resembled a single silver concaved plate.

The creature smiled and shook its head. "You pitiful fools. You think you can outmatch the intelligence and skill of Grand Queen Vitriol?"

Floyd asked, "Who?"

"Me, you idiot," she spat. "And what are those pathetic weapons on your arms?"

Dusty held up his hand. "Hamster guns, ma'am."

"Ha! What a joke. Leave it to an ignoramus species to use a rodent to attempt to overtake my mightiest battle cruiser."

Floyd said, "We'll see about that." He raised his hamster gun, aimed, and fired.

As if she predicted the laser bolt, the moment it was fired Grand Queen Vitriol slashed the incoming laser with the silvery plate at the end of the broomstick. The laser deflected and bounced back to Floyd, smacking him square in his face.

Floyd hit the deck.

"Floyd!" Boone yelled. He fired his weapon.

Grand Queen Vitriol slashed the broomstick again.

Boone yelped and crumpled to the ground.

Dusty called, "Take that!"

Again, Grand Queen Vitriol swung her plate, impacted the laser, but Dusty rolled and dodged the reflected bolt.

Dusty laughed, "Missed me!" He kept rolling and smacked his head on a wall. He grunted and fell unconscious.

Grand Queen Vitriol rolled her eyes. "Idiot." She stepped forward and peered behind a console. "Ah, who is this? Quinto and Bastle? And yet another human. How did I know you two would be fraternizing with these disgusting creatures?"

Quinto, Bastle, and Colt slowly stood, facing the Grand Queen.

The queen smirked. "Luck must have been with you when you outmaneuvered the squads I sent to Earth. But now it looks like your luck has run out."

A line of armed Zammarians marched up the corridor, guns aimed at Quinto, Bastle, and Colt.

"So sad, human." Grand Queen Vitriol smiled at Colt. "You chose to team with these fools when you could have lived out the rest of your life as a dog. I imagine such inferior creatures live a splendid life. You could have been dumb and happy. Now, you will be vaporized alongside these clumsy nincompoops." She angled her head. "Any last thoughts?"

Colt gritted his teeth. "Sammy."

She straightened. "What?"

"He was my best friend. And because of you, he's…he's dead."

She rested her broomstick on one shoulder. "I haven't the slightest what you're talking about. But no matter." She sauntered off. "Troops. Make quick work of these three fools."

The Zammarians raised their guns.

"No!" Colt yelled and stroked his hamster.

Red light.

Laser blasts.

One by one, the Zammarians fell. The surviving ones fired back. Colt dove and dodged.

Quinto and Bastle ducked, knocking their heads against each other. They toppled over unconscious.

Colt kept firing, knocking out another Zammarian. Then another. Then another. Tears welled, but he was able to see enough to aim and hit the bumbling aliens.

Colt nearly had victory in his grasp, then Grand Queen Vitriol stepped in, intercepted one of Colt's laser blasts, and deflected it back to him.

Colt spun from the bolt, but it hit his wrist. His hamster gun disintegrated, and he fell to the deck, his head landing on Quinto's body. He grabbed his aching hand. Burn marks scarred his wrist and his watch appeared smashed. He cried.

Grand Queen Vitriol, the last standing, surveyed her fallen troops. "I can't believe it. That little runt took you all out. I'm truly surrounded by imbeciles."

Colt grunted, and pulled himself upright, cradling his injured hand.

"You." Grand Queen Vitriol stomped closer to the boy. "How dare you be a far better marksman than my entire garrison of troops." She looked over the fallen troops again, then turned back to Colt. "Ever consider working for me?"

"I'll never join you."

"Come, come. We have a decent mentoring program here. I could take you under my wing, show you the ropes."

"No! You're not my mother."

She waved a hand. "Whoa. Slow it down. I'm not the motherly type. I'm just offering a fulltime position. Consider the job offer a compliment. Besides, the Zammarian military gets great benefits, like a savings program that's out of this world and a killer retirement package." She glanced at the fallen troops. "Should you survive to retirement age, that is."

Quinto groaned and shifted. Bastle hadn't powered down Quinto's hamster. Colt grabbed Quinto's arm, tickled the hamster, and pointed it at the queen.

Grand Queen Vitriol looked up just as the red laser bolt struck her chest.

She flew back and slammed against the wall. "You cursed brat! Look what you've done!" She gazed down at the smoldering hole in her chest, a trickle of smoke rising from it. She gasped. "Oh, what a world! What a world! Who would have imagined a little kid like you could destroy my beautiful wickedness?" She gasped again. "Killed by a hamster." She strained. "Stupidest…death…ever…" Her head slumped to the side.

A fresh batch of Zammarian troops stormed into the corridor, their weapons drawn.

Colt gripped the hamster gun, still on Quinto's wrist, and readied himself to fire it.

The Zammarians caught sight of the dead queen and gasped. Captain Duds, leading the group, looked to Colt. "You killed her. She's dead."

Colt hesitated, firing the hamster gun.

Captain Duds asked, "What's your name, human?"

"Uh…Colt."

"Hail to Colt! The wicked queen is dead!"

The troops raised their weapons above their heads and echoed, "Hail to Colt, the wicked queen is dead!"

Captain Duds grabbed the queen's broomstick. "Here's her broomstick. Please, take it with you."

Colt's forehead wrinkled. "Why would I want her broomstick?"

The troops parted and another brown gecko-like creature strode in. She glanced at the queen. "Wowa. Like, Auntie Vitriol is totally fried."

"She's…" Colt tried to speak up. "She's your aunt?"

"Totally, little dude." She smiled and chomped on her bubble gum. "You're a cutie. Guess you're the hero or something. Like, we didn't like my aunt. She was a total bummer, you know what I mean. Besides, with her gone, I'm, like, the de facto ruler of Zammar. So, like, slap a crown on me and call me queen, right? Queen Fanny. I totally like the sound of that." She chomped on her gum again.

Dusty began to stir. "Man…" He rubbed his head. "I'm gonna feel that in the morning."

"Dusty!" Colt shot over to his stepdad. "You okay?"

"Right as rain, Colt." He struggled to sit up and saw the surrounding troops. "Whoa. Are we prisoners or something?"

"Heck no," Queen Fanny said. "Like, I think humans are super cool. Especially your malls. I'm totally gaga over shopping."

Colt asked, "What about all the people?"

"What people?"

"On Earth. The ones that are acting like dogs now?"

"Oh, right." Queen Fanny stepped up to Quinto and Bastle and nudged them with her foot. "Like, wake up. You guys gotta change those big guns out there to zap humans back to normal."

Quinto and Bastle moaned and slowly opened their eyes. "Uh?" Bastle said. "Did we win?"

Queen Fanny said, "You got a new queen. And…*tsk*!" She stared at her nails. "I totally chipped a nail. It was all that button pressing I had to do for auntie." She looked up. "You all don't know a good place to get nails done, do you?"

"Actually," Colt spoke up. "I do."

10. Back Home

BACK ON EARTH in Colt's living room, Colt's mom sat in a chair at a small table across from Queen Fanny. The new queen said, "You've, like, totally been going at my nails."

"Well," Mom started, "they were pretty rough, *ruff-ruff*! Oh, excuse me." She touched her lips. "I don't know why I keep doing that."

Mom finished filing the last of Queen Fanny's nails, then shook a tiny bottle of nail polish and unscrewed the lid. "You're going to love this color."

"Lemme see." Queen Fanny leaned toward the bottle. "Oh, hot pink! Totally my color." She held out her fingers. "Paint away." She giggled.

Meanwhile, Colt paced the room, trying to ignore the pungent stench of fresh nail polish.

Bastle opened the front door.

Colt looked to the door and demanded. "Is he done?"

Bastle stepped aside. "See for yourself."

Colt bolted outside.

There, standing in the middle of the yard stood a large white duck, feathers flapping at the sight of Colt. "Quack, quack!"

Colt ran to him and wrapped his arms around him.

"Quack, quack!" Sammy repeated.

"Thank you," Colt said with a huge smile. "Thank you, Bastle."

Quinto stepped up from behind, wiping sweat from his brow. "Hey. I helped, too."

"You too, Quinto." Colt said, excitedly. "Thank you!"

"Well, well, well," Dusty moseyed up. "You got your duck back. I guess you'll be busy with more writing."

Colt frowned. "More writing?"

"Sure. Ain't Sammy your writing buddy? Besides. The world's gotta know how Colt saved the world again from the evils lurking in the cosmos."

Quinto pouted. "Zammarians do not lurk."

Dusty shrugged. "Besides, Colt is still under contract to make that movie. And you know them movie folks love themselves a sequel. That's where the real money is made."

"Well…" the slow drawl drew everyone's attention as Floyd strode up from behind. "I wouldn't put too much stock in them Hollywood types. They've been in cahoots with the government since day one. Puttin' subliminal messages in them movie pictures so you ain't got no choice but to buy yourself a twenty-dollar popcorn and sodas that make you loyal to just one political party."

"And the candy," Boone stepped up.

Floyd shook his head. "Now, don't get me started on candy. Peanut M&Ms? Don't make me laugh. We know what they're really puttin' in them chocolate and candy cases. Mind-controlling chips. That's what."

So wrapped up in listening to Floyd's rant, no one noticed the cardboard box at the far end of the yard just behind Quinto and Bastle's toolchest. Tucked away in the box were Quinto and Bastle's most fantastical inventions, the Subservience Instantiator and Atomic Pulverizer.

In the bottom corner of the box was a sizeable hole, recently gnawed by sharp teeth. The owners of these teeth wiggled their hamster bodies through the hole, located the two devices, and gave each other a knowing wink as they made off with them.

Author's Notes—John Hope

Heroism

UNLIKE COLT, not many people get the opportunity to combat an alien invasion or zip into the space to blast away said aliens with hamster weaponry. But we all have moments in our lives when we're challenged to step up and be the hero.

True heroism is not always as fun as laser hamsters. It's often boring like giving a speech in class or completing a big project for school. Heroes step into situations when the odds are against them, when things are hard, when things aren't going well, and there's a high likelihood of failure—yet they do it anyhow. They face horrible situations in times when whining is preferred. Remember, complaining is always easier than stepping up and doing something hard.

Like Colt in this story, you can be a hero. Sometimes, all you need is a reason, a purpose to drive you forward. It won't be easy. It may even hurt. And you may fail. But if you do, get back up and try again. If you do this, congratulations—you are a hero.

~JH

In the Land of Pigs, the Butcher is King

Greg Stanina

No sooner after a forced emergency landing on this extraterrestrial planet had we began to scout out our newfangled environment when we were suddenly beset upon by a deranged slaughterhouse pig, wielding his (its?) hefty meat cleaver.

As was typical with most farmers on *any* planet, he didn't take kindly to strangers trespassing on his land, and with us being Earthlings, and this clearly not being Earth, we were not only strangers, but illegal aliens to boot.

The slaughterhouse pig was a towering bipedal musclebound giant, clad in a black, rubber smock smeared with encrusted crimson stains and a various assortment of questionable fluids. Oh, and green Wellington boots.

He had a thick metal ring pierced through his snout and a most sour disposition. This irascible temperament, combined with the pointy tusks that protruded from his face had me surmising he was either a razorback or wild boar. But the fact he was gamboling about on two legs, clothed, and brandishing a weapon, was a real head scratcher, indeed.

We took refuge behind an enormous, randomly placed bale of hay, knowing that this sanctuary of forage would be fleeting at best. As we fought quickly to catch our breath, we attempted to make some sort of sense out of what exactly was going on here.

There was me, Lieutenant Robert "Rack" Hansen, Colonel Colette Boudreaux, and Admiral Pickett Smith. We were astronauts aboard a top-secret space station nestled within the moon's shadow, currently on day 407 of the Nemesis Mission. That location, for better or worse, afforded us a near perfect view of Earth's decimation via nuclear warfare.

Call it what you will: World War Three, Armageddon, Dooms-day. But we watched in shock and horror as everything we knew and everyone we loved was wiped out by a myriad of mushroom clouds.

It all happened so fast. A matter of minutes, maybe? Though it's hard to keep track of time when you're 238,855 miles from your home base.

Why? How? There was nary a moment to react, weep, seethe, or to even just let the verisimilitude of the unfortunate circumstances sink in before one of the dozens of red buttons on the ship's console began to flash and beep.

Fuel Bay Four.

Smith suggested it could be a leak in the gas line. He grabbed his tool belt to evaluate the situation, but before he could fully wrap it around that ever-expanding midsection of his, a byproduct of too much (407 days' worth, to be exact) freeze-dried ice cream, the rest of the buttons began to blink and bleep, the console now a metallic discotheque of strobing lights and cacophonous discord. Then we felt the ship lurch and totter, and the interior cabin whirred and trembled, a surefire indication that the rocket boosters had been initiated.

Smith discarded his tool belt and leapt at the helm, tugging both joysticks tightly in a futile attempt to keep the ship steady. Something had triggered the vessel into E.C.M. (Emergency Crash-Land Mode), and when that happened, you had no choice but to strap in and hold on. Granted we had practiced for a scenario like this numerous times at Space Camp, but this was the real deal and we were all operating in a state of sheer panic. The world we knew was now extinct, and our ship was more than likely going to descend us right into the heart of that apocalyptic hell. Who knew what sort of bedlam awaited us. Heavily armed savages? Cannibalistic humanoid underground dwellers? Zombies!?

Before securing myself into the leather bucket seat that had been my domicile for well over a year, I opened the tiny cage that rested atop one of the computer monitors and retrieved my white and black-spotted rodent sidekick. Affectionately known as Harvey The Wonder Hamster, I named him after the Weird Al Yankovic song from years past.

Harvey was *actually* a dwarf guinea pig, according to the pet store owner, bearing all the characteristics of the domestic cavy only in miniature form. This made him the ideal travel companion (the first dwarf guinea pig in space) since I could tuck him securely into the breast pocket of my shirt and parade him around, much like a Beverly Hills socialite would gallivant about with their miniature poodles stowed in grossly overpriced handbags like some sort of wardrobe accessory. And that's precisely what I did, dropping him into my shirt pocket, after kissing him softly on his nose and assuring him everything was going to be okay. Then I sat down, buckled up, and awaited our descent.

The next few minutes played out exactly how you'd expect them to.

Eyes clamped shut.

Hands tightly gripping the sides of the chair.

Praying.

Riding out the twists and turns and drops as though this were some sort of catastrophic roller coaster ride of terror.

More praying.

Hoping against hope that we would survive the inevitable collision.

Obviously, we made it. Harvey, too. But upon emerging from the wreckage of our ship, though this planet resembled Earth, there was an unsettling feeling in the pit of my stomach that it was not, in fact, the planet we had come to know and love. After what he had witnessed a few short hours ago, Earth would have been reduced to a cinder, a fiery dystopian wasteland swathed in smoke, soot, and ash, and most certainly overrun with roving mutant marauders. But this place was fertile farmland, with crops and pastures extending in all directions for as far as the eyes could see.

A ramshackle house stood off in the near distance, flanked by a barn and silo. Beyond that was a cold, foreboding metal structure that resembled something akin to a meat-packing plant or slaughter-house, which would explain the acrid stench of death that wafted in the breeze.

Smith took a minute or two to assess the ship's damage, taking note that exhaust was bellowing from orifices that probably shouldn't be spewing fumes.

"What do you think?" I asked him.

Though his face bore a mask of dire straits, Smith did his best to remain optimistic. "With the right materials, I might be able to get her to fly again."

We wandered over to the rickety house in search of help, food, answers, and anything else the inhabitants would be willing to bestow upon these weary, disoriented space travelers.

Assuming they're human.

Not sure why that phrase popped into my head at that exact moment, but was it beyond reason to assume that this particular planet could be occupied by a species that wasn't human?

Several knocks on the wooden front door went unanswered. Colette wiped away several layers of dust and dirt from one of the windows with her shirt sleeve, then attempted to peer inside. After a few seconds, she shook her head and said, "It doesn't look like anyone's lived here in a while."

"Impossible," Smith retorted. "*Someone's* been tending to this land."

I added, "And judging from that smell, I'd say someone's been working in the slaughterhouse."

Feeling more than a tad brazen, Smith turned the brass handle and the wooden door proceeded to creak open with just the slightest touch, and the three of us were instantly greeted with the pervasive smell of must, fermented milk, and sweat. Gag-inducing, in other words, so much so that Colette dry heaved, if only for a moment.

"Hello?" I called out into the expanse, but just like our gentle tapping earlier, my greeting went unanswered.

We crept inside, bobbing and weaving around the cobwebs that were strewn about. As the outside of the dwelling implied, the house was in a desperate state of disarray. Furniture was coated in filth, overturned or altogether destroyed, windowpanes fractured or shattered, and the floor littered with shards of broken plates and dishes which cracked and splintered beneath our boots as we traversed this treacherous terrain. Additionally, the windows had been haphazardly boarded up, so light in the house was scant.

"No one's here," Colette reiterated.

I nodded in agreement, having zero desire to explore the night-marish recesses of this abode any further than we already had. "There was a barn around the side. Perhaps there's something in there we can use to repair the ship."

Smith scoffed, "I wouldn't bank on it."

"It's worth a shot," I turned toward the door and motioned for them to follow.

Harvey the Wonder Hamster, my dwarf guinea pig crony, was getting restless in my pocket, poor thing. He needed to stretch his legs for a bit, maybe have a bite to eat.

"Hey, come check this out." It was Colette, knelt down beside a chest of drawers, gazing into a glass aquarium which sat upon it. Whatever was inside surely had her intrigued.

Smith and I strode over to where she stood and spied the crea-ture inside. It *was* a creature, after all: A chameleon, I believe. A *big* one.

Slowly munching on a lettuce leaf, it was very much alive, which only served to cement the claim Smith and I had made about this area *not* being as devoid of life as it seemed.

Now, there was nothing necessarily out of the ordinary regarding this particular chameleon, other than the fact it was wearing some sort of armor, like a bomb squad robot, resembling a four-legged tank with a lizard's head. Strapped to its back was what appeared to be a laser cannon. How it operated the cannon was anyone's guess, and I didn't really care to find out.

I backed away and again motioned Colette and Smith toward the door. "I say we go back to the ship and try sending out a distress call."

"The radio's fried," Smith lamented. "And anyway, who would we call? Earth is gone, man. No one's coming for us."

"I don't like this place," Colette said, almost as an aside, as she tiptoed over to one of the precipitously boarded up windows and scanned the outside through two rotting planks.

I couldn't say I disagreed with her. Had no one heard the crash? Was anyone curious enough to come out and investigate? The live chameleon was a dead giveaway that this planet, at least *this* sector, wasn't desolate. Sure, the house needed a bit of spit and polish, but someone or *something* resided here.

Smith picked up a fallen picture frame from the floor and polished away a coating of grime with his thumb. Then, with a smidge of awestruck concern in his voice: "Get a load of this."

He handed me the frame and I surveyed the photograph inside. It was old, browned with age as photos tend to do, but I could make out the image just fine, though my eyes couldn't believe what they were seeing. It was two strapping pig-men wearing denim overalls, each carrying a fishing rod and proudly holding up their prized catch: a red snapper. Their eyes were alight with celebratory pride.

I shook my head in disbelief. Clearly, these burly *men* must be wearing masks. Extremely lifelike swine masks.

Suddenly, from outside, a thunderous screeeeech-thud startled the three of us. It sounded like a heavy metal sliding door being thrust open with vigor, reverberating the entire house.

From her perch at the window, Colette harshly whispered, "The slaughterhouse."

Smith and I joined her and through the two wooden beams we saw a thickset pig-man emerge from the slaughterhouse's antechamber, outfitted in a bloody apron and schlepping a giant meat cleaver.

"What is it?" Colette queried.

It *had* to be one of the two *people* in the old photograph.

Listen, I was never one to judge a book by its cover, as they say, but the sight of this ghastly man-beast sent a shiver down my spine, especially when he tilted his head to the sky and his snout took discerning whiffs of the air around him. He had caught a scent, our scent, and the way his brow furrowed, it was obvious he was not content to have visitors.

With the slaughterhouse door open wide, *we* were blasted with a scent as well, the putrid stink of blood and flesh, death and decay.

I shuddered again. What sort of livestock was being butchered within the confines of that abattoir? I highly doubted he was processing ham and bacon, all things considered. Could that explain the lifelessness of this place? Were humans being rounded up and slaughtered like cattle?

A giggle erupted in my stomach. Human cattle? Apparently, I had been exposed to an unhealthy dose of science-fiction movies as a kid. Then again, we were stranded on a planet with literal pig-men. If that wasn't the epitome of science-fiction turned science-fact, then I don't know what was.

He turned and those beady eyes seemed to home in on the window we were all hidden behind. He couldn't see us, could he? Perhaps he sensed our presence.

"We're not safe here," Colette stating the obvious.

The slaughterhouse pig started to snort and wave its arms about madly, much like a rattlesnake sounding its rattle to warn intruders that they were about to have a *very* bad day.

"We're not safe here," Colette again, this time her voice riddled with panic.

She was right, and when the slaughterhouse pig let loose an ear-piercing, blood-curdling squeal, an obvious battle cry, *that* was our cue to get out of Dodge, scrambling to our feet and rushing out the door, into the open, and in the direction that led us away from the slaughterhouse.

The pig-man galumphed in hot pursuit, surprisingly limber and swift for such a hulking monstrosity.

Despite my brain being ablaze with fear, a morbidly humorous recollection from my past infiltrated its way inside. It was of the summer spent on my grandparent's farm, pawned off on the septu-agenarian couple as a means for my parents to save money on daycare, wherein I chased their pot-bellied pigs around merely for fun. Now I knew how those piglets felt, except we weren't being chased for fun. Our pursuer's temperament and bloodied meat cleaver showed us he had nothing but ill intent. Though, come to think of it, we may have actually eaten one or more of those pigs. Alas.

We took refuge behind the giant bale of hay, to catch our breath and rest our legs, when we realized we were fast approaching three tiny buildings. Actually, they seemed more like shacks or sheds. Either way, they would provide us a safe haven from the rampaging slaughterhouse pig, if only momentarily.

One was made of straw, the other sticks, and the third with bricks. Why did that seem oddly familiar to me?

Each shed only had capacity for one person each, so we expeditiously made our choices: me, the straw, Colette, the sticks, and Smith, the bricks.

Doors slammed shut and locked, and sighs of relief were breathed. We were safe, but for how long?

Not long at all, apparently, as the pig-man reared up and hewed at my straw dwelling with his mighty meat cleaver. Several times that deadly blade came dangerously close to lopping my face off. Straw was no match for a razor-sharp weapon that was typically used to mince and slice meat, bones and sinew.

Eventually the hacking stopped and I heard what sounded like the slaughterhouse pig inhaling deeply, filling his lungs with as much oxygen as he could muster. Then he leaned forward and unleashed a gale force caliber exhalation of breath that threatened to topple my hay hideout. Basically, he was huffing, puffing, and blowing my little house in. My goose was cooked.

I resigned myself to this inevitable fate. After all, Earth was gone. I had no home. No family. I had nothing. Then I felt that my shirt pocket also had nothing in it.

Harvey the wonder hamster had escaped!

I was fine with *my* life being on the proverbial chopping block, but I had to make sure Harvey was safe. Where could he have gone?

Another puff from the big, bad pig (who clearly had his fairy tales mixed up) tore the roof from my shed. If only I had a weapon of some kind. There *were* guns in our space station, but we clambered out with such haste, worried that the ship would explode, that we left the firearms behind.

One final puff of exhaled air and my straw façade was gone. I was going to assume a karate stance of some sort, though I knew nothing about martial arts, but the pig-man gripped me around the throat with his behemoth hands and threw me across the field like a rag doll. I landed hard, the wind knocked from my sails.

The pig-man turned and began the cleaver hackity-hackity

followed by the huff and puff routine on Colette's stick sanctum, which eventually tumbled like a deck of cards.

Colette screamed as the man-beast lunged for her, but he stopped dead in his tracks when his eyes befell upon her face. Then, rather than seizing her by the throat, as he had done with me, he grabbed hold of the front of her shirt and pulled her close to him, uncomfortably close, and snuffled up and down her neck with that hairy snout of his, soaking in her aroma. The psychopathic slaughterhouse pig was noticeably a fan of the fairer sex, even human ones. Colette cringed in disgust.

Colette was cute, I guess, sort of a homelier Sigourney Weaver, but far from a fetching beauty. Then again, who knew when the pig-man had last seen a female, and his attraction for her was enough to keep him from rending her limb from limb.

He dropped the meat cleaver and hoisted Colette over one shoulder, despite her kicks and screams of protest. Then he turned on his heel and marched off toward the slaughterhouse.

I rushed up to Smith's brick quarters just as he was exiting and he shrieked, "Dear God, he's going to mate with her!"

I climbed to my feet just as the admiral unlatched the brick house door and retreated from his confinement. "We've got to save her," he urged.

"Not so fast," I grabbed him by the arm. "He's too strong. We need a weapon."

Smith pointed to the pig-man's discarded meat cleaver. "Will *that* do?"

I grabbed hold of the handle and attempted to pick it up. The damned thing weighed a ton. Smith offered assistance, and between the two of us, we were able to at least upheave it, but it was seriously like two mortals trying to lift Thor's Hammer.

Grunting, straining, sweating, with our muscles stressed to the max, we tugged on the handle of the weighty meat cleaver and followed after Colette.

The pig-man set Colette down at the entrance to the slaughterhouse and shoved her inside, the girl crashed to her knees. He then slid the giant metal door shut with monster truck force.

Smith and I reached the front of the ruinous house and collapsed, fatigued and out of breath.

"We're never going to make it," Smith panted.

I took a moment to ponder our options. Even if we were to make it inside the slaughterhouse, there was zero chance we could appropriately employ that mammoth meat cleaver in a way that would inflict any sort of harm to the beast-man.

We *could* attempt to recoup our guns from the downed spaceship, but by then Colette could be dead...or worse.

It was then that I heard a squeak, a recognizable squeak, the squeak of the one and only Harvey, the Wonder Hamster. He was pecking about near the front door of the house, searching for food and water probably. Geez, I'm the worst dwarf guinea pig father on the planet. Feeding and hydrating him should have been my top priority, prior to running for our lives from the crazed pig-man.

Whilst on my knees, I slowly crawled toward him, careful not to frighten him away. He wasn't typically skittish, but with this being a new and scary world, there was no telling what was going through that tiny brain of his.

His whiskered nose twitched as I drew near, detecting my snail's pace approach. I just hoped that he recognized me as a friend and not a foe, because if he fled into the house he could very possibly wedge himself into some nook or cranny and I'd never be able to retrieve him.

He was just within my reach when he did exactly that, his four legs scurrying away from me and into that pigsty. I let an expletive or two rip, then stood up and ran in after him, Smith on my boot heels. Then, together we closed the door behind us.

Fortunately, Harvey hadn't gone too far. He was poking around the chest of drawers that acted as a base for the chameleon's aquarium.

The heavily armored chameleon.

The chameleon with a laser cannon attached to its back.

"Harvey, you genius," I said, proudly, as I scooped him up and placed him into my shirt's pocket. I turned to Pickett Smith. "You're familiar with laser guns, right?"

Smith nodded, "Sure. It's been a while, though."

I pried the lid from the top of the aquarium, reached in and carefully procured the lizard from inside. With the armor and cannon affixed to him, he definitely had some physical heaviness to him, but nothing even close to the weight of the meat cleaver.

After handing the lizard to Smith, the Admiral inspected the creature up and down, left and right, top to bottom, head to toe. Then the chameleon emptied its bladder, the stream missing Smith's boots by mere inches.

Regarding his initial findings, "Looks like it's powered by Kyber Crystals. Trigger mechanism is near the sternum. High magnification sniper scope with night vision capabilities."

All Greek to me.

"Will it stop that pig-man?"

Smith nodded, "I have no doubt that this baby could incinerate a yak from 200 yards away."

"Good enough. Let's go save Colette."

Confident in the fact that we finally had a weapon, and thus a fighting chance against our cretin nemesis, I kicked open the wooden front door as though I were Chuck Norris, and the two of us stepped into the sunlight, ready and raring to do battle.

I tugged on the giant metal sliding door of the slaughterhouse but it failed to budge.

"We're going to need the power of Hercules to get that door open," I said.

"Or this," Smith patted the top of his chameleon laser cannon. "Step aside."

I did as instructed, Smith aimed the laser at the vexatious door, locked his feet into place, just in case the cannon had any recoil, then squeezed the trigger.

The cannon, and I'm guessing the lizard, too, began to hum and pulse. Then the cannon itself began to glow a bright lime green and the metal heated up.

"You might want to avert your eyes," Smith warned, shouting over the thrumming, the volume of which seemed to crescendo.

A green photon beam projected forth and bored a hole into the slaughterhouse door, emitting a blinding spectrum of lights as it did so.

Smith held his finger on the trigger as long as he could, until the hole in the door was large enough for us to enter through, and until the heat of the cannon reached a temperature that was no longer comfortable for his hands. The chameleon seem unfazed and bored.

"Let's go," I darted toward the door and carefully entered through the newly formed hole, knowing full well that the metal was hot enough to scald and perhaps even melt skin. Smith followed behind and we found ourselves in a fully operational meat-packing plant, where animals were ushered in and brutally butchered for their flesh and organs. Which animals was still anyone's guess. I suppose I was sticking with my human cattle theory, though the place was quiet as a tomb. A massive, metal, blood-soaked tomb. No moos from cows. No bleats from sheep. No oinks from pigs. No screams from humans.

Colette. Where was she?

I called out her name and it seemed to echo endlessly. She responded with a scream, and that too echoed for what seemed like an eternity. This made it difficult to pinpoint her actual whereabouts.

"Where are you?" I shouted.

Where are you?
Where are you?
Where are you?

Silence.

Then we heard the squeal of the pig-man. I don't speak pig squeal, but you could sense from the overall tone that he was not pleased that we were invading his territory.

He, too, was hard to pinpoint. The slaughterhouse was like a giant resonating wall of sound. The screams and squeals seemed to come from everywhere and nowhere all at once.

Then, to add insult to injury, and make our rescue mission all the more difficult, every machine in the building suddenly came to life. Hydraulics, saws, conveyer belts, water pumps, air hoses, all working in tandem, and creating migraine-inducing dissonance, stifling Colette's cries for help.

The slaughterhouse pig stepped out from behind a wash basin and stood in the center of the walkway that led toward the back of the building. We could read it plainly on his face that he was *not* a happy camper. He was breathing heavy, his hairy snout snorting, clenching his fists and flexing the muscles in his arms and neck until the veins threatened to burst.

"Torch this creep," I said to Smith, my voice booming with bravado.

Smith aimed and squeezed the trigger of the chameleon laser cannon but nothing happened. He squeezed the trigger again, and again. Same result.

The pig-man tramped toward us, fully intending to tear us into tiny little pieces.

"Umm,"

"I know, I know," Smith panicked, beads of sweat bursting forth from seemingly every pore on his forehead. "I think the laser has to power up again."

"We don't have time for that," my voice was shaky and hoarse.

The pig-man was closing in, and fast.

Three more trigger pulls, to no avail.

"Distract him," Smith suggested.

"Distract him? How?"

"Wow him with your juggling act,"

How could Smith be cracking jokes at a time like this? Although my juggling skills *were* top notch.

The pig-man was close enough now that we could actually smell the body odor emanating from his armpits. Dread was setting in, and my fight or flight response was charged up and ready to go. Then I felt shuffling in my shirt pocket.

Harvey the Wonder Hamster!

I grabbed hold of my furry friend and set him loose.

"Go!"

Just as I had hoped, the dwarf guinea pig took off like a torpedo and scuttled right between the pig-man's legs, stopping the goliath swine cold.

He unleashed an angry squeal, unhappy that a rodent was loose in a facility where meats were being processed, then turned and toddled after Harvey, who had just tunneled beneath a hydraulic skinning machine.

The pig-man grabbed hold of the machine and gave it a mighty shake, hoping to scare the dwarf guinea pig from beneath it. To no avail, of course. Harvey was no dummy.

"I think I got it," Smith said, victoriously.

"Fire!" I roared.

Smith aimed the chameleon, pulled the trigger, and that glorious photon beam burst from the cannon's barrel and made direct contact with the slaughterhouse pig's muscly back, searing the flesh and perforating a hole as it scorched through bone and lungs and ultimately that inhuman heart.

The pig-man unleashed a truly horrible, pain wracked squeal so loud that it actually drowned out the sounds of the slaughterhouse's killing machines. Then he fell to his knees and threw his arms up in the air as the laser burned through his ribcage and exploded his chest and stomach.

Smith released the trigger, silencing the chameleon laser cannon, and he and I watched as the pig-man gurgled one final bloody squeal, which was more of a croak at this point, then crumpled to the cold, hard floor. Dead.

No time for celebration as Colette still needed rescuing. Smith ran off to find her, while I hunted for and ultimately found the button to cease all of the noisy equipment.

It was while basking in the sweet sound of silence that I heard Harvey's squeak, and his little whiskered muzzle peeked out from beneath the machine he had been hiding under. I happily held out my hand, the dwarf guinea pig crawled inside, and I returned him to the protection of my shirt's breast pocket.

Smith returned with a drowsy Colette, one arm around her waist, slowly helping her toward the exit.

"She okay?" I asked.

"I'll live," she answered for herself. "Let's just get out of here."

The sun was setting as we left the slaughterhouse and stopped to mull over our next move.

Earth was still a wasteland. Our ship was still beyond repair. This planet, save for the pig-man and the chameleon, seemed lifeless.

But we had each other. We had Harvey. We had the chameleon laser cannon that Smith had christened Lazarus.

We were alive, and that was more than we could say for the inhabitants of the rock we once called home. We would just have to take things one day at a time and let fate runs its course.

Then I remembered that there were actually two pig-men in the photograph Smith had found in the house earlier.

Author's Notes–Greg Stanina

QUENTIN TARANTINO PEPPERS HIS SCRIPTS/FILMS with ideas, concepts and plot-lines "borrowed" from movies that he holds near and dear to his heart, tweaked just enough to make them his own, and thus paying homage to said movies. He's also considered a genius in his field.

The idea of an enormous pig-man, swathed in a bloody apron, walking on two legs and wielding a meat cleaver came to me in a fever dream, much in the way the metallic endoskeleton terminators appeared to director James Cameron whilst he was in the throes of influenza. I knew I had to build a story around this character and when the "Amazing Pets" project was presented to me, I suddenly had the platform I needed.

An amazing pet was added, in this case a dwarf guinea pig named Harvey, and for the central core I took a page from Tarantino and sprinkled my story with some elements from a 1984 low-budget sci-flick called DEF-CON 4.

In that film, a trio of astronauts return to earth after a nuclear exchange between the United States and the Soviet Union, but rather than being beset upon by bloodthirsty pig-men, they must contend with humans crazed by radiation poisoning and starvation in a savage wasteland.

My trio of space explorers crash land on an alien planet that resembles earth, but isn't, and are tormented by the aforementioned pig-man who we can only assume is breeding and slaughtering humans like cattle. Then I gave my tale a nifty title and the rest, as they say, is history. So, as you can see, I'm basically like Quentin Tarantino...just without all that genius baggage.

~GS

Linked

Elle Andrews Patt

E*very dog must have his day.*
                    —*Jonathon Swift*

IN THE MIDDLE of nowhere South Carolina, with only Lieutenant Colonel Tate Addamson at his side, Major Sargeant Jack Downey's midnight mission went sideways fast.

They were AWOL from the safe house they, unimaginatively, called "Failure to Unlink Island". Downey had landed there several months ago when his temporal headset failed to unlink his mind from his host, military K9642, a German Shepherd named River. The program was disbanded, not for the first time. The Colonel was an unlink failure from a previous foray into linking the minds of military specialists to animal hosts.

Both their human bodies lay in a hospital in Columbia, waiting for unlink.

Downey's used-to-be-friend-with-benefits—who was now just a woman friend due to his current status as a dog—had brought ice cream, not part of their mandated diets, to the island three weeks ago and now they had a craving.

But a man stood inside their mission target, a 24/7 convenience store gas station with a grill, a couple of booths, and, most importantly, a twelve-flavor ice cream counter. Tate had looked up the location and hours and here they were, out on the darkest edge of the parking lot on a moonless night. But here, too, was someone robbing the place. And now, an old pick-up truck pulling in.

And them. AWOL.

Without backup.

Well, kind of without backup. Tate didn't have a GPS tracker because his gorilla host, a hulking silverback named Bomassa, was supposedly in secure lock-up for the night. Downey's host, River, free to roam the island within its dog-proof confines, had a tracker the size of a rice grain embedded in the skin between his shoulders.

But no one knew they were gone, so yeah, no backup.

The truck's headlights faded in the glare of the two security lights on either side of the parking lot, the overheads mounted on either end of the two gas pump islands, and the floodlights on the store itself. Neither the gunman nor the middle-aged woman clerk crying in front of him noticed the truck as the driver parked in a spot near the door. Worse, the young man stocking the coolers had dropped to the ground when the gunman stalked in and was now working his way toward the registers, apparently intent on getting himself killed.

Downey willed River into taking deep breaths, suppressing the K9's growing excitement and anxiety at seeing a man with an outstretched gun. River had been trained for this. So had Downey.

Tate stood up from his knuckle-walking stance and dropped his backpack on the crumbling black asphalt. Downey shook River's head. Really? He wanted to talk now? Tate settled on his jeans-covered haunches, snatched up the backpack, and whipped out his iPad. It was always on. Under Tate's direction, Bomassa's massive but nimble fingers flew over the enlarged keyboard.

"Stop the driver. I'll stop the robbery," the iPad said in a male voice with a British accent.

Downey opened River's throat and barked. They were top-secret projects. They had a plan that should work on a middle-of-the-night foray for ice cream, but once the cops were involved, Tate couldn't hide behind his huge, 100 XX whatever, custom-made black hoodie and a faded pair of jeans, with the hope his bare gorilla feet wouldn't be noticed.

The pick-up's driver door opened.

The clerk dropped her hands to fumble with the register.

The stock boy crept another three feet down the aisle.

Well, shit.

Tate shoved the iPad in his pack and stuck a strap in his mouth. He could walk upright but not fast. He was terrifyingly speedy running on all fours. Deep inside, Downey sighed. It's not like there was a world where he'd let anything happen to these people if he could stop it. He'd gone into spec ops and Delta Force for a reason. He was stuck in River as a special reconnaissance research project because of his own drive to help innocent people terrorized by the not-so-innocent.

Downey let River go, aiming him at the bearded driver who'd just jumped out of his truck and closed the door. He stopped River just three feet short and let his growling snarl loose.

The driver spun, holding both hands up, palms out. "Whoa, doggy, it's okay, calm down there."

Downey circled River around the man, keeping his attention away from Tate, now knuckle-walking up onto the sidewalk in front of the store.

The man stepped backward, up against the truck door. "Who's a good doggy?" he said, feeling for the door handle with his right hand. "You're a good doggy, good doggy."

The door handle clicked.

Downey walked River forward. The driver whipped the door

open, scrambled inside and slammed the door shut. Downey rushed the closed door, throwing River's front paws up on the window, and ferociously barking, spit flying from their mouth.

The driver started the truck. Downey turned River's head, spotting both the gunman and the clerk, cash in her hands, looking out the window at him. The driver jerked the truck backwards. Downey dropped down and jumped sideways to avoid the front tire as the driver turned out of the spot.

Tate closed Bomassa's hand on the closest door handle, waiting.

Still barking, Downey ran at the store's large front window to keep the clerk and gunman's attention.

Tate snapped the store door open and went roaring in. The gunman fired two wild shots before Tate and Bomassa knocked him over. Downey leaped and hit the window high enough to see the gun slid across the stained tile floor. The clerk screamed. Cash flew into the air. When they landed back on the sidewalk, Downey ran River the short distance to the store's out-door and pushed through it.

Tate picked the gunman up and dropped him on his belly.

The clerk disappeared beneath the counter.

The smell of urine drifting from Downey's right overpowered the human fear, sweat, and a thousand other scents hitting River's nose and tongue. The stock boy had wet himself.

The clerk stood up, a short-barreled Mossberg shotgun in her unsteady hands. "Everybody freeze," she shouted, her voice louder and stronger than Downey expected.

River crouched and before Downey could stop him, leaped for the woman's arm, powerful jaws open. Downey clamped his jaws shut in mid-air. His eighty pounds knocked the woman sideways. The shotgun boomed. Shot peppered the ceiling, sending shards of insulated ceiling tile down over them like confetti.

River was confused with nowhere to put his energy. Downey parked him over the woman, panting his moist breath onto her hands where they covered her face. After a long moment, River shimmied his body and thumped his tail against his sides, wagging it with his whole butt, Downey along for the ride.

On the other side of the counter, Bomassa's low, continuous growl ceased.

Downey lifted River's head to see what he could see through River's eyes.

Tate was balanced upright on Bomassa's large feet, the gunman's Glock held in his right hand. Tate grunted and waved Bomassa's left hand toward the door. The gunman popped up off the floor and scuttled out of the store as fast as he could.

Downey's mood lightened. Maybe they could still keep this little mission to themselves if no cops were called. A bell rang. Tate pointed outside. Downey took that to mean someone was pulling up to the pumps. Tate disappeared the Glock in one of his voluminous hoodie pockets.

Downey moved River off the woman.

Tate opened the store's door, setting off a low buzz Downey hadn't noticed earlier. He only leaned out, Bomassa's long arm hanging onto the door to keep it open and snagged the backpack he'd left on the sidewalk. The stock boy was creeping backwards. Downey leaped onto and off of the counter. The boy started to run but slipped on his own wet spot.

Downey trotted River down the adjacent aisle and around the end cap to block the boy's retreat. His face bright red, the boy climbed to his feet. Tate stood at the clerk's counter now, taking his iPad out of his backpack. He typed. The iPad spoke, but the volume was turned down too low. Tate picked it up and fiddled with it. Bomassa's head inside the hoodie turned toward the window. He held the iPad up. "Incoming customer," it announced.

That wasn't good.

Downey spotted a mop bucket on wheels, the mop propped inside, parked in the short hallway for the restrooms. He trotted over to it, River's nails clicking in the silence of the store under the constant lulling drone of a Muzak playlist meant to calm the masses and encourage a relaxed shopping experience.

"It's okay," the iPad said. "The robber's gone. I'm Tate."

Downey tugged the bucket out by the handle using River's teeth, then tried to drag it along. The water sloshed.

"I can't speak due to a physical condition," the iPad's British man voice said.

Downy let go of the handle, went around the bucket, and pushed it forward with River's head. River wasn't sure about that, but didn't outright refuse.

"Please get up,' the iPad said to the clerk. "Incoming customer."

The boy had gathered his courage. He again bolted for the stockroom door, slipping and sliding around the end cap, and tripped headlong over the mop bucket, dumping the contents across the floor. River backed away and Downey let him.

"Barry!" the clerk suddenly yelled. "You okay?"

Movement above him drew Downey's attention to the curved mirror mounted from the ceiling in the corner of the store past the stockboy, drenched and spread eagle on the floor. In the mirror's reflection, the clerk stood on her side of the counter. Tate hunched over to pick something...cash...off the floor.

"Barry!"

"Yeah," the stock boy sputtered. "I'm fine, Sheila."

The buzzer buzzed. A blonde woman in a red jacket entered.

Sheila gathered the loose cash on the counter, plucked a bill off the top of the lottery ticket display.

"Oh!" the woman in red said. She bent down.

Tate passed the cash he'd gathered to Sheila. She wasn't happy, but also not terrified.

Barry rolled over onto his hands and knees.

The woman in red stood up, holding something...cash...in both hands. She click-clacked in her heels to Tate's side and placed the cash on the counter.

"Fan fell over," Sheila said. "Blew all that cash plumb outta the drawer."

"Too bad it wasn't manna from heaven," Red Jacket said.

"I wish," Sheila said. "I just hope we got it all. Boss likes the drawer closed out even at the end of each shift."

"Lordy, tell me about it! I worked at Tarjay until I retired last year."

"You go ahead and get what you need, honey. Just watch the chip aisle, the mop bucket went over back there."

Barry, having levered himself up, grabbed the mop.

Red Jacket giggled. "Y'all having a bad night, aren't you?"

"Naw, it's just mid-shift."

"I get that, too," Red Jacket said. "I shore do." She patted Tate's forearm. "My, you're a big fella, aren't you? And I like your toe-y shoes! My friend has a pair, we call them her gorilla feet, but hers don't have the fur tops. I'll have to tell her to get some!"

Tate nodded, slow and exaggerated.

She click-clacked away, saying "That's just so fun!"

Downey wasn't sure what to do, so he sat and watched the mirror. Barry got to mopping. Tate was tapping on the iPad, Sheila counting cash into the drawer. Spec Ops could use more quick thinkers like her. He glanced at Barry. Barry was glancing at him. They both looked away.

Red Jacket made her way to the drink coolers via the back coffee aisle. "Aww, what a pretty dog! And you get to bring him to work!"

The alcohol on her breath smelled sweet. Before he knew what she intended, her hand landed on the top of River's head and started scratching. River leaned into it. Damnnnn...that felt good.

Barry made some sort of sound that meant nothing, his knuckles white on the mop handle.

"Sweet dog." She gave him a final pat. "I'm just gonna tip-toe over here for Cokes."

He and Barry watched her collect her drinks, an apple and a couple of nut bars already tucked in the crook of her elbow. When she click-clacked away, Downey followed her up the next dry aisle to the register. Sheila closed the drawer with a decisive shove and the register beeped.

Tate shuffled over to study the lottery tickets, a twenty in his hand, to give Red Jacket room to dump her purchases on the counter. A couple of minutes later, she sang out, "Good night!" and sashayed out the door to the older man waiting for her in a vintage powder blue Mercedes SL.

The mop bucket rattled closer. Barry cleared his throat. "Uh, your dog, sir. He, uh, seems real smart."

Tate typed on the iPad he'd set back down on the counter. "He's almost human," the iPad said.

Ha-ha. Downey opened River's throat and barked. He sometimes used a stylus to communicate on the iPad or Tate's massive computer set-up at the safe house, but it was slow and frustrating. He'd learned to be a man of very few words and good canine body language.

"Was all the money there?" The Brit on the iPad asked.

"I'll have to check against the receipts, but it appears so."

Tate typed some more. Hit the text to talk again. "Will your boss understand about the ceiling, or do you need to call the cops?"

She peered into the depths of Tate's hoodie and then shot a look at River before looking back down at Bomassa's hands on the iPad. "Just a couple of ceiling tiles. I think it'll be fine. I doubt that ass comes back around again, thanks to the both of you."

Tate typed. "We just came in for ice cream."

"Well, let me treat you," Sheila said. She smiled and it transformed her face from guarded to quite beautiful.

River sat, his mouth dropping open, and panted.

"It's okay," Tate said through the iPad. "We can pay."

"It's okay," Sheila said. "I won't get in trouble. I own the place."

Tate hooted, a gorilla chuckle. Downey figured Shelia could see enough of his face to see Bomassa's play face, his mouth open and tannin-blackened teeth hidden.

"Come on down to the counter and pick your poison."

"Uh," Barry said. "Dogs can't eat ice cream. They're lactose-intolerant."

That explained the squirts last time. But ice cream was worth the discomfort.

"Barry, honey, pull a T-shirt from inventory. At least you'll be half-dry."

Barry threw River a sideways look and Downey doggy-grinned in return. Mop water may not smell good, but, to the human nose, it probably went a long way toward covering the smell of pee. Not really his original intention, but if it helped, Barry could think it was. Barry flushed again and headed to the back, steering the mop bucket with both hands on the mop.

They'd just made the ice cream counter when the door buzzed. All three of them turned to look. A Sheriff's deputy stepped just inside, eyeing River.

"What's wrong, Josh?" Sheila asked.

"Got a 911 call about a dangerous animal at this location."

They all looked at River.

"Don't look too dangerous to me," Sheila said.

Josh pushed his hat back on his head. "No, not at the moment. But you know he can't be in here since y'all serve food."

"This man's disabled, Josh. This here's his service dog."

"That so?"

Tate still had the iPad in his hands. He tapped on it with one finger. "Yes, sir."

He walked closer to them, sizing them up, before he stopped again. "He's not got a service dog vest on."

"That what you gonna tell the judge," Sheila said, fists on her hips, "when the Humane Society and ACLU both come down on you?"

Apparently sensing this line of questioning could go on a while, Tate placed the iPad on the shiny silver of the ice cream counter, knocking over the cone display, which crashed to the floor. River ducked away to avoid being hit. Downey sat him back down a foot away. Even on his own, River would be too well-trained to go for the cone still rocking near his left front paw.

"Not required," the iPad said. Tate kept typing. "Sorry about that, Sheila."

"No worries, honey."

"We still have a leash law county-wide."

"Oh, Josh," Sheila said with a sigh. "This is private property."

"He's gonna have to leave this store at some point."

Tate was typing again. "Not required due to my disability."

Downey wondered how much research Tate did before agreeing to abscond with him for ice cream. It never occurred to him that they might need more thorough cover at midnight in nowhere. Of, course, he expected to wait outside and let Tate bring him his ice cream. River also ran waaaay faster than Bomassa if they had to escape the situation.

Tate was fond of holding Bomassa's opposable thumbs and better-organized brain structure over Downey's head. But he might have a point. Without non-frustrating access to the internet or a phone, Downey was taking more pleasure in the moment and, possibly, maybe, not thinking ahead quite like he used to.

The deputy's jaw was jutting out now as he thought.

"You may ask what tasks my dog has been taught to perform." The iPad Brit sounded prim.

The deputy nodded. "All right, then, what tasks does this animal perform for you?"

"He monitors my blood sugar."

Ah! That was a good one. No way to demonstrate.

The deputy took a deep breath and let it out in a huge sigh. He shrugged. "Okay."

Tate had been typing since the last message. Now the iPad said, in that just-so voice Downey decided to hate, "He's well-trained off-leash. Since I don't always have a voice device available, he responds to signals."

Sheila cocked her head with a considering expression. The deputy smiled.

Great. A trained poodle act. That no one asked for. Tate had been a test pilot. Like Downey, he was used to being part of an elite unit that worked hard and played hard. He'd agreed to mind-meld with Bomassa in order to go into space. Part of an experiment to test manned spacecraft without the men. Or women, for that matter. He'd been lonely. Now he had Downey.

Without turning from the counter, Tate lowered his left hand flat.

Downey opened River's mouth and pretend-yawned with a strangled whine. River knew that signal though, and laid them belly flat to the floor, his interest piqued. He liked ice cream as much as Downey did, so his motives were suspect. Downey felt better though about subjecting River to the squirts just for the flavor of something bad for him. Besides, it was only a temporary discomfort and practically a patriotic service to his country for helping Downey get his fix...

Tate turned around.

Downey could see the light rimming Bomassa's large, angled nostrils and the curve of his slightly open muzzle with his teeth showing—gorilla smile. Downey narrowed River's eyes at him in warning. River caught his play-fight vibe and lifted his top lip in a flash of fang while dropping his front end to the floor, hind end wagging in the air with a contagious joy lighting them up inside.

Tate held his right hand out flat with the palm down then turned it up. Downey rolled River onto his back, belly up, paws dangling in the air. Tate stuck Bomassa's index finger out and rolled it twice. Downey rolled all the way over and then rolled over again.

Sheila made an 'Ooo' sound.

Tate held his finger upright. River knew that one. He jumped up into a sit before Downey figured it out. Tate pointed left, lifted his finger upright again, and spun his whole hand. Downey dutifully trotted River over to the two booths on the back coffee aisle and then lapped the store, trotting past Barry, standing in the open doorway of the stockroom with all sorts of tantalizing scents wafting out. River, remaining true to his training, focused only on Downey's directed movement of their body. He ignored the deputy, too, all cologne and car leather, and gun oil, and midnight in nowhere South Carolina, and returned to his spot in front of Tate, where they sat again.

"Good boy!" Sheila burst out with a little clap of her hands.

Watching him, Tate touched the iPad screen without looking. The Brit voice said, "Excuse me in advance, Sheila, but here's a good one."

Uh, oh.

"River," the voice continued, "Lick your own..."

Downey stood River up, his hackles rising, and growled at Tate.

"...paws."

The deputy barked out a laugh. "That was funny! Thought you were going to ask something else there for a second."

"You should film that for Tik-Tok, hon," Sheila said, shaking her head, then nodding decisively. "You'd get a lot of views."

"Okay, nothing to see here, I guess," the deputy said, already turning for the door. "Try not to terrorize the other customers."

Tate typed. "Would never cross my mind, sir," the iPad said.

Downey snorted internally. River sneezed in reaction. Yeah. He'd only terrorize innocent Delta Force members stuck inside military K9s.

"Wait, Josh!" Sheila left them to open the sliding hot counter window. She scooped some potato wedges that had been sitting under the warmer into a red and white cardboard fry tray, dropped the tray into a white paper bag and held it out to the deputy. "Here you go. I know you love these! Thanks for checking in on me."

The deputy took the bag with a broad smile. "Just call if you need me."

"I've got you on speed dial."

They watched him leave, his rear tires spinning on the crumbly parking lot pavement before he shot back out onto U.S. 1.

"Warm fries with your ice cream?" Sheila asked.

Tate nodded, making the motion loud. Downey and River barked as one.

"He really is almost human," Sheila said.

Tate took the bag of fries, held four fingers up, and pointed at the pistachio ice cream.

"Four scoops, you got it, hon."

While Sheila scooped the ice cream into a cup, Tate pointed at each flavor for Downey's benefit. He knew chocolate was out because of River. He barked when Tate touched the Strawberry label.

On some level Downey was just beginning to get used to after months of living inside him, River had remained aware of Barry's smell and footsteps, his location in the store, even his approach in the last couple of minutes, but Downey was still startled when

Barry spoke. "He can't see inside the freezer. Does he read English?"

Tate looked over his shoulder at the boy and shrugged.

Barry frowned at River, like he might see inside him if he tried hard enough. Downey looked away and yawned. He trotted to the booths, jumped up onto the farthest bench where he could watch the action, and sat waiting to be served.

"Napkins are on the table. Y'all enjoy your snacks," Sheila said. "Barry, honey, could you bring our guests two bottles of water?"

Tate set Downey's ice cream in front of River. They licked the top, the cup sliding around on the table, River's eyes half-closed as they both enjoyed the cold, creamy sweetness. Tate placed half the fries on a napkin. They smelled divine. The warmth and salt exploded on their cold tongue. When the fries were gone, they dove back into the ice cream. Tate reached Bomassa's hand out and held the cup. Downey decided to love him again despite the poodle tricks.

The gas pump bell rang.

A minute later, the door buzzed. It had to be getting on to one A.M. now. The bar and sports crowds would be swinging in over the next hour, making Sheila's overnight shift worth keeping the store open. Downey remembered well the recon time he'd spent outside convenience stores while tracking down high-value targets.

Licking the strawberry dregs out of the cup, River's nose and ears gave Downey male, boots, the subtle swish of jeans. He was a half-second behind when River recognized the man and started wiggle butt wagging, still focused on the last smear of ice cream in the bottom lining of the cup.

Bomassa gave a very soft hoot.

Chris. Tate and Bomassa's handler, and head of security at "Failure to Unlink Island", which, to be fair, was not just a safe house, but a secure 220-acre compound. Secure against threats, at least, just not as secure as previously thought against two unlink failures determined to go AWOL on a midnight mission for ice cream.

The ice cream gone, River didn't object to Downey lifting their head. Chris was alone, but there would be, no doubt, two MPs in civilian clothes waiting with the van he could see at the pumps. Chris put his hands on his hips and shook his head in exaggerated disappointment, then lifted his chin at Bomassa. "You still eating, Colonel?

Tate nodded.

Chris turned back to Sheila, working on something at the register. "Miss? Could I get some ice cream?"

"Barry!" Sheila called out. "Ice cream!"

Barry popped out of one of the aisles. "What can I get you, sir?"

"Scoop of Fudge Ripple in a cone," Chris said without even looking. He'd been in before, obviously. Not enough to be a regular, but enough to be familiar with the offerings.

"I'll bring it to you."

Correctly ascertaining Downey as the greater flight risk, Chris sat, crowding an enthusiastic River over while Downey kept the K9 from greeting him with licks. "You boys have a nice Great Escape outing?"

Downey woofed. Tate shrugged. Barry delivered Chris's cone. Chris wrinkled his brow, his lips pursing as he considered Barry's state of half-dry half-wet dishevelment. The bell on the gas pumps rang again as the MPs drove over the line and parked out of sight of the store windows.

Between bites of his ice cream, Chris asked, "Anyone shoot video?"

Downey hadn't seen either Sheila or Barry with a phone. There must be security cameras, though. Tate shook Bomassa's head.

"There's cameras, though."

Tate typed. The iPad said, "I'll take care of it."

Chris looked dubious, but Tate still outranked him despite being trapped inside Bomassa. He crunched through his cone while Tate, and Bomassa, Downey was sure, savored the last couple of spoonfuls of their ice cream. Then Chris cleared their debris into the nearby trash can and they made their way to the front of the store.

Sheila looked up and smiled. "No charge, folks. Thanks for your help."

Chris and Downey hung back while Tate took his iPad to the register. He typed. "Thanks, Sheila. Could I ask another favor?"

"Sure thing, sweetie."

It took a long moment for Tate to frame his request before he once more hit the text to talk. "Could my friend here review and erase the security footage? He'll make sure that man never bothers you again."

Sheila eyed Chris, then River, then Tate, tilting her head a little to peer beneath his hoodie. Coming to a decision, she nodded. "Yes, sir. Thank you for your service, Colonel. I won't tell nobody you were here. And neither will Barry."

Downey turned River's head just enough to glimpse Barry eavesdropping on the edge of an aisle. The boy saw him looking and crossed his heart before making a zipper motion over his lips before pointing at his pants and mouthing, thank you. Downey dipped River's eye closed, giving Barry a slow canine wink. Barry's face lit up, he clapped both hands over his mouth, spun on his heel, and disappeared.

Downey's glee at the boy's reaction translated through River, their front paws dancing just a bit. Chris had slid behind the counter and was tapping through Sheila's security footage. It only took a few minutes and then Tate lifted Bomassa's hand in goodbye and Sheila waved them out the door.

In the van, Tate and Downey sat in the middle row by themselves. It'd been a month since Downey's last official mission inside River. Even feeling like a chastised pre-teen, he was more relaxed for having been on an adventure. Outside the van windows, the dark countryside was that familiar, but always startling, dark-dark without streetlights or a full moon. The air vents brought the scent of cows and grass and exhaust and a hundred other things Downy hadn't learned to identify yet to River's nose to occupy their back brain. Turned down low, Duran Duran wailed about being hungry like the wolf on the oldies station.

River's stomach gurgled.

Tate and Bomassa both, Downey was pretty sure, gave him a unified side-eye.

The second gurgle sounded like a clogged drain emptying.

Oh, shit. Downey looked out the front window, trying to decide if they could make it back to the island in time.

Driving, Chris met Downey's panicked gaze in the rearview mirror. "You know," he said, "dogs are lactose intolerant."

He knew. He knew.

Author's Notes—Elle Andrews Patt

ALTHOUGH MIND LINKING and GPS tracking by injectable microchip does not yet (as far as I know!) exist, writers and companies have been trying to make a working version for years. Voss-Mauser and Lightning GPS tried for quite a while. Don't open any links on the page attached to Lightning GPS as someone has hacked it and installed malware (ask me how I know!)

What I do know well is the counties deep in the South Carolina interior. And the delicious food and treats offered at those with grills. And the kind people who inhabit them. With all four military branches present in South Carolina, it seemed like an ideal location for this little story.

I hope you enjoyed it! These characters will be back in a longer story!

~*EAP*

About the Authors

PARKER FRANCIS
SCOTT MICHAEL POWERS
KRISTIN DURFEE
KEN PELHAM
BRIA BURTON
J.C. BRUCE
JADE KERRION
JOHN HOPE
GREG STANINA
ELLE ANDREWS PATT

PARKER FRANCIS

Award-winning author Parker Francis, aka Victor DiGenti, writes in multiple genres, including mystery, thriller, speculative fiction, and nonfiction. Together, the cloned pair has written six novels, a collection of short stories, and 12 nonfiction books. His novels include the *Windrusher* trilogy of adventure fantasies featuring a four-legged feline protagonist and the Quint Mitchell Mystery series. Victor DiGenti (the name you'll find on his passport) works as a ghostwriter and biographer. He's penned biographies and family histories for many clients, including WWII veterans, jazz musicians, entrepreneurs, and retired corporate executives. Vic has also edited and published books for other individuals through his imprint Windrusher Hall Press.

As a working author and publisher, Vic has taught writing classes at the University of North Florida and workshops at writers' groups and conferences throughout Florida. He's a longtime member and former Executive Vice President of the Florida Writers Association, a member of the Association of Ghostwriters, International Thriller Writers, and serves on the Board of the Beaches Museum based in Jacksonville Beach. Vic lives and works in Ponte Vedra Beach, Florida, with his wife and four frisky cats.

Visit him at **www.windrusherhallpress.com**

SCOTT MICHAEL POWERS

Scott Michael Powers' first sci-fi thriller novel, **The Roswell Swatch**, was published in 2016 by *Off*-University Press. His second sci-fi thriller novel, **The Murder Plague**, was published in 2024 by Black Rose Writing. Both earned awards and rave reviews.

*"**The Murder Plague** is a chilling bloodbath that you'll binge from the edge of your seat."* — *IndiesToday.com*
   The Roswell Swatch *is "Part thriller, part science fiction, with dynamic pacing and a clever plot. Highly recommended."—Brian Kaufman, author.*

Scott is working on his third and fourth novels, promising that his third will be his best yet, and that his fourth will be his best yet. He also has published short stories.

Scott built a distinguished, 40-year career as a journalist in Texas, Ohio, and Florida, covering beats that included local, state, and national politics, the environment, tourism, business, higher education, NASA and Kennedy Space Center. His work attracted numerous journalism awards, though his real fame arose from his being locked in a fundraiser's closet by then-Vice President Joe Biden's advance team in 2011.

After retiring from journalism in 2022, Scott turned full-time to fiction writing. He and his wife live in an Orlando, Florida, neighborhood full of big trees and cops.

Visit Scott at **www.scottmichaelpowers.com** for updates on his work, and his ruminations on writing, stories, and being an indie author.

KRISTIN DURFEE

Kristin Durfee grew up outside of Philadelphia where an initial struggle with reading blossomed into a love and passion for the written word.

Kristin currently resides outside of Orlando, FL, and when not enjoying the theme parks or Florida sun, she spends most of her time with her husband, son, and their quirky rescue dogs.

Shot - A female homicide detective in prohibition-era New York City hunts for a serial killer before her hidden pregnancy forces her out of the department.

> *"A compelling and intriguing tale, layered with suspense, loaded with treachery deep from within. What more could you ask for?" —NY Times and USA Today bestselling author Steve Berry*

Mass - A teenager experiencing visions from God, possibly caused by a brain tumor, takes her parents to court with the help of a cult to become medically emancipated to continue having the visions, risking everything for her connection.

> *"A moving, worldly-wise tale of a teen on a spiritual roller-coaster ride." — Kirkus Review*

> *Winner of the 2021 Royal Palm Literary Awards Gold Young Adult Novel*

The Other Kimmy Brown - A recently single journalist wrongly on a family's email chain decides to crash their Thanksgiving and ends up going on a journey she never expected.

Visit Kristin at **www.kristindurfee.com** to keep up to date on all her works.

KEN PELHAM

Ken Pelham has won eleven Royal Palm Literary Awards for both fiction and nonfiction. A member of International Thriller Writers, his novels **Brigands Key** and **Place of Fear** both won first-place RPLAs. His nonfiction book, **Out of Sight, Out of Mind: A Writer's Guide to Mastering Viewpoint,** was named Royal Palm 2015 Published Book of the Year, and his book exploring the evolution of genre fiction, **Gumshoes, Fangs, Rockets, & Spies**, won the 2021 RPLA Gold for History.

Fans of Sherlock Holmes, check out the thrilling novelette, **The Riddle of the Forgeries**, winner of the 2025 RPLA Gold for Novelette.

More short stories are collected in **Borderlands: Tales of Mystery & Imagination**.

Brigands Key is ". . . a perfect storm of menace . . . breathtaking."—The Florida Weekly

For more, visit Ken at **www.kenpelham.com**

BRIA BURTON

Award-winning author Bria Burton lives in St. Pete, Florida. Her fiction has appeared in over twenty anthologies and magazines. At the 2019 Royal Palm Literary Awards, *Her Midnight Ride* won the Silver Award for novelette. *The Running Girls* was a 2017 RPLA Finalist. *Little Angel Helper* won a 2016 RPLA for novella.

> *"**Little Angel Helper** is a well-told, uplifting novella that readers looking for a truly inspirational, heartwarming story are sure to love." —Judge, 25th Annual Writer's Digest Self-Published Book Awards*

While Bria writes, her cat does his best to distract her, which is why he and his late brother-from-another-mother Lance the dog star in her family-friendly short story collection and podcast, *Lance & Ringo Tails*. At St. Pete Running Company, she's a blogger and customer service manager. As a member of the Florida Writers Association, she leads a local critique group.

She's thrilled to contribute to another project by the authors of the Alvarium Experiment. Her past contributions include "On Both Sides" (The Prometheus Saga), "Her Midnight Ride" (The Prometheus Saga 2), "AOB" (Return to Earth), "The Count of the Alician Apocalypse" (The Masters Reimainged), "The Eyes of Mona Lisa" (The Masters Reimainged 2), and "Backlash/Front-lash\Whiplash" (The Light Fantastic).

Visit her website for links to her books and stories: **www.briaburton.com**

J.C. BRUCE

J.C. Bruce is an award-winning journalist and author who enjoys dual citizenship in the United States of America and Florida. His six-book series, **The Strange Files,** has won numerous awards. The latest, **Strange Timing**, was named Published Book of the Year in the Royal Palm Literary Awards as well as winning gold medals in the Thriller and Science Fiction categories. The stories recount the misadventures of Alexander Strange, America's preeminent weird-news reporter.

In addition to books, he writes the Essential News column in Florida Weekly and is a prolific blogger and social media blabbermouth. When he's not writing, he's in training for the Florida Man Underwater Ping-Pong Championships. Among countless (math is not his thing) honors, he was recently awarded a doctorate from Miami's Lightgate Institute for Extranormal Studies, a think tank he totally made up for his latest book.

You can find links to his novels on his website, **www.JCBruce.com,** where you can also subscribe to his wildly popular monthly newsletter, which will make you the smartest person in the room—or the Zoom. The newsletter is 100 percent organic, hypoallergenic, and calorie-free.

The books of The Strange Files series are, in order: **The Strange Files, Florida Man, Get Strange, Strange Currents, Mister Manners, Strange Timing**

Short stories include:
    The Code
    Cool as a Moose Egg

Some actual journalism:
    Tour of Duty
    JCBruce.com

JADE KERRION

At 3 a.m., when her husband and three sons are asleep, USA Today best-selling author Jade Kerrion weaves unforgettable characters into unexpected stories.

Her debut science fiction novel, **Perfection Unleashed**, won six literary awards and launched the **Double Helix** series which blends cutting-edge genetic engineering and high-octane action with an unforgettable romance between an alpha empath and an assassin.

Readers continue their adventures in this dystopian Earth with the spin-off futuristic thriller series **Double Helix Case Files**, starting with **Miriya**.

The **Daughter of Air** and **Lord of the Ocean** series, beginning with **Cursed Tides**, blends fairy tales and mythology into urban fantasy. It's the story you always wanted to read: The Little Mermaid finally kicks ass!

Jade's award-winning fantasy novel, **Eternal Night**, draws you in the post-apocalyptic world of **Aeternae Noctis** where humans —victims of a war between immortals—are about to tip the balance.

Jade's devious plan for world domination begins with making all her readers as sleep deprived as she is.

Visit Jade at **www.jadekerrion.com**

JOHN HOPE

Mr. Hope is an award-winning short story, children's book, middle grade, young adult, science fiction, fantasy, and historical fiction writer. His work appears in paperback, hardback, audiobook, and short story collections. Mr. Hope, a native Floridian, loves to travel with his wife, Jaime, and two kids. He enjoys suffering through long distance running adventures. He gives informational and inspirational presentations to schools, writing groups and clubs, and various conferences. And in his spare time, he flips his offspring on their heads for his personal enjoyment.

You can read more from John Hope, as well as download free presentations, color pages, and other goodies from **www.johnhopewriting.com**, including:

Laser Hamsters (The Light Fantastic: A Speculative Fiction Anthology)

Middle-Grade Novels
> **Scott Free**
> **Silencing Sharks**
> **Father's Violin**
> **Secret Adventures of Foxfire: Fixing Walls**
> **No Good**
> **Colby in the Crosshairs**

Children's Books
> **Book 1 – Pankyland**
> **Book 2 – Pankyland: The Movie**
> **Book 3 – Pankyland: Be Little World**

Short Stories
> **Fairy Tales, the Sequel**

GREG STANINA

Greg Stanina has been described as a human breeze, a fluffy nimbus, a gasser and a gasseroo, a soothing sauna, a cool cucumber, a tonic fizz, a sunset sail, a shrug, a wink, and a whistle. He also dabbles in writing fantastical fiction and may or may not suffer from acute Stendhal Syndrome.

Greg's short stories and story collections can be found on his Amazon author page: **www.amazon.com/stores/Greg-Stanina/author/B0086KEZMU**

ELLE ANDREWS PATT

As a hybrid author, Elle Andrews Patt publishes novels independently, short stories traditionally, and audio in partnership with Podium Audio. Her work has been recognized by the National Indie Excellence, Silver Falchion, and Royal Palm Literary Awards, among others. When not writing, she can be found working out or hunting bourbon with her hubby.

Novels
The Archivist series: Ghost, Spirit, Wraith
Following an accident, Archivist Andrea Kelley's eyes are opened to the existence of ghosts.
Blind Mice Bite: *A blind former investigator is detained for murder but the name the police are using is his deepest cover identity, a name only he knows.*

Short Fiction
Missing: Prelude to a Murder Conviction
Skinned (Summer of Sci-fi and Fantasy)
Becoming (Summer of Sci-fi and Fantasy 2)
Regarding Mr. Bulkington (The Masters Reimagined)
Among the Blue Horses (The Masters Reimagined 2)
Someday Loyal (Return to Earth)
Manteo (The Prometheus Saga)
Remuda (The Prometheus Saga 2)

Visit Elle at **www.elleandrewspatt.com**

www.ingramcontent.com/pod-product-compliance
Lightning Source LLC
Chambersburg PA
CBHW020419260626
47156CB00007B/2461